## *Story Telling at its Finest*

Written by one of the most widely acclaimed authors of the present generation, these are witty, warmly human, sometimes startling stories about a large and varied gallery of people:

> A bewildered young man experiences a series of weird and hilarious adventures on his first trip to the big city . . .

> An embittered woman stops at nothing, even murder, to get what she wants . . .

> A frightened young girl stumbles into an affair with a carnival performer . . .

These are a few of the personalities you will meet in this superlative group of tales by an author who has been labeled by the critics as:

> "A hugely gifted artist."—*The Atlantic*

> "The human warmth keeps bubbling up through the satire."—*New York Times*

> " . . . performs miracles with the language."—*The Saturday Review*

---

The New Cross Section of
Current World Literature and Criticism

# NEW WORLD WRITING

**First Mentor Selection** of *New World Writing*
(#Ms73) presents contributions by Christopher Isherwood, Tennessee Williams, Thomas Merton, Gore Vidal, others.

**Second Mentor Selection** of *New World Writing*
(#Ms79) includes selections by James Jones, Norman Mailer, Pablo Picasso, Dylan Thomas, W. H. Auden, etc.

**Third Mentor Selection** of *New World Writing*
(#Ms85) presents new writing by Alberto Moravia, Peter Matthiessen, Edith Sitwell, Ignazio Silone, and others.

**Fourth Mentor Selection** of *New World Writing*
(#Ms96) includes contributions by William Sansom, Nadine Gordimer, Shelby Foote, Eric Bercovici, Theodore Roethke, Susanne K. Langer, etc.

**Fifth Mentor Selection** of *New World Writing*
(#Ms106) offers exciting contributions by Dylan Thomas, Ralph Ellison, William Carlos Williams, Samuel Beckett, John Lehmann, and drawings by Tom Keogh.

**Sixth Mentor Selection** of *New World Writing*
(#Ms118) includes a play by Saul Bellow, a chapter from Louis Armstrong's life, calligraphic drawings and poems from Japan, and other fiction, poetry and criticism.

**Seventh Mentor Selection** of *New World Writing*
(#MD130) presents a play by Reuel Denney, new poems from England and Brazil, a special section on Dylan Thomas, cartoons by Bobo Leydenfrost, etc.

**Eighth Mentor Selection** of *New World Writing*
(#MD146) presents a puppet play by Federico Garcia Lorca, drawings from Africa, a unique sampling of Dutch poetry, a provocative essay on modern American prose, etc.

**Ninth Mentor Selection** of *New World Writing*
(#MD170) includes the work of seven Korean poets, two stories from India, a play by Ionesco, stories from Italy, France, and the United States, poetry selected by John Ciardi, and articles on literature, music and art.

## EACH VOLUME 50c

*Dylan Thomas*

# Adventures
## in the
# Skin Trade
### and other stories

**A SIGNET BOOK**

Published by THE NEW AMERICAN LIBRARY

*SIGNET BOOKS are published by
The New American Library of World Literature, Inc.
501 Madison Avenue, New York 22, New York*

PRINTED IN THE UNITED STATES OF AMERICA

# Contents

# Note

The title of this volume could be considered misleading on a couple of counts. The title piece itself is not a "short story," as such things are defined. "Adventures in the Skin Trade" was called by its author a novel-in-progress, and there are other prose pieces here that would be ruled out of any properly run short story contest.

Dylan Thomas' magical prose was not easily confined to literary categories and prescribed lengths. His talent was too prodigal; his quickened awareness, his extravagant humor, his conjuring skill with words brought people and places alive, revealed mystery, but they also overflowed bounds. Not long before he was fatally stricken in New York in November, 1953, Dylan Thomas had spoken of further adventures he expected to set down for his young hero in this unfinished story. But if Thomas had gone on with it, there is no certainty that he would have ended up with a novel, in the accepted sense, although the new parts undoubtedly would have had the same enchantment and debonair satisfaction.

The publisher, therefore, makes no apology for using the word "story" in its broadest sense in regard to this unfinished novel, or for some other pieces in this book which might better be called "fictions." He believes that everything in the book will find its own justification in what it will give readers; and there are even a few stories that have the classic attributes of suspense and surprise and will bid fair to become classics of the short story.

The aim of this book was to gather together all stories by Dylan Thomas that were not permanently available in book form. Some had been published in volumes long out of print such as *The World I Breathe* (New Directions, 1939), of which only 700 copies were ever printed. Others are new. As the editors collected the texts, they found references to other stories and went searching for them.

Dylan Thomas was also prodigal of manuscripts and publication; and some stories turned up in relatively unknown "little magazines." The result is that this volume is both bigger and richer than was expected; about half of its contents has never received book publication before; a number of stories have not previously been published on this side of the Atlantic; and three can be said to be given their first open publication.

In this search many people have been helpful; and the publisher wishes to signalize particular gratitude to Mr. David Higham, for many years Dylan Thomas' literary agent and now one of the three trustees of his estate, and his able assistant, Miss I. F. Mayes, both of whom have been untiring in their search for texts; to Mr. Daniel Jones of Swansea, Wales, a composer and close friend of Dylan Thomas, who approved the texts used; to Constantine Fitz Gibbon, the novelist and former editor of *Yellow Jacket,* who supplied photostats of stories which had never been published elsewhere; and to Mr. Donald M. Allen, formerly on the staff of New Directions, who did research and made contributions way beyond what was expected of him.

# Adventures in the Skin Trade

## I. A FINE BEGINNING

That early morning, in January 1933, only one person was awake in the street, and he was the quietest. Call him Samuel Bennet. He wore a trilby hat that had been lying by his bedside in case the two house-breakers, a man and a woman, came back for the bag they had left.

In striped pyjamas tight under the arms and torn between the legs, he padded barefoot downstairs and opened the breakfast-room door of his parents' six-room house. The room smelt strong of his father's last pipe before bed. The windows were shut fast and the curtains drawn, the back door was bolted, the house-breaking night could not enter anywhere. At first he peered uneasily into the known, flickering corners of the room, as though he feared that the family might have been sitting there in silence in the dark; then he lit the gaslight from the candle. His eyes were still heavy from a dream of untouchable city women and falling, but he could see that Tinker, the aunt-faced pom, was sleeping before the burned-out fire, and that the mantelpiece clock between hollow, mock-ebony, pawing horses, showed five to two. He stood still and listened to the noises of the house: there was nothing to fear. Upstairs the family breathed and snored securely. He heard his sister sleeping in the box-room under the signed photographs of actors from the repertory theater and the jealous pictures of the marriages of friends. In the biggest bedroom overlooking the field that was called the back, his father turned over the bills of the month in his one dream; his mother in bed mopped and polished through a wood of kitchens. He closed the door: now there was nobody to disturb him.

But all the noises of the otherwise dead or sleeping, dark early morning, the intimate breathing of three invisible relations, the loud old dog, could wake up the neighbors.

And the gaslight, bubbling, could attract to his presence in the breakfast-room at this hour Mrs. Probert next door, disguised as a she-goat in a nightgown, butting the air with her kirby-grips; her dapper, commercial son, with a watch-chain tattooed across his rising belly; the tubercular lodger, with his neat umbrella up and his basin in his hand. The regular tide of the family breath could beat against the wall of the house on the other side, and bring the Baxters out. He turned the gas low and stood for a minute by the clock, listening to sleep and seeing Mrs. Baxter climb naked out of her widow's bed with a mourning band round her thigh.

Soon her picture died, she crawled back grieving to her lovebird's mirror under the blankets, and the proper objects of the room slowly returned as he lost his fear that the strangers upstairs he had known since he could remember would wake and come down with pokers and candles.

First there was the long strip of snapshots of his mother propped against the cut-glass of the windowsill. A professional under a dickybird hood had snapped her as she walked down Chapel Street in December, and developed the photographs while she waited looking at the thermos flasks and the smoking sets in the nearest shopwindow, calling "Good morning" across the street to the shopping bags she knew, and the matrons' outside costumes, and the hats like flowerpots and chambers on the crisp, permed heads. There she was, walking down the street along the windowsill, step by step, stout, safe, confident, buried in her errands, clutching her handbag, stepping aside from the common women blind and heavy under a week's provisions, prying into the looking-glasses at the doors of furniture shops.

"Your photograph has been taken." Immortalized in a moment, she shopped along forever between the cut-glass vase with the permanent flowers and the box of hairpins, buttons, screws, empty shampoo packets, cotton-reels, flypaper, cigarette cards. At nearly two in the morning she hurried down Chapel Street against a backcloth of trilbies and burberries going the other way, umbrellas rising to the first drops of the rain a month ago, the sightless faces of people who would always be strangers hanging half-developed behind her, and the shadows of the shopping center of the sprawling, submerged town. He could hear her shoes click on the tramrails. He could see, beneath the pastelled silk scarf, the round metal badge of Mrs. Rosser's Society, and the grandmother's cameo brooch on the vee of the knitted clover jumper.

The clock chimed and struck two. Samuel put out his hand and took up the strip of snaps. Then he tore it into pieces. The whole of her dead, comfortable face remained on one piece, and he tore it across the cheeks, up through the chins, and into the eyes.

The pom growled in a nightmare, and showed his little teeth. "Lie down, Tinker. Go to sleep, boy." He put the pieces in his pyjama pocket.

Then there was the framed photograph of his sister by the clock. He destroyed her in one movement, and, with the ripping of her set smile and the crumpling of her bobbed head into a ball, down went the Girls' School and the long-legged, smiling colts with their black knickers and bows; the hockey-legged girls who laughed behind their hands as they came running through the gates when he passed, went torn and ruined into his pyjama pocket; they vanished, broken, into the porch and lay in pieces against his heart. Stanley Road, where the Girls' School stood, would never know him again. Down you go, Peggy, he whispered to his sister, with all the long legs and the Young Liberals' dances, and the boys you brought home for supper on Sunday evenings and Lionel you kissed in the porch. He is a solicitor now. When I was eleven years old and you were seventeen I heard you, from my bedroom, playing the Desert Song. People were downstairs all over the world.

Most of the history sheets on the table were already marked and damned in his father's violet writing. With a lump of coal from the dead fire, Samuel marked them again, rubbing the coal hard over the careful corrections, drawing legs and breasts in the margins, smudging out the names and form numbers. History is lies. Now take Queen Elizabeth. Go ahead, take Alice Phillips, take her into the shrubbery. She was the headmaster's daughter. Take old Bennet and whip him down the corridors, stuff his mouth with dates, dip his starched collar in his marking ink and hammer his teeth back into his prim, bald, boring head with his rap-across-the-knuckle ruler. Spin Mr. Nicholson on his tellurion until his tail drops off. Tell Mr. Parsons his wife has been seen coming out of the Compass piggyback on a drunk sailor, catching pennies in her garters. It's true as History.

On the last sheet he signed his name several times und a giant pinman with three legs. He did not scribble on t top sheet. At a first glance was no sign of interferenc Then he threw the coal into the grate. Dust drifted up in cloud, and settled down again on the pom's back.

If only he could shout at the ceiling now, at the da circle made by the gas, at the cracks and lines that ha always been the same faces and figures, two bearded me chasing an animal over a mountain edge, a kneelin woman with faces on her knees: Come and look at Samue Bennet destroying his parents' house in Mortimer Stree off Stanley's Grove, he will never be allowed to come back Mrs. Baxter, have a dekko from under the cold sheets Mr. Baxter, who worked in the Harbor Trust Office, ca never come back either. Mrs. Probert Chestnuts, you billygoat is gone, leaving a hairy space in the bed; Mr. Bel the lodger coughs all night under his gamp; your son cannot sleep, he is counting his gentlemen's three and eleven-three halfhose jumping over the tossed blankets. Samuel shouted under his breath, "Come and see me destroying the evidence, Mrs. Rosser, have a peep from under your hairnet. I have seen your shadow on the blind as you undressed, I was watching by the lamp-post next to the dairy, you disappeared under a tent and came out slim and humped and black. I am the only gooseberry in Stanley's Grove who knows that you are a black woman with a hump. Mr. Rosser married to a camel, every one is mad and bad in his box when the blinds are pulled, come and see me break the china without any noise so that I can never come back."

"Hush," he said to himself, "I know you."

He opened the door of the china pantry. The best plates shone in rows, a willow tree next to an ivied castle, baskets of solid flowers on top of fruits and flower-coiled texts. Tureens were piled on one shelf, on another the salad-bowls, the finger-bowls, the toast-racks spelling Porthcawl and Baby, the trifle-dishes, the heirloom mustache-cup. The afternoon tea-service was brittle as biscuits and had gold rims. He cracked two saucers together, and the horn-curved spout of the teapot came off in his hand. In five minutes he had broken the whole set. Let all the daughters of Mortimer Street come in and see me, he whispered in the close pantry: the pale young girls who help at home, calculating down the pavement to the rich-smelling shops, screwing up their straight, dry hair in their rooms at the top of the house; their blood is running through them like salt. And I hope the office girls knock on the door with the stubs of their fingers, tap out Sir or Madam on the glass porch, the hard, bright babies who never go too far. You can hear them in the lane behind the post office as you tiptoe along, they are saying, "So he said and I said and he said and Oh yeah I said," and the just male voices are agreeing softly. Shoo them in out of snoring Stanley's Grove, I know they are sleeping under the sheets up to their fringes in wishes. Beryl Gee is marrying the Chamber of Commerce in a pepper-and-salt church. Mrs. Mayor's Chain, Madame Cocked Hat, Lady Settee, I am breaking tureens in the cupboard under the stairs.

A tureen-cover dropped from his hand and smashed.

He waited for the sound of his mother waking. No one stirred upstairs. "Tinker did it," he said aloud, but the harsh noise of his voice drove him back into silence. His fingers became so cold and numb he knew he could not lift up another plate to break it.

"What are you doing?" he said to himself at last, in a cool, flat voice. "Leave the Street alone. Let it sleep."

Then he closed the pantry door.

"What are you doing, ranting away?"

Even the dog had not been wakened.

"Ranting away," he said.

He would have to be quick now. The accident in the cupboard had made him tremble so much that he could hardly tear up the bills he found in the sideboard drawer and scatter them under the sofa. His sister's crochetwork was too difficult to destroy, the doilies and the patterned tea-cosies were hard as rubber. He pulled them apart the best he could, and wedged them up the chimney.

"These are such small things," he said. "I should break the windows and stuff the cushions with the glass." He saw his round soft face in the mirror under the Mona Lisa. "But you won't," he said, turning away, "you're afraid of the noise." He turned back to his reflection. "It isn't that. You're afraid she'll cut her hands."

He burnt the edge of his mother's sunshade at the gas-mantle, and felt the tears running down his cheeks and dropping onto his pyjama collar.

Even in the first moment of his guilt and shame, he remembered to put out his tongue and taste the track of the tears. Still crying, he said, "It's salt. It's very salt. Just like in my poems."

He went upstairs in the dark, with the candle shaking, past the box-room to his own room, and locked the door on the inside. He put out his hands and touched the walls and his bed. Goodmorning and goodbye, Mrs. Baxter. His window, facing her bedroom, was open to the windless, starless early morning, but he could not hear her breathe or sleep. All the houses were quiet. The street was a close grave. The Rossers and the Proberts and the Bennets were still and safe and deep in their separate silences. His head touched the pillow, but he knew that he could not sleep again. His eyes closed.

Come down into my arms, for I shan't sleep, girls asleep on all sides in the attics and spare rooms of the square, red houses with the bay windows looking out on the trees behind the railings. I know your rooms like the backs of my hands, like the backs of your heads in the pictures when you are leaning over onto the next door shoulders. I shan't sleep again. Tomorrow, today, I am going away by the 7:15 train, with ten pounds and a new suitcase. Lay your curling-pins on my pillow, the alarm at six-thirty will hurry you back to draw the blinds and light the fires before the rest come down. Come down quickly, the Bennets' house is melting. I can hear you breathe, I can hear Mrs. Baxter turn in a dream. Oh, the milkmen are waking!

He was asleep with his hat on still, and his hands clenched.

2

The family awoke before six o'clock. He heard them, from a sunken half-sleep, bothering on the landing. They would be in dressing gowns, stale-eyed and with ragged hair. Peggy might have put two blushes on her cheeks. The family rushed in and out of the bathroom, never stopping to wash, and collided on the narrow top of the stairs as they nagged and bustled to get him ready. He let himself sink deeper until the waves broke round his head again, and the lights of a city spun and shone through the eyes of women walking in his last remembered dream.

From the lapping distance he heard his father shout like a man on the opposite shore:

"Have you put the sponge bag in, Hilda?"

"Of course I have," she answered from the kitchen.

Don't let her look in the china-pantry. Samuel prayed among the women walking like lampposts. She never uses the best china for breakfast.

"All right, all right, I just asked."

"Where's his new hairbrush?"

"That's right, shout my head off. Here it is. How can I give it to you if you're in the kitchen. It's the brush with the initials—S.B."

"I know his initials."

"Mother, does he want all these vests? You know he never uses them."

"It's January, Peggy."

"She knows it's January, Hilda. You haven't got to tell the neighbours. Can you smell something burning?"

"It's only mother's sunshade," Samuel said in the locked bedroom.

He dressed and went down. The gas in the breakfast ·oom was on again. His mother was boiling an egg for him on the gas-stove. "We'll have our breakfast later," she said, "you mustn't miss the train. Did you sleep well?"

"No burglars last night, Sam," his father said.

His mother brought the egg in. "You can't expect them every night."

Peggy and his father sat down in front of the empty grate.

"What do you think you'll do first when you get there, Sam?" said Peggy.

"He'll get himself a nice room, of course, not too central. And don't have an Irish landlady." His mother brushed his collar as he ate. "Go and get yourself settled straightaway, that's the important thing."

"I'll get myself settled."

"Don't forget to look under the wallpaper for bugs."

"That's enough of that, Peggy. Sam knows a clean place when he sees one."

He saw himself knocking at a lodging-house in the very centre of the city, and an Irishwoman appearing at the door. "Goodmorning, madam, have you a cheap room?" "Cheaper than sunlight to you, Danny Boy." She would not be more than twenty-one. "Has it got bugs?" "All over the walls, praise be to God." "I'll take it."

"I'll know what I'm doing," he said to his mother.

"Jenkins' motor isn't here yet," Peggy said. "Perhaps there's a puncture."

If he doesn't come soon, they'll notice everything. I'll cut my throat on a piece of china.

"Remember to call on Mrs. Chapman. Give her all our love from 42."

"I'll call on her tomorrow, mother."

The taxi drew up outside. The corners of bedroom blinds would be lifted all over the street.

"Here's your wallet. Don't put it in your handkerchief pocket now. You never know when you'll be wanting to blow your nose."

"You'll be scattering largesse," Peggy said. She kissed him on the forehead.

Remind me to wipe it off in the cab.

"You're kissing the editor of the *Times* now," said his mother.

"Well, not quite that, Sam. Not yet, eh?" His father said, "Rungs of the ladder," and then looked away.

"Write tomorrow morning sharp. Send us the news."

"You send me your news, too. Mr. Jenkins is blowing his horn."

"Better than blowing your trumpet," Peggy said. "And there's never any news in Mortimer Street."

You wait, slyboots. Wait till the flames touch the doilie with the herons on it.

He came down to pat Tinker.

"Come on, don't fuss over the old dog, he's all fleas. It's gone seven."

Peggy was opening the door of the taxi for him. His father shook him by the hand. His mother kissed him on the mouth.

"Goodbye, Mortimer Street," he said, and the cab was off. "Goodbye, Stanley's Grove."

Through the back window he saw three strangers waving. He pulled down the blind.

3

Sitting with his bag in the lavatory of the moving train, for all the compartments were full, he read through his

notebook and tore out the pages in order. He was dressed
in a brand-new brown tweed overcoat, a brown town-
suit, a white starched shirt with a woollen tie and a tiepin,
and black, shining shoes. He had put his hard brown hat
in the washbasin. Here was Mrs. Chapman's address next
to the telephone number of a Mr. Hewson who was going
to introduce him to a man who worked on a newspaper;
and under these the address of the Literary Institute that
had once awarded him a guinea for a poem in a competi-
tion: Will Shakespeare at the Tomb of the Unknown
Warrior. He tore the page out. Then the name and address,
in red ink, of a collected poet who had written him a letter
thanking him for a sonnet-sequence. And a page of names
that might help.

The lavatory door half opened, and he shut it quickly
with his foot.

"I beg your pardon."

Hear her apologizing down the corridor, full as an egg.
She could turn every handle the whole length of the train,
and in every closet a fully-clothed man would be sitting
with his foot against the door, lost and alone in the long,
moving house on wheels, travelling in silence with no
windows, at sixty miles an hour racing to another place
that did not want him, never at home wherever the train
stopped. The handle turned again, and Samuel coughed
somebody away.

The last page of the notebook was the only one he kept.
Under a drawing of a girl with long hair dancing into an
address, he had written: Lucille Harris. A man he met on
the Promenade had said as they sat on a bench, looking
at the legs passing: "She's okay. She's a girl I know. She's
the best in the world, she'll take care of you. Give her a call
when you're up. Tell her you're Austin's friend." That
page he placed in his wallet between two one-pound notes.

The rest of the pages he picked up from the floor,
bunched together, and threw down between his legs into
the bowl. Then he pulled the chain. Down went the helping
names, the influential numbers, the addresses that could
mean so much, into the round, roaring sea and on to the
rails. Already they were lost a mile behind, blowing over
the track now, over the glimpses of hedges into the
lightning-passing fields.

Home and help were over. He had eight pounds ten and
Lucille Harris' address. Many people have begun worse,

he said aloud. I am ignorant, lazy, dishonest, and sentimental, I have the pull over nobody.

The handle turned again.

"I bet you're dancing," he said to the person on the
other side of the locked door.

Footsteps pattered away down the train.

First of all, when I reach there, I'll have a Bass and a
stale sandwich, he decided. I'll take them to a table in a
corner, brush off the cakecrumbs with my hat, and prop
my book against the cruet. I must have all the details right
at the beginning. The rest must come by accident. I'll be
sitting there before noon, cool and calm, my hat on my
knees, my glass in my hand, looking not a day under
twenty, pretending to read and spying from the corners of
my eyes at the waiting, drinking, restless people busily
alone at the counter. The other tables will be crowded.
There will be women, beckoning without moving, over their
cold coffee; old, anonymous men with snuff on their
cheeks, trembling over tea; quiet men expecting no one
from the trains they wait for eagerly every hour; women
who have come to run away, to take a train to St. Ives or
Liverpool or anywhere, but who know they will never
take any train and are drinking cups of tea and saying to
themselves, "I could be catching the twelve o'clock but
I'll wait for the quarter past"; women from the country
with dozens of children coming undone; shop girls, office
girls, street girls, people who have nothing worse to do, all
the unhappy, happy in chains, bewildered foreign men and
women in the station buffet of the city I know from cover
to cover.

The door rattled. "You there," a voice said outside.
"You've been there for hours."

He turned on the hot water tap. It spurted cold water
into the basin before he could take his hat out. "I'm a
director of the company," he said, but his voice sounded
weak to him and without assurance.

When the footsteps had faded again, he gathered up his
cases and walked out of the lavatory and down the corridor.
Standing outside a first-class compartment, he saw a man
and a ticket-inspector come to the door and hammer on it.
They did not try the handle.

"Ever since Neath," the man said.

Now the train was losing speed, running out of the lost
country into the smoke and a tunnel of factories, puffing

past the district platforms and the high houses with broken windows and underclothes dancing in the dirty yards. Children at the windows never waved their hands to the train. It might have been the wind passing.

A crowd of people stood arguing outside the door as the train drew up under a great glass roof.

## 4

"Nip of Bass, please, and a ham sandwich." He took them to a table in a corner, brushed off the crumbs with his wet hat, and sat down just before noon. He counted his money: eight pound nine and a penny, nearly three pounds more than he had ever seen. Some people had this every week. It had to last him until he was dead. At the next table sat a plump, middle-aged man with a chocolate brown birthmark over his cheek and chin like the half of a beard. He was propping his book against an empty bottle when a young man walked over from the counter.

"Hullo, Sam."

"Hullo, Ron. Fancy seeing you."

He was Ronald Bishop who used to live in the Crescent off Stanley's Grove.

"Been up in the smoke for long, Sam?"

"Just arrived, how's tricks?"

"Same as me, we must have been on the same train. Oh, so so. Still at the old game, Sam?"

"Yeah, up on a bit of business. You at the usual?"

"Yeah."

They had never had anything to say to each other.

"Where you staying, Ron?"

"Usual. Strand Palace."

"Daresay I'll be seeing you, then."

"Okay, make it tomorrow in the bar, about seven-thirty."

"Okay."

"It's a date, don't forget."

"No fear."

They both forgot it at once.

"Well, be seeing you."

"Be good."

As Ronald Bishop walked off, Samuel said silently into his glass: A fine beginning. If I go out of the station and turn round the corner I'll be back in 42. The little Proberts will be playing doctor outside the Load of Hay.

The only stranger anywhere near me is a businessman with a stained face, reading the palms of his hands. No, here comes a woman in a fur coat, she's going to sit next to me. Yes, no, no. I smelt her as she passed: eau de cologne and powder and bed.

The woman sat down two tables away, crossed her legs, powdered her nose.

This is the beginning of an advance. Now she is pretending not to notice that her knees are uncovered. There's a lynx in the room, lady. Button your overcoat. She's rattling her spoon on her saucer to attract my attention, but when I stare at her hard, without smiling, I see she is looking down gently and innocently into her lap as though she had a baby there. He was glad she was not brazen.

Dear mother, he wrote with his finger on the back of an envelope, looking up, between every few invisible words, at the unnoticing woman opposite, this is to tell you that I arrived safely and that I am drinking in the buffet with a tart. I will tell you later if she is Irish. She is about thirty-eight years old and her husband left her five years ago because of her carryings on. Her child is in a home, and she visits him every other Sunday. She always tells him that she is working in a hat shop. You need not worry that she will take all my money as we liked each other on first sight. And you need not worry that I shall break my heart trying to reform her, because I have always been brough' up to believe that Mortimer Street is what is right, and I would not wish that on anybody. Besides, I do not want to reform her. Not that I think she is nasty. Her business is very hard on stockings, so I am going to pay the first week's rent for our little room in Pimlico. Now she is going across to the counter to buy another cup of coffee. I hope you will notice that she is buying her own. Everybody in the buffet is unhappy except me.

As she came back to her table, he tore up the envelope and stared at her, unsmiling, for a full minute by the Bovril clock. Once she raised her eyes to his, then looked away. She was tapping her spoon on the side of her cup, then opening and closing the clasp of her handbag, then turning her head round slowly to face him and then looking away again, quickly through the window. She must be new, he thought with a sudden compassion, but he did not stop staring. Should I wink? He tilted his hard, wet hat over one eye, and winked: a long, deliberate wink that screwed up his face and made his burning cigarette nearly touch the blunt end of his nose. She snapped her handbag, pushed two pennies under the saucer, and walked right out of the room, never looking at him as she passed.

She's left her coffee, he thought. And then: My God, she was blushing.

A fine beginning.

"Did you speak?" asked the man with the birthmark, spying up. His face was red and purple where it was not brown, faintly shabby and unshaved, shiftily angry about the eyes as though his cunning were an irritation impossible to bear.

"I think I said it was a fine day."

"Stranger in town?"

"Yes, I've just come up."

"How do you like it?" He did not appear to care at all.

"I haven't been outside the station yet."

Now the woman in the fur coat would be telling a policeman, "I have just been winked at by a short boy wearing a wet hat." "But it isn't raining, madam." That would settle her.

He put his hat under the table.

"There's plenty to see," the man said, "if that's what you want. Museums, art galleries." Without speaking, he went through a list of names of other attractions, but rejected them all. "Museums," he said after a long pause. "There's one at South Kensington, and there's the British Museum, and there's one at Whitehall with guns. I've seen them all," he said.

Now every table was occupied. Cold, stiff people with time to kill sat staring at their tea and the clock, inventing replies to questions that would not be asked, justifying their behaviour in the past and the future, drowning every present moment as soon as it began to breathe, lying and wishing, missing all the trains in the terror of their minds, each one alone at the terminus. Time was dying all over the room. And then all the tables except the one next to Samuel's were unoccupied again. The lonely crowd went out in a funeral procession, leaving ash and tea-leaves and newspapers.

"You must move out of the station sometime, you know," the man said, returning to a conversation that held no interest for him. "If you want to see around. It's only fair. It's not fair to come up in a train and sit in the buffet and then go back and say you've seen London, is it?"

"I'm going out now, quite soon."

"That's right," the man said, "give London a chance."

He is so tired of talking to me that he is nearly losing his temper, Samuel thought.

He looked around him again, at the mourners fidgeting to the counter, at the quick whisky drinkers in a knot by the tea-urn, at the waitresses listlessly busy with cardboard cakes and small change.

"Otherwise, it's like not getting out of bed, isn't it?" the man said. "You've got to walk round, you know, you've got to move some time. Everybody does it," he said in a sudden, dull passion.

Samuel bought another nip of Bass from a girl like Joan Crawford.

"This is the last one, then I'm going," he said when he had returned to his table.

"Do you think I care how many more you have? You can stay here all day, why should I mind?" The man was looking at the palms of his hands again as his temper mounted. "Am I my brother's keeper?"

Ronald Bishop still stood at the counter.

Mortimer Street has tracked me down, Samuel thought bitterly, even into this lopsided quarrel with a palmist in a station restaurant. There was no escape. But it was not escape he wanted. The Street was a safe hole in a wall behind the wind in another country. He wanted to arrive and be caught. Ronald stood there like a fury with a rolled umbrella. Come in, Mrs. Rosser, in your fawn and beige antimacassar coat, with your tribal hat on your waves, and scream the news of the Street across the table in your whist-drive voice. I could not escape your fury on a birds' rock, you would be mincing and pinching down to the fishy sea with your beak gaped open like a shopping bag.

"I hate a nosey parker," the man said, and got up. On his way to the counter he passed the table where the Irish prostitute had sat and removed the pennies from under the plate.

"Stop, thief!" Samuel said softly. No one could hear. There is a waitress with a consumptive husband who needs those pennies. And two children. Tristram and Eve. He changed the names quickly. Tom and Marge. Then he walked over and put a sixpence under the plate just as a waitress came to the table.

"It fell on the floor," he said.

"Oh yeah?"

As he walked back, he saw that the waitress was talking to three men at the counter and nodding her head in his direction. One man was Ronald Bishop. One was the man with the birthmark.

Oh, fine, fine! If he had not broken the china he would have caught the next train back. The pieces would be swept up by now, but the tears would be running all over the house. "Mother, mother, he's put my crochetwork up the chimney," he heard his sister scream in a guard's whistle. Herons, flower baskets, palm trees, windmills, Red Riding Hoods, stuffed up in the flames and soot. "Get me a rubber to rub out coal, Hilda. I shall of course lose my position. That is only to be expected." "Oh my teapot, oh my blue set, oh my poor boy." He refused to look at the counter where Ronald Bishop inaudibly reviled him. The waitress knew as soon as she saw him that he stole from the begging tins of the blind and led them by the arm into thick traffic. The birthmarked man said that he had shown a certain postcard to a customer in a fur coat. The voices of his parents condemned above the clattering of the cups. He stared hard at his book though the print climbed and staggered as if the tears of the left house had run down after him along the rails and flowed into this hot, suspicious room over the tea-stained air into his eyes. But the image was false and the book was chosen for strangers. He did not like or understand it.

"My bills." "My doilies." "My willowplate."

Ronald Bishop went out on to the platform.

"Be seeing you, Ron."

Ronald Bishop's face was flushed with the embarrassment of not noticing him.

One pleasure is, Samuel said to himself, that I do not know what I expect to happen to me. He smiled at the waitress behind the counter, and she stared away at once as guiltily as though he had discovered her robbing the till. I am not so innocent as I make out, he thought. I do not expect any old cobwebbed Fagin, reeking of character and stories, to shuffle out of a corner and lead me away into his grand, loud, filthy house; there will not be any Nancy to tickle my fancy in a kitchen full of handkerchiefs

and beckoning, unmade beds. I did not think a choir o
loose women immediately would sing and dance around the
little tables, in plush cloths and advertised brassieres, as
walked into London for the first time, rattling my fortune
fresh as Copperfield. I could count the straws in my hair
with one hand.

Hush! I know you, he said, cheater at Patience, key-
hole peeper, keeper of nail-clippings and earwax, lusting
after silhouettes on Laburnam's blind, searching for thighs
in the Library of Classical Favourites, Sam Thumb in the
manhole prying up on windy days.

I am not like that at all, he said, as the man with the
birthmark came over to his table and sat down opposite
him.

"I thought you were going," the man said. "You told me
you were going. You've been here an hour now."

"I saw you," Samuel said.

"I know you saw me. You must have seen me, mustn't
you, because you were looking at me," the man said.
"Not that I want the twopence, I've got a houseful of
furniture. Three rooms full to the ceiling. I've got enough
chairs for everyone in Paddington to have a sit down.
Twopence is twopence," he said.

"But it was twopence to the waitress, too."

"She's got sixpence now, hasn't she? She's made four
pence clear. It doesn't do any harm to you just because she
thinks you were trying to nip it off her."

"It was my sixpence."

The man raised his hands. The palms were covered
with calculations in ink. "And they talk about equality.
Does it matter whose sixpence it was? It might have been
mine or anybody's. There was talk of calling the man-
ageress," he said, "but I put my foot down there."

They were both silent for several minutes.

"Made up your mind where you're going when you
move out of here?" the man said at last. "Because move
you must, some time, you know."

"I don't know where I'm going. I haven't any idea in
the world. That's why I came up to London."

"Look here," the man said, controlling his voice, "there's
sense in everything. There's bound to be. Otherwise we
wouldn't be able to carry on, would we? Everybody knows
where he's going, especially if he's come by train. Other-

wise he wouldn't move from where he took the train from, that's elementary."

"People run away."

"Have you run away?"

"No."

"Then don't say it. Don't say it." His voice trembled; he looked at the figures on his palms. Then gently and patiently he began again. "Let's get the first thing straight. People who have come must go. People must know where they're going, otherwise the world could not be conducted on a sane basis. The streets would be full of people just wandering about, wouldn't they? Wandering about and having useless arguments with people who know where they're going. My name is Allingham, I live in Sewell Street off Praed Street, and I'm a furniture dealer. That's simple, isn't it? There's no need to complicate things if you keep your head and know who you are."

"I'm Samuel Bennet. I don't live anywhere at all. I don't do any work, either."

"Where are you going to go, then? I'm not a nosey parker, I told you my business."

"I don't know."

"He doesn't know," Mr. Allingham said. "Don't think you're anywhere now, mind. You can't call this place anywhere, can you? It's breathing space."

"I've been wondering what was going to happen. That's what I've been discussing with myself. I came up really to see what would happen to me. I don't want to make anything happen myself."

"He was discussing it with himself. With a boy of twenty. How old are you?"

"Twenty."

"That's right. Discussing a question like that with a boy just out of his teens. What did you expect to happen?"

"I don't know. Perhaps people would come up and talk to me at the beginning. Women," Samuel said.

"Why should they talk to you? Why should I talk to you? You're not going anywhere. You're not doing anything. You don't exist," he said.

But all Samuel's strength was in his belly and his eyes. He should veil his eyes or the marble-topped counter might melt and all the clothes of the girls behind them peel away and all the cups chip on the shelves.

"Anyone might come up," he said. Then he thought of his fine beginning. "Anyone," he said without hope.

A clerk from the Crescent a dozen doors away; a cold, ordinary woman from Birmingham, driven off by a wink; anybody, anybody; a deacon from the Valleys on a mean blind, with his pocketbook sewn in his combs; an elderly female assistant on holiday from a flannel and calico shop where the change hums on wires. Nobody he had ever wanted.

"Oh, anyone of course. Janet Gaynor," Mr. Allingham said. "Marion Davies and Kay Francis and . . ."

"You don't understand. I don't expect that kind of person. I don't know what I do expect at all, but it isn't that."

"Modest."

"No, I'm not modest either. I don't believe in modesty. It's just that here I am and I don't know where to go. I don't want to know where to go."

Mr. Allingham began to plead, leaning across the table, pulling softly at Samuel's collar, showing the sums on his hands. "Don't say you don't want to know where to go. Please. There's a good boy. We must take things easy, mustn't we? We mustn't complicate things. Take one simple question. Now don't rush it. Take your own time." He gripped a teaspoon with one hand. "Where will you be tonight?"

"I don't know. I'll be somewhere else but it won't be anywhere I've chosen because I'm not going to choose anything."

Mr. Allingham put the knotted teaspoon down.

"What do you want, Samuel?" he whispered.

"I don't know." Samuel touched his breast pocket where his wallet was. "I know I want to find Lucille Harris," he said.

"Who's Lucille Harris?"

Then Mr. Allingham looked at him.

"He doesn't know," he said. "Oh, he doesn't know!"

A man and a woman sat down at the next table.

"But you promised you'd destroy him," the woman said.

"I'll do it, I'll do it," the man said. "Don't you worry. You drink your tea. Don't you worry."

They had lived a long time together, and had grown to resemble one another with their dry, bunched faces and their nibbling mouths. The woman scratched herself as she drank, as she gripped the edge of the cup with her grey lips and shook it.

"Twopence she's got a tail," Samuel said in a low voice, but Mr. Allingham had not noticed them arrive.

"That's right," he said. "You have it your own way. And she's covered all over with fur."

Samuel put his little finger in the neck of the empty bottle.

"I resign myself," Mr. Allingham said.

"But you don't understand, Mr. Allingham."

"I understand enough," he said loudly. The couple at the next table stopped talking. "You don't want to make things happen, don't you? I'll make them happen all right. You can't come in here and talk to me like you've been talking. Lucille Harris. Lucy da monk!"

The man and the woman began whispering. "And it's only half-past one," the woman said. She shook her cup like a rat.

"Come on. We're going." Mr. Allingham scraped back his chair.

"Where to?"

"Never you mind. It's I'm making things happen, isn't it?"

"I can't get my finger out of the bottle," Samuel said.

Mr. Allingham lifted up the suitcases and stood up. "What's a little bottle?" he said. "Bring it with you, son."

"Father and son, too," the woman said as Samuel followed him out.

The bottle hung heavily on his finger.

"Where now?" Outside in the roaring station.

"You follow me. And put your hand in your pocket. It looks silly."

As they walked up the slope to the street, Mr. Allingham said, "I've never been with anybody with a bottle on his finger before. Nobody else has ever had a bottle on his finger. What'd you want to put your finger in the bottle for?"

"I just pushed it in. I'll be able to get it off with soap, there's no need to make a fuss."

"Nobody else has ever had to get a bottle off with soap, that's all I'm saying. This is Praed Street."

"It's dull, isn't it?"

"All the horses have gone away," Mr. Allingham said. "This is my street. This is Sewell Street. It's dull isn't it?"

"It's like the streets at home."

A boy passed them and shouted "Ikey Mo" to Mr. Allingham.

"This is 23. See? There's the sign, 23."

Mr. Allingham opened the front door with a key. "Second floor, first on the right."

He gave three knocks. "Mr. Allingham," he said, and they walked in.

The room was full of furniture.


## II. PLENTY OF FURNITURE


Every inch of the room was covered with furniture. Chairs stood on couches that lay on tables; mirrors nearly the height of the door were propped, back to back, against the walls, reflecting and making endless the hills of desks and chairs with their legs in the air, sideboards, dressing tables, chests-of-drawers, more mirrors, empty bookcases, washbasins, clothes cupboards. There was a double bed, carefully made, with the ends of the sheets turned back, lying on top of a dining table on top of another table; there were electric lamps and lampshades, trays and vases, lavatory bowls and basins, heaped in the armchairs that stood on cupboards and tables and beds, touching the ceiling. The one window, looking out on the road, could just be seen through the curved legs of sideboards on their backs. The walls behind the standing mirrors were thick with pictures and picture frames.

Mr. Allingham climbed into the room over a stack of mattresses, then disappeared.

"Hop in, boy." His voice came up from behind a high kitchen dresser hung with carpets; and, climbing over, Samuel looked down to see him seated on a chair on a couch, leaning back comfortably, his elbow on the shoulder of a statue.

"It's a pity we can't cook here," Mr. Allingham said. "There's plenty of stoves, too. That's a meatsafe," he said, pointing to one corner. "Just under the bedroom suite."

"Have you got a piano?"

"There used to be one," he said. "I think it's in the other room. She put a carpet over it. Can you play?"

"I can vamp. You can tell what tunes I'm doing, easily. Is the other room like this?"

"Two more rooms, but I think the piano's locked. Yes, there's plenty of furniture," Mr. Allingham said, looking round with distaste. "Whenever I say 'That's enough now,' in she comes with her 'Plenty more room, plenty more room.' She'll find she can't get in one day, that's what'll happen. Or she can't get out, I don't know which would be the worst. It gets you sometimes, you know," he said, "all this furniture."

"Is she your wife, Mr. Allingham?"

"She'll find there's a limit to everything. You get to feel kind of trapped."

"Do you sleep here?"

"Up there. It's nearly twelve foot high. I've measured. I can touch the ceiling when I wake up."

"I like this room," Samuel said. "I think it's perhaps the best room I've ever seen."

"That's why I brought you. I thought you'd like it. Proper little den for a man with a bottle on his finger, isn't it? I told you, you're not like anybody else. Nobody else can bear the sight of it. Got your cases safe?"

"They're there. In the bath."

"You keep your eye on them, that's all. I've lost a sofa. One more suite and I'll lose my bed. And what happens when a customer comes? I'll tell you. He takes one peek through the door and off he trots. You can only buy what's on the top at the moment, see."

"Can you get into the other rooms?"

"You can," Mr. Allingham said. "She takes a dive in, head-first. I've lost all interest in the other rooms, myself. You could live and die in there and nobody'd know. There's some nice Chippendale, too. Up by the skylight."

He rested his other elbow on a hallstand.

"I get to feel lost," he said. "That's why I go down to the buffet, there's only tables and chairs there."

Samuel sat on his perch, swinging the bottle and drumming his feet against the side of a bath mounted yards above the floor of mattresses. A carpet behind him, laid out flat and wide along the air, having no visible support, bore a great earthenware jar dangerously upon the backs of its patterned birds. High over his head, in the tall room, a rocking-chair balanced on a card-table, and the table's thin legs rested on the top of a cupboard standing up straight among pillows and fenders, with its mirrored door wide open.

"Aren't you frightened of things falling? Look at that rocking-chair. One little prod and over she comes."

"Don't you dare. Of course I'm frightened," Mr. Allingham said. "If you open a drawer over there, a washstand falls down over here. You've got to be quick as a snake. There's nothing on the top you'd like to buy, is there?"

"I like a lot of the things, but I haven't any money."

"No, no, you wouldn't have money. That's right. Other people have money."

"I like the big jar. You could hide a man in that. Have you got any soap for my finger?"

"Of course, there's no soap, there's only washbasins. You can't have a bath, either, and there's five baths. Why do you want a jar big enough to hide a man in? Nobody I've ever met wants to hide a man in a jar. Everybody else says that jar's too big for anything. Why do you want to find Lucille Harris, Sam?"

"I didn't mean I wanted to hide a man in it. I mean that you could if you wanted to. Oh, a man I know told me about Lucille, Mr. Allingham. I don't know why I want to find her, but that's the only London address I kept. I put the others down the lavatory in the train. When the train was moving."

"Good, good." Mr. Allingham put his hand on the thick, white neck of the naked statue, and tightened his fingers.

The door opened onto the landing. Two people came in, and climbed up the mattresses without a word. The first, a fat short woman with black hair and a Spanish comb, who had painted her face as though it were a wall, took a sudden dive toward the corner behind Samuel and disappeared between two columns of chairs. She must have landed on cushions or a bed, for she made no sound. The second visitor was a tall, youngish man with a fixed smile; his teeth were large, like a horse's, but very white; his glistening fair hair was done in tight curls, and it smelt across the room. He stood on a spring mattress just inside the door, bouncing up and down. "Come on, Rose, don't be sulky," he said. "I know where you've gone." Then, pretending to see Samuel for the first time, "Good gracious, you look like a bird up there," he said. "Is Donald hiding anywhere?"

"I'm not hiding," Mr. Allingham said. "I'm by the statue. Sam Bennet, George Ring."

George Ring bowed and bounced, rising a foot from the mattress.

He and Mr. Allingham could not see each other. Nobody could see the woman with the Spanish comb.

"I hope you've excused the room to Mr. Bennet," George Ring said. He bounced a few steps in the direction of the hidden statue.

"I don't think it needs any excusing, Mr. Ring," Samuel said. "I've never seen such a comfortable room."

"Oh, but it's terrible." George Ring was moving up and down rapidly now. "It's very kind of you to say it's comfortable, but look at the confusion. Just think of living here. You've got something on your finger, did you know that? Three guesses. It's a bottle." He shook his curls and laughed as he bounced.

"You don't know anything yet," said Mr. Allingham's voice. The heavy bouncing had shaken down a carpet on to the hallstand and he was hidden as though in another, lower room. "You don't know anything about him. You wait. What are you bouncing for, George? People don't go bouncing about like a ball as soon as they come into a room."

"What I don't know about you!" In one leap George Ring was standing directly below Samuel, craning up his curls.

"He doesn't know where he's going, for one thing. And he's looking for a girl he doesn't know called Lucille."

"Why are you looking for her?" George Ring's head touched the bath. "Did you see her picture in the paper?"

"No, I don't know anything about her, but I want to see her because she's the only person I know by name in London."

"Now you know two more, don't you? Are you sure you don't love her?"

"Of course I'm sure."

"I thought perhaps she might be a sort of Holy Grail. You know what I mean. A sort of ideal."

"Go on, you big pussycat," Mr. Allingham said. "Get me out of here."

"Is this the first time you've come to London? I felt

like that when I came up first, too. Years and years ago I felt there was something I must find. I can't explain it Something just round the corner. I searched and searched. I was so innocent. I felt like a sort of knight."

"Get me out of here," Mr. Allingham said. "I feel like the whole room's on top of me."

"I never found it." George Ring laughed and sighed and stroked the side of the bath. "Perhaps you'll be lucky," he said. "You'll walk round the corner and there she'll be. Lucille. Lucille. Is she on the telephone?"

"Yes. I've got her number in my book."

"Oh, that makes it easier, doesn't it? Come on, Rose," he said. "I know exactly where you are. She's in a pet."

Samuel rocked softly on his box in the middle of the furniture. This was the fullest room in England. How many hundreds of houses had been split in here, tables and chairs coming in on a wooden flood, chests and cupboards soaring on ropes through the window and settling down like birds. The other rooms, beyond that jostled door, would be taller and darker even than this, with the mute, black shape of the locked piano mountainous under a shroud of carpets and Rose, with her comb like the prow of a ship driving into their darkness and lying all night motionless and silent where she struck. Now she was dead still on a sunk bed between the column of chairs, buried alive, soft and fat and lost in a grave in a house.

"I'm going to buy a hammock," George Ring said. "I can't bear sleeping under all this furniture."

Perhaps the room was crowded at night with people who could not see each other, stretched under chairs, under sofas, dizzily asleep on the tops of raised tables, waking up every morning and crying out, "Earthquake, earthquake!"

"And then I'll go to bed like a sailor."

"Tell Rose to come and get me out of here," Mr. Allingham said, behind the cloaked hallstand, "I want to eat."

"She's sulking, Donald. She's mad about a Japanese screen now."

"Do you hear that, Sam? Isn't there enough privacy in this room? Anybody can do anything, nobody can see you. I want to eat. I want to have a snack at Dacey's. Are you sleeping here tonight?"

"Who?" Samuel asked. "Me?"

"You can doss down in one of the other rooms, if you

think you can get up again. There's enough beds for a harem."

"Harem," George Ring said, pronouncing it another way. "You've got company, Rose darling. Do come out and be introduced."

"Thank you, Mr. Allingham," Samuel said.

"Didn't you really have any idea at all?" George Ring bounced, and for a moment his scented head was level with Samuel's. One wide, bright, horse-toothed smile, and the head was gone. "About sleeping and things. I think it's awfully brave. You might have fallen in with all kinds of people. 'He fell among thieves.' Do you know Sir Henry Newbolt's poem?"

"He flung his empty revolver down the slope," Samuel said.

The day was moving carelessly on to a promised end and in a dark room full of furniture where he'd lie down with his bunch of wives in a crow's-nest bed or rock them in a hammock under the ceiling.

"Goodie goodie! It's so exciting to find someone who knows about poetry. 'The voices faded and the hills slept.' Isn't that beautiful? The voices faded . . . ? I can read poetry for hours, can't I, Donald? I don't care what kind of poetry it is, I love it all. Do you know, 'Is there anybody there, said the traveller?' Where do you put the emphasis, Mr. Bennet? Can I call you Sam? Do you say, 'Is there *anybody* there' or 'Is there anybody *there*?'"

"It isn't natural," Mr. Allingham said, "for a man not to be able to see anybody when he's sitting right next to them. I'm not grumbling, but I can't see anything, that's all. It's like not being in the room."

"Oh, do be quiet, Donald. Sam and I are having a perfectly serious discussion. Of course you're in the room, don't be morbid."

"I think I'd put about the same emphasis on all the words," Samuel said.

"But don't you find it tends to make the line rather flat? '*Is* there anybody there, said the traveller,'" George Ring murmured, pacing the mattresses, his head on one side. "I feel you do want a stress somewhere."

Will I be alone tonight in the room with the piano, Samuel wondered. Alone like a man in a warehouse, lying on each bed in turn, opening cupboards and putting my hand in, looking at myself in mirrors in the dark.

"Don't call me morbid, George Ring," Mr. Allingham said. He tried to move, but the statue fell against his chair. "I remember once I drank forty-nine Guinnesses straight off and I came home on top of a bus. There's nothing morbid about a man who can do that. Right on the top of the bus, too, not just in the upper deck."

Or will the room be full as a cemetery, but with the invisible dead breathing and snoring all around me, making love in the cupboards, drunk as tailors in the dry baths? Suddenly a warm body might dive in through the door and lie in my bed all night without a name or a word.

"I think forty-nine Guinnesses is piggish," said George Ring.

"It was raining," Mr. Allingham said, "and I never get truculent. I may sing and I may have a bit of a dance, but I never get nasty. Give me a hand, Sam."

Samuel took the carpet off the hallstand and pushed the statue away. It had fallen between Mr. Allingham's legs. He came up slowly into sight and rubbed his eyes like a man waking.

"I told you," he said, "you get trapped. Coming to Dacey's, George?"

"I'll have to stay for hours, you know that," George Ring said. "You know I'm the only person who can humor Rosie when she's in one of her states. Oh, come on Rosie, don't be temperamental. It's ninety per cent temper and ten per cent mental. Just because you're an actress you think you can stay under the furniture all the afternoon. I'll count five . . ."

Samuel followed Mr. Allingham to the door.

"Five, six, seven," George Ring said, as Mr. Allingham slammed the door hard, and his voice was lost in the noise of furniture falling. They went down the stairs into the hallway that smelt of cabbage, and out onto the grey street.

"I think it must have been the rocking-chair," Samuel said.

"Mrs. Dacey's is just round the corner," Mr. Allingham said. "There you are. See the Cadbury sign?"

## 2

Mrs. Dacey's front window was whitewashed from inside, and the words "High Class" had been scrawled across it. " 'Susan Dacey, licensed to sell tobacco,' " Samuel read aloud. "Is it a restaurant too?"

"You must tell her that," Mr. Allingham said, opening the door. A bell rang. "It hasn't been called that before." He held his foot against the door so that the bell kept ringing. "She's a woman in a thousand."

A tall, thin, dignified woman came through the private door at the back of the shop, her hands clasped in front of her. She was dressed in black almost down to the ankles, with a severe white collar, and she held her head primly as though it might spill. God help the other nine hundred and ninety-nine. But she smiled then, and her eyes were sharp and light; the dullness raced from her mouth, leaving it cruel and happy.

"Take your trotter off the door," she said.

The bell stopped.

"That's better. You made enough noise to wake the dead." She was a well-spoken woman, clear and precise, like a schoolmistress.

"Keeping well, Mrs. Dacey? This is a new friend, Sam Bennet. Two pies and two coffees, please. Where's Polly?"

"Up to no good," said Mrs. Dacey, stepping behind the counter. Her grand dress floated around her. "You're from the country," she said, over her shoulder, as she turned the coffee tap on the brass urn. "How did you find Ikey Mo?"

"That's me." Mr. Allingham blushed on one side of his face.

"I'm not from the country really." Samuel told her where he came from. "I met Mr. Allingham in the station. I'm going to sleep in his flat tonight."

"I'd sooner sleep in an ashpit," she said.

The coffee was thick and white and tasteless. They took their cups to a cubicle and Samuel brushed off the crumbs from his chair with his sleeve. His hat was gone. There were small pellets of dirt in the dust at his feet.

"You've got a bottle on your finger," she said.

"There, you see, everybody notices. Why don't you take it off, Sam? It isn't a decoration, it isn't useful, it's just a bottle."

"I think my finger must have swollen, Mr. Allingham. The bottle's much tighter now."

"Let me have a look at you again." Mrs. Dacey put on a pair of spectacles with steel rims and a hanging chain. "He's only a baby."

"I'm twenty."

"Ikey Mo, the baby farmer." She walked carefully to the back of the shop and called, "Polly, come down here. Polly. Polly."

A girl's voice called back from high up the house, "What for, ma?"

"Come and get a gentleman's bottle off."

"It sounds like a Russian composer, doesn't it, darling?" George Ring said, at the door. "What a marvelous dress, you look like a murderess."

He sat down next to Samuel.

"I couldn't get Rose to move. She's going to lie there all day in a tantrum. Do tell me what's happening, everybody."

"It's that bottle again," Mr. Allingham said, "Why didn't he put his finger in a glass or something? I don't know what he was poking his finger about for in the first place. It's an enigma to me."

"Everything's an enigma to you. You can't understand the slightest touch of originality. I think it must be awful not to have any imagination. It's like a sense of humour."

"I'm just saying that not to be able to go in and buy a bottle of Bass without having to leave with the bottle on your finger seems to me like a kind of nightmare. That's all I'm saying."

Samuel heard Mrs. Dacey's daughter running downstairs. Then he saw her hand on the edge of the door. In the second she took to push the door open and come in, he made her a hundred faces; he made her talk and walk in all the disguises of his loves at night; he gave her golden hair, black hair, he knew that she would be gypsy-skinned and white as milk. Polly come and put the kettle on with your white, slender, brown broad hands, and see me waiting like a grenadier or a caliph in the mousey cubicle.

"It's like one of those nightmares when you're playing billiards and the cue's made of elastic," Mr. Allingham said.

In came a girl with a long, pale face and glasses. Her hair was not any of Samuel's colours but only dark and dull.

"Go and help to pull his bottle off," said Mrs. Dacey.

Polly sat down on the table and took his hand. "Does it hurt? I've never done it before." She pulled at his finger.

"I hope you won't ever have to do it again, either," Mr. Allingham said. "I don't care if I haven't got any imagination. I'm glad I'm like I am without anything on my finger."

Polly bent over Samuel's hand and he saw down her dress. She knew that he was looking, but she did not start back or spread her hand across the neck of her dress; she raised her head and stared at his eyes. I shall always remember this, he said to himself. In 1933 a girl was pulling at a bottle on the little finger of my left hand while I looked down her dress. It will last longer than all my poems and troubles.

"I can't get it off," she said.

"Take him up to the bathroom then and put some soap on it," said Mrs. Dacey, in her dry, neat voice. "And mind it's only his bottle."

George Ring said as they got up to go, "Scream if you want me, I'll be up in a wink. She's the most terrible person, aren't you, darling? You wouldn't catch little George going up there all alone."

Polly led the way upstairs.

"I'm not complaining," Mr. Allingham said, "I'm just making a statement. I'm not saying it isn't all as it should be. He's got a bottle on his finger and I've got a tooth in my pie."

His voice faded.

### 3

Someone had drawn the ragged curtains in the bathroom to shut out the damp old day, and the bath was half full of water with a rubber duck floating on it. As Polly closed and locked the door birds began to sing.

"It's only the birds," she said. She put the key down her dress. "You needn't be frightened."

Two cages hung from the ceiling.

But Samuel had looked frightened when she turned the key and put it away where he never wanted to find it, not when the room grew suddenly like a wood in the tangled shadows of the green curtains.

"It's a funny place to have birds," he said.

"They're mine." Polly let the hot water run and the birds sang more loudly as though they heard a waterfall. "Mr. Allingham comes here for a bath on Wednesdays and he says they sneer at him and blow little raspberries all the time he's washing. But I don't think he washes very much. Doesn't Mr. Allingham make you laugh too?"

He expected her to be smiling when she turned to him, but her face was still and grave, and all at once he saw that she was prettier than any of the girls he made up in his mind before she opened the door downstairs. He distrusted her prettiness because of the key. He remembered what Mrs. Dacey had said when Mr. Allingham asked where Polly was. "Up to no good." He did not think she was going to put her arms around him. That would have been different. If she tried to put his head under the water he'd shout for George Ring and up he'd come like a horse, neighing and smelling of scent.

"I only locked the door because I don't want George Ring to come in. He's queer. He puts scent all over his underclothes; did you know that? The Passing Cloud, that's what we call him. The Passing Cloud."

"You didn't have to put the key where you put it, though," Samuel said. "I might push you down and fish for it, I might be that sort."

"I don't care."

If only she would have smiled at him when she said that. But she looked as though she really did not care whether he pushed her down or whether he sat on the edge of the bath and touched the duck with his bottle.

The duck floated in circles on the used, greasy water.

"What's your name?"

"Sam."

"Mine's Mary. But they call me Polly for short."

"It isn't much shorter, is it?"

"No, it's exactly the same length."

She sat by his side on the edge of the bath. He could not think of anything to say. Here was the locked door he had often made up in stories and in his head, in bed in Mortimer Street, and the warm, hidden key, and the girl who was willing for anything. The bathroom should be a bedroom and she should not be wearing glasses.

"Will you take off your glasses, Polly?"

"If you like. But I won't be able to see very far."

"You don't have to see very far, it's only a little room," he said. "Can you see me?"

"Of course I can. You're right next to me. Do you like me better now?"

"You're very pretty, I suppose, Polly."

"Pretty Polly," she said, without a smile.

Well, he said to himself, here you are, here she is without any glasses on.

"Nothing ever happens in Sewell Street." She took his hand and let his finger with the bottle on it lie in her lap.

Here you are, he said, with your hand in her lap.

"Nothing ever happens where I come from, either. I think things must be happening everywhere except where one is. All kinds of things happen to other people. So they say," he said.

"The man who was lodging next door but one cut his throat like this," she said, "before breakfast."

On his first free day since he was born Samuel sat with a loose girl in a locked bathroom over a teashop, the dirty curtains were drawn, and his hand lay on her thighs. He did not feel any emotion at all. O God, he thought, make me feel something, make me feel as I ought to, here is something happening and I'm cool and dull as a man in a bus. Make me remember all the stories. I caught her in my arms, my heart beat against hers, her body was trembling, her mouth opened like a flower. The lotus of Osiris was opening to the sun.

"Listen to the old birds," she said, and he saw that the hot water was running over the rim of the washbasin.

I must be impotent, he thought.

"Why did he cut his throat like that, Polly? Was it love? I think if I was crossed in love I'd drink brandy and whisky and crème de menthe and that stuff that's made with eggs."

"It wasn't love with Mr. Shaw. I don't know why he did it. Mrs. Bentley said there was blood everywhere, everywhere, and all over the clock. He left a little note in the letter rack and all it said was that he'd been meaning to do it ever since October. Look the water'll drip right through into the kitchen."

He turned it off. The birds stopped singing.

"Perhaps it was love, really. Perhaps he loved you, Polly, but he wouldn't say so. From a distance."

"Go on, he had a limp," she said. "Old Dot and Carry. How old are you?"

"Twenty."

"No you're not."

"Well, nearly."

"No you're not."

Then they were silent, sitting on the bath, his hand in her lap. She trailed her pale hand in the water. The birds began again.

"Pale hands I love," he said.

"Beside the Shalimar. Do you, Sam? Do you love my hands? That's a funny thing to say." She looked dully at the long, floating weed in the water and made a wave. "It's like the evening here."

"It's like evening in the country," he said. "Birds singing and water. We're sitting on a bank by the river now."

"Having a picnic."

"And then we're going to take our clothes off and have a swim. Gee, it'll be cold. You'll be able to feel all the fish swimming about."

"I can hear the 47 bus, too," she said. "People are going home to tea. It's cold without any clothes on, isn't it? Feel my arm, it's like snow, only not so white. Pale hands I love," she began to sing. "Do you love me altogether?"

"I don't know. I don't think I feel anything like that at all. I never do feel much until afterwards and then it's too late."

"Now it isn't too late. It isn't too late Sam. We're alone. Polly and Sam. I'll come and have a swim with you if you like. In the dirty old river with the duck."

"Don't you ever smile, Polly? I haven't seen you smile once."

"You've only known me for twenty minutes. I don't like smiling much, I think I look best when I'm very serious, like this." She saddened her eyes and mouth. "I'm a tragedienne. I'm crying because my lover's dead."

Slowly tears came to her eyes.

"His name was Sam and he had green eyes and brown hair. He was ever so short. Darling, darling, darling Sam, he's dead." The tears ran down her cheeks.

"Stop crying now, Polly. Please. Stop crying. You'll hurt yourself."

But she was crying pitifully.

"Stop it, Polly, pretty Polly." He put his arm round her shoulders. He kissed her on the cheek. It was warm and wet. "Nobody's dead, Polly darling," he said. She cried and moaned his name in the abandon of her made grief, tore at the loose low neck of her dress, threw back her hair and raised her damp eyes to the birds in their cages and the cracked heavens of the ceiling.

"You're doing it fine," he said in despair, shaking her shoulders. "I've never seen such fine crying. Stop now, please, Polly, please, while you can stop."

Ninety-eight per cent of the human body is water, he thought. Polly Dacey is all salt water. She sat by his side like a flood in an apron.

"I'll do anything you like if you'll only stop," he said. "You'll drown yourself, Polly. I'll promise to do anything in the world."

She dried her eyes on her bare arm.

"I wasn't really breaking my heart, silly. I was only depicting. What'll you do, then? Anything? I can depict being glad because my lover's not really dead, too. The War Office made a mistake."

"Anything," he said. "I want to see you being glad tomorrow. You mustn't do one after the other."

"It's nothing to me, I can do them all in a row. I can do childbirth and being tight and—"

"You do being quiet. Do being a quiet lady sitting on a bath, Polly."

"I will if you'll come and have a swim with me. You promised." She patted her hair into place.

"Where."

"In the bath. You get in first, go on. You can't break your promise."

George Ring, he whispered, gallop upstairs now and bite your way through the door. She wants me to sit with my overcoat on and my bottle on my finger in the cold, greasy bath, in the half-dark bathroom, under the sneering birds.

"I've got a new suit," he said.

"Take it off, silly. I don't want you to go in the bath with your clothes on. Look, I'll put something over the window so you can undress in the dark. Then I'll undress too. I'll come in the bath with you. Sam, are you frightened?"

"I don't know. Couldn't we take our clothes off and not go in the bath? I mean, if we want to take them off at all. Someone might come in, it's terribly cold, Polly. Terribly cold."

"You're frightened. You're frightened to lie in the water with me. You won't be cold for long."

"But there's no sense in it. I don't want to go in the bath. Let's sit here and you do being glad, Polly."

He could not move his hand, she had caught the bottle between her legs.

"You don't want to be frightened. I'm not any older than you are," she said, and her whispering mouth was close to his ear. "As soon as you get in the bath I'll jump on top of you in the dark. You can pretend I'm somebody you love if you don't like me properly. You can call me any name." She dug her nails into his hand. "Give me your coat, I'll hang it over the window. Dark as midnight," she said, as she hung the coat up, and her face in the green light through the curtains was like a girl's under the sea. Then all the green went out, and he heard her fumbling. I do not want to drown. I do not want to drown in Sewell Street off Circe Street, he whispered under his breath.

"Are you undressing? I can't hear you. Quick, quick, Sam."

He took off his jacket and pulled his shirt over his head. Take a good look in the dark, Mortimer Street, have a peek at me in London.

"I'm cold," he said.

"I'll make you warm, beautifully warm, Sam." He could not tell where she was, but she was moving in the dark and clinking a glass. "I'm going to give you some brandy. There's brandy, darling, in the medicine cupboard. I'll give you a big glass. You must drink it right down."

Naked, he slipped one leg over the edge of the bath and touched the icy water.

Come and have a look at impotent Samuel Bennet from Mortimer Street off Stanley's Grove trembling to death in a cold bath in the dark near Paddington Station. I am lost in the metropolis with a rubber duck and a girl I cannot see pouring brandy into a tooth-glass. The birds are going mad in the dark. It's been such a short day for them, Polly.

"I'm in the bath now."

"I'm undressing too. Can you hear me?" she said softly. "That's my dress rustling. Now I'm taking my petticoat off. Now I'm naked." A cold hand touched him on the face. "Here's the brandy, Sam. Sam, my dear, drink it up and then I'll climb in with you. I'll love you, Sam. I'll love you up. Drink it all up then you can touch me."

He felt the glass in his hand and he lifted it up and drank all that was in it.

"Christ!" he said in a clear, ordinary voice. "Christ!"

Then the birds flew down and kicked him on the head, carefully between the eyes, brutally on each temple, and he fell back in the bath.

That was all the birds singing under the water, and the sea was full of feathers that swam up his nostrils and into his mouth. A duck as big as a ship sailed up on a drop of water as big as a house and smelt his breath as it spurted out from broken, bleeding lips, like flames and water-spouts. Here came a wave of brandy and birds, and Mr. Allingham, naked as a baby, riding on the top with his birthmark like a rainbow, and George Ring swimming breaststroke through the open door, and three Mrs. Daceys gliding in yards above the flowing ground.

The darkness drowned in a bright ball of light, and the birds stopped.

4

Voices began to reach him from a great distance, travelling in lavatories in racing trains along a liquid track, diving from the immeasurably high ceiling into the cold sea in the enormous bath.

"Do you see what I see?" That was the voice of the man called Allingham, who slept under the furniture. "He's taking a little dip."

"Don't let me look, Donald, he's bare all over." I know him, Samuel thought. That's George Ring the horse. "And he's ill too. Silly Sam."

"Lucky Sam. He's drunk, George. Well, well, well, and he hasn't even got his bottle off. Where's Polly?"

"You look over there," Mrs. Dacey said. "Over there on the shelf. He's drunk all the eau de cologne."

"He must have been thirsty."

Large, bodiless hands came over the bath and lifted him out.

"He's eccentric," Mr. Allingham said, as they laid him on the floor, "that's all I'm saying. I'm not preaching, I'm not condemning. I'm just saying that other people get drunk in the proper places."

The birds were singing again in the electric dawn as Samuel fell quietly to sleep.

He sank into the ragged green water for the second time and, rising naked with seaweed and a woman under each arm and a mouthful of broken shells, he saw the whole of his dead life standing trembling before him, indestructible and unsinkable, on the brandy-brown waves. It looked like a hallstand.

He opened his mouth to speak, but a warm wave rushed in.

"Tea," said Mrs. Dacey. "Tea with plenty of sugar every five minutes. That's what I always gave him and it didn't do a bit of good."

"Not too much worcester, George, don't bury the egg."

"I won't," Samuel said.

"Oh, listen to the birds. It's been such a short night for the birds, Polly."

"Listen to the birds," he said clearly, and a burning drink drowned his tongue.

"They've laid an egg," Mr. Allingham said.

"Try some Coca Cola, Donald. It can't do any harm, he's had tea and a prairie oyster and angostura and Oxo and everything."

"I used to pour the tea down by the pint," Mrs. Dacey said affectionately, "and it came up, lump sugar and all."

"He doesn't want a Coca Cola. Give him a drop of your hair oil. I knew a man who used to squeeze boot-blacking through a veil."

"You know everybody piggish. He's trying to sit up, the poor darling."

Samuel wrestled into the dry world and looked around a room in it, at Mrs. Dacey, now miraculously divided into one long woman, folding her black silk arms in the doorway, at George Ring arching his smile and hair toward the rusty taps, at Mr. Allingham resigned above him.

"Polly's gone," he said.

It was then that he understood why the three persons in the bathroom were so tall and far. I am on the floor, looking up, he said to himself. But the others were listening.

44

"You're naked too," Mr. Allingham said, "under the blanket."

"Here's a nice wet sponge." George Ring dabbed and smoothed. "Keep it on your forehead. There, like that. That better?"

"Eau de cologne is for outside the body," said Mrs. Dacey without disapproval, "and I'll give our Polly such a clip. I'll clip her on the earhole every time she opens her mouth."

Mr. Allingham nodded. "Whisky I can understand," he said. "But eau de cologne! You put that on handkerchieves. You don't put whisky on handkerchieves." He looked down at Samuel. "I don't."

"No, mustn't suck the sponge, Sam."

"I suppose he thinks red biddy's like bread and milk," Mr. Allingham said.

They gathered his clothes from the side of the bath and hurriedly dressed him. And not until he was dressed and upright, shivering along the landing to the dark stairs, did he try to speak again. George Ring and Mr. Allingham held his arms and guided him toward the top of that winding grave. Mrs. Dacey, the one mourner, followed with a rustle of silk.

"It was the brandy from the medicine cupboard," he said, and down they went into the coarse, earthlike silence of the stairs.

"Give me furniture polish," Mr. Allingham said. "Crack. Mind your head. Especially when I'm out of sorts in the bath."

The darkness was settling like more dirt and dust over the silent shop. Someone had hung up a sign, "Closed," on the inside of the window, not facing the street. "Meths is finicky," Mr. Allingham said.

They sat Samuel down on a chair behind the counter and he heard Mrs. Dacey, still on the stairs, calling for Polly up into the dark, dirty other floors and caves of the drunken house. But Polly did not answer.

She would be in her locked bedroom now, crying for Sam gone, at her window staring out onto the colourless, slowly disappearing street and the tall houses down at heel; or depicting, in the kitchen, the agony of a woman in childbirth, writhing and howling round the crowded sink; or being glad at a damp corner of the landing.

"Silly goose," said George Ring, sitting long-legged on

the table and smiling at Samuel with a ferocious coyness. "You might have been drowned. Drownded," he said again, looking slyly up from under the spider line of his eyebrows.

"Lucky you left the door open," Mr. Allingham said. He lit a cigarette and looked at the match until it burned his finger. "I suppose," he said, his finger in his mouth.

"Our maid at home always said 'drownded,'" said George Ring.

"But I saw Polly lock the door. She put the key down her dress." Samuel spoke with difficulty from behind the uncertain counter. The words came out in a rush, then reversed and were lost, tumbling among the sour bushes under his tongue. "She put it down her dress," he said, and paused at the end of each word to untie the next. Now the shop was almost entirely dark.

"And chimbley. You know, for chimney. Well, my dear, the door was open when we went up. No key, no Polly."

"Just a boy in the bath," Mr. Allingham said. "Do you often get like that, Sam? The water was up to your chin."

"And the dirt!"

"It wasn't my dirt. Someone had been in the bath before. It was cold," Samuel said.

"Yes, yes." Samuel could see Mr. Allingham's head nodding. "That alters the situation, doesn't it? Dear God," he said, "you should have gone in with your clothes on like everybody else."

"Polly's gone," said Mrs. Dacey. She appeared out of nowhere in the wall and stood behind the counter at Samuel's side. Her rustling dress brushed against his hands, and he drew them sharply back. I touched a funeral, he said to the dazed boy in his chair. Her corpse-cold hand fell against his cheek, chilling him out of a moment's sleep. The coffin has walked upright into my sitting bed.

"Oooh," he said aloud.

"Still cold, baby?" Mrs. Dacey bent down, creaking like a door, and mothered him about the hair and mouth.

There had been little light all day, even at dawn and noon, mostly the close, false light of bedroom and restaurant. All day he had sat in small, dark places, bathroom and travelling lavatory, a jungle of furniture, a stuffed shop where no one called except these voices saying:

"You looked so defenseless, Sam, lying there all cold and white."

"Where was Moses when the light went out, Mrs. Dacey?"

"Like one of those cherubs in the Italian Primitives, only with a bottle on your finger, of course."

"In the dark. Like this."

"What did our Polly do to you, the little tart?" Mrs. Dacey said in her tidy, lady's voice.

Mr. Allingham stood up. "I'm not listening. Don't you say a word, Sam, even if you could. No explanations. There he was, gassed in the bath, at half-past four in the afternoon. I can stand so much."

"I want to go out," Samuel said.

"Out the back?"

"Out."

Out of the blind, stripping hole in a wall, aviary and menagerie, cold water shop, into the streets without locks. I don't want to sleep with Polly in a drawer. I don't want to lie in a cellar with a wet woman, drinking polish. London is happening everywhere, let me out, let me go. Mrs. Dacey is all cold fingers.

"Out then. It's six o'clock. Can you walk son?"

"I can walk okay, it's my head."

Mrs. Dacey, unseen, stroked his hair. Nobody can see, he said silently, but Mrs. Susan Dacey, licensed to sell tobacco, is stroking my hair with her lizards; and he gave a cry.

"I've got no sympathy," said Mr. Allingham. "Are you coming, Sue?"

"Depends where you're going."

"Taking the air down the Edgware Road. He's got to see around, hasn't he? You don't come up from the provinces to drink eau de cologne in the bath."

They all went out, and Mrs. Dacey locked the shop.

It was raining heavily.

2

"Fun!" George Ring said.

They walked out of Sewell Street into Praed Street arm-in-arm.

"I'm a fool for the rain." He shook his clinging curls and danced a few steps on the pavement.

"My new brown overcoat's in the bathroom," Samuel said, and Mrs. Dacey covered him with her umbrella.

"Go on, you're not the sort that puts a coat on in the rain, are you? Stop dancing, George."

But George Ring danced down the pavement in the flying rain and pulled the others with him; unwillingly they broke into a dancing run under the lampposts' drizzle of light, Mrs. Dacey, black as a deacon, jumping high over the puddles with a rustle and creak, Mr. Allingham, on the outside, stamping and dodging along the gutter, Samuel gliding light and dizzy with his feet hardly touching the ground.

"Look out. People," cried Mr. Allingham, and dragged them, still dancing, out onto the slippery street. Caught in a circle of headlights and chased by horns they stamped and scampered onto the pavement again, clinging fast to each other, their faces glistening, cold and wet.

"Where's the fire, George? Go easy, boy, go easy." But Mr. Allingham, one foot in the gutter, was hopping along like a rabbit and tugging at George Ring's arm to make him dance faster. "It's all Sam's fault," he said as he hopped, and his voice was high and loud like a boy's in the rain.

Look at London flying by me, buses and glowworms, umbrellas and lampposts, cigarettes and eyes under the watery doorways, I am dancing with three strangers down Edgware Road in the rain, cried Samuel to the gliding boy around him. Light and without will as a suit of feathers, he held onto their arms, and the umbrella rode above them like a bird.

Cold and unsmiling, Mrs. Dacey skipped by his side, seeing nothing through her misted glasses.

And George Ring sang as he bounced, with his drenched hair rising and falling in level waves, "Here we go gathering nuts and may, Donald and Mrs. Dacey and George and Sam."

When they stopped, outside the Antelope, Mr. Allingham leaned against the wall and coughed until he cried. All the time he coughed he never removed his cigarette.

"I haven't run for forty years," he said, his shoulders shaking, and his handkerchief like a flag to his mouth. He led them into the Saloon Bar where three young women sat with their shoes off in front of the electric log fire.

"Three whiskies. What's yours, Sam? Nice drop of Kiwi?"

"He'll have whisky, too," Mrs. Dacey said. "See, he's got his color back."

"Kiwi's bootpolish," one of the young women whispered, and she bent, giggling, over the grate. Her big toe came out of a hole in her stocking, suddenly, like a cold inquisitive nose, and she giggled again.

This was a bar in London. Dear Peggy, Samuel wrote with his finger on the counter, I am drinking in a bar called the Antelope in Edgware Road with a furniture dealer, the proprietoress of a tea-shop, three young women and George Ring. I have put these facts down clearly because the scent I drank in the bath is still troublesome and people will not keep still. I am quite well but I do not know for how long.

"What're you doing, Sam? Looks like you're drawing. I've got a proper graveyard in my chest, haven't I? Cough, cough," Mr. Allingham said, angrily between each cough.

"It wasn't that cough that carried him off," the young woman said. Her whole plump body was giggling.

Everything is very trivial, Samuel wrote. Mr. Allingham is drunk on one whisky. All his face goes pale except his mark.

"Here we are," Mr. Allingham said, "four lost souls. What a place to put a man in."

"The Antelope's charming," said George Ring. "There's some real hunting prints in the private bar." He smiled at Sam and moved his long, blunt fingers rapidly along the counter as though he were playing a piano. "I'm all rhythm. It's like a kind of current in me."

"I mean the world. This is only a little tiny bit in it. This is all right, it's got regular hours; you can draw the curtains, you know what to expect here. But look at the world. You and your currents," Mr. Allingham said.

"No, really it's rippling out of me." George Ring tap-danced with one foot and made a rhythmical, kissing noise with his tongue against the roof of his mouth.

"What a place to drop a man in. In the middle of streets and houses and traffic and people."

The young woman wagged her finger at her toe. "You be still." Her friends were giggling now, covering their faces and peeping out at Mr. Allingham between their fingers, telling each other to go on, saying "hotcha" and "hi de ho" and "Minnie the Moocher's Wedding Day" as George Ring tapped one narrow, yellow buckskin shoe and strummed on the counter. They rolled their eyes and said, "Swing it, sister," then hissed again into a giggle.

"I've been nibbling away for fifty years now," Mr. Allingham said, "and look at me. Look at me." He took off his hat.

"There's hair," whispered the young woman with the hole in her stocking.

His hair was the color of ferrets and thin on the crown; it stopped growing at the temples but came out again from the ears. His hat had made a deep, white wrinkle on his forehead.

"Here we are nibbling away all day and night, Mrs. Dacey. Nibble nibble." His brown teeth came over his lip. "No sense, no order, no nothing, we're all mad and nasty. Look at Sam there. There's a nice harmless boy, curly hair and big eyes and all. What's he do? Look at his bloody bottle."

"No language," said the woman behind the bar. She looked like a duchess, riding, rising and sinking slowly as she spoke, as though to the movements of a horse.

"Tantivy," Samuel said, and blushed as Mr. Allingham pointed a stained finger.

"That's right. Always the right word in the right place. Tantivy! I told you, people are all mad in the world. They don't know where they're going, they don't know why they're where they are, all they want is love and beer and sleep."

"I wouldn't say no to the first," said Mrs. Dacey. "Don't pay any attention to him," she said to the woman behind the counter, "he's a philosopher."

"Calling everybody nasty," said the woman, rising. "There's people live in glass houses." Over the hurdle she goes, thought Samuel idly, and she sank again onto the hidden saddle. She must do miles in a night, he said to his empty glass.

"People think about all kinds of other things." George Ring looked at the ceiling for a vision. "Music," he said, "and dancing." He ran his fingers along the air and danced on his toes.

"Sex," said Mr. Allingham.

"Sex, sex, sex, it's always sex with you, Donald. You must be repressed or something."

"Sex," whispered the young woman by the fire.

"Sex is all right," Mrs. Dacey said. "You leave sex alone."

"Of course I'm repressed. I've been repressed for fifty years."

"You leave sex out of it." The woman behind the counter rose in a gallop. "And religion," she said.

Over she goes, clean as a whistle, over the hedge and the waterjump.

Samuel took a pound out of his wallet and pointed to the whisky on the shelf. He could not trust himself yet to speak to the riding woman with the stuffed, enormous bosom and two long milk-white loaves for arms. His throat was still on fire; the heat of the room blazed up his nostrils into his head, and all the words at the tip of his tongue caught like petrol and gorse; he saw three young women flickering by the metal logs, and his three new friends thundered and gestured before him with the terrible exaggeration of people of flesh and blood moving like dramatic prisoners on a screen, doomed forever to enact their pettiness in a magnified exhibition.

He said to himself: Mrs. Antelope, pouring the whisky as though it were four insults, believes that sex is a bed. The act of love is an act of the bed itself; the springs cry "Tumble" and over she goes, horse and all. I can see her lying like a log on a bed, listening with hate and disgust to the masterly voice of the dented sheets.

He felt old and all-knowing and unsteady. His immediate wisdom weighed so heavily that he clutched at the edge of the counter and raised one arm, like a man trapped in the sea, to signal his sinking.

"You may," Mrs. Dacey said, and the room giggled like a girl.

Now I know, thought Samuel beneath his load, as he struggled to the surface, what is meant by a pillar of the church. Long, cold Mrs. Dacey could prop Bethesda on the remote top of her carved head and freeze with her eyes the beetle-black sinners where they scraped below her. Her joke boomed in the roof.

"You've dropped a fiver, Sam." Mr. Allingham picked up a piece of paper and held it out on the sun-stained palm of his hand.

"It's Lucille Harris's address," Samuel said.

"Why don't you give her a ring? The phone's on the

stairs, up there." George Ring pointed. "Outside the Ladies."

Samuel parted a curtain and mounted.

"*Outside* the Ladies," a voice said from the sinking room.

He read the instructions above the telephone, put in two pennies, dialed, and said, "Miss Harris? I'm a friend of Austin's.

"I am a friend of nobody's. I am detached," he whispered into the buzzing receiver. "I am Lopo the outlaw, loping through the night, companion of owls and murderers. Tu wit tu woo," he said aloud into the mouthpiece.

She did not answer, and he shuffled down the stairs, swung open the curtain, and entered the bright bar with a loping stride.

The three young women had gone. He looked at the grate to see if their shoes were still there, but they had gone too. People leave nothing.

"She must have been out," he said.

"We heard," said Mr. Allingham. "We heard you talking to her owl." He raised his glass and stared at it, standing sadly and savagely in the middle of the room like a man with oblivion in his hand. Then he made his choice, and drank.

"We're going places," he said. "We're taking a taxi and Sam is going to pay for it. We're going to the West End to look for Lucille."

"I knew she was a kind of Holy Grail," George Ring said when they were all in the darkness of the taxi rattling through the rain.

Samuel felt Mrs. Dacey's hand on his knee.

"Four knights at arms, it's terribly exciting. We'll call at the Gayspot first, then the Cheerioh, then the Neptune."

"Four lost souls."

The hand ached on along the thigh, five dry fishes dying on a cloth.

"Marble Arch," Mr. Allingham said. "This is where the fairies come out in the moon."

And the hurrying crowd in the rain might have had no flesh or blood.

"Park Lane."

The crowd slid past the bonnet and the windows, mixed their faces with no features and their liquid bodies under a sudden blaze, or vanished into the streaming light of a tall door that led into the bowels of rich night London

"No vest," he said in surprise, but the girl had turned away.

"It's a Sunday School," Mr. Allingham said. "Tasted your wine yet, Sam? This horse's unfit to work. A regular little bun dance. You could bring the vicar's wife in here."

Mrs. Cotmore-Richards, four foot one and a squeak in her stockinged trotters.

"A regular little vestry," Mr. Allingham said. "See that woman dancing? The one who fell in the flour bin. She's a bank manager's niece."

The woman with the dead white face smiled as she passed them in the arms of a padded boy.

"Hullo, Ikey."

"Hullo, Lola. She's pretendin', see. Thinks she's Starr Faithfull."

"Is she a prostitute, Mr. Allingham?"

"She's a manicurist, Sammy. How's your cuticles? Don't you believe everything you see, especially after it's dark. This is all pretending. Look at Casanova there with the old girls. The last time he touched a woman he had a dummy in his mouth."

Samuel turned around. George Ring whinnied in a corner with several women. Their voices shrilled and rasped through the cross noise of the drums.

"Lucy got a beating the last time I see her," said a woman with false teeth and a bald fur. "He said he was a chemist."

"Lucille," George Ring said, impatiently shaking his curls. "Lucille Harris."

"With a clothesbrush. He had it in a little bag."

"There's a chemist," said a woman wearing a picture hat.

"He doesn't mean Lucy Wakefield," another woman said.

"Lucy Wakefield's in the Feathers with a man from Crouch End," said the bank manager's niece, dancing past. The boy who danced with her was smiling with his eyes closed.

"Perhaps he got a leather belt in his little bag," said the woman with the fur.

"It's all the same in a hundred years," said the woman in the picture hat. She went down to her white wine, widening her legs like an old mule at a pool, and came up gasping. "They put hair oil in it."

This was all wrong. They spoke like the women who

wore men's caps and carried fishfrails full of empties in the Jug and Bottle of the Compasses at home.

"Keeps away the dandruff."

He did not expect that the nightclub women under the pavement should sing and twang like sirens or lure off his buttons with their dangerous, fringed violet eyes. London is not under the bedclothes where all the company is grand and vile by a flick of the cinema eye, and the warm linen doors are always open. But these women with the shabby faces and the comedians' tongues, squatting and squabbling over their mother's ruin, might have lurched in from Llanelly on a football night, on the arms of short men with leeks. The women at the tables, whom he had seen as enamouring shapes when he first came in dazed from the night, were dull as sisters, red-eyed and thick in the head with colds; they would sneeze when you kissed them or hiccup and say Manners in the dark traps of the hotel bedrooms.

"Good as gold," he said to Mr. Allingham. "I thought you said this was a low place, like a speakeasy."

"Speak easy yourself. They don't like being called low down here." Mr. Allingham leant close, speaking from the side of his mouth. "They're too low for that. It's a regular little hellhole," he whispered. "It's just warming up. They take their clothes off soon and do the hula hula; you'll like that."

"Nobody knows Lucille," George Ring said. "Are you sure she isn't Lucy? There's a lovely Lucy."

"No, Lucille."

" 'She dwells beside the springs of Dove.' I think I like Wordsworth better than Walter de la Mare sometimes. Do you know 'Tintern Abbey'?"

Mrs. Dacey appeared at Samuel's shoulder. "Doesn't baby dance?" He shuddered at the cold touch of her hand on his neck. Not here. Not now. That terrible impersonal Bethesda rape of the fingers. He remembered that she had carried her umbrella even while she danced.

"I got a sister in Tintern," said a man behind them.

"Tintern Abbey." George Ring pouted and did not turn round.

"Not in the Abbey, she's a waitress."

"We were talking about a poem."

"She's not a bloody nun," the man said.

The music stopped, but the two boys on the little platform still moved their hands and lips, beating out the dance in silence.

Mr. Allingham raised his fist. "Say that again and I'll knock you down."

"I'll blow you down," the man said. He puffed up his cheeks, and blew. His breath smelt of cloves.

"Now, now." Mrs. Dacey levelled her umbrella.

"People shouldn't go around insulting nuns then," Mr. Allingham said as the ferrule tapped his waistcoat.

"I'll blow you down," the man said. "I never insulted any nun. I've never spoken to a nun."

"Now, now." The umbrella drove for his eyes, and he ducked.

"You blow again," said Mrs. Dacey politely, "I'll push it up your snout and open it."

"Don't you loathe violence," George Ring said. "I've always been a terrible pacifist. One drop of blood and I feel slimy all over. Shall we dance?"

He put his arm round Samuel's waist and danced him away from the bar. The band began again though none of the couples had stopped dancing.

"But we're two men," Samuel said. "Is this a waltz?"

"They never play waltzes here, it's just self-expression. Look, there's two other men dancing."

"I thought they were girls."

"My friend thought you were a couple of girls," George Ring said in a loud voice as they danced past them. Samuel looked at the floor, trying to follow the movements of George Ring's feet. One, two, three, turn around, tap.

One of the young men squealed, "Come up and see my Aga Cooker."

One, two, three, swirl and tap.

"What sort of a girl is Polly Dacey, really? Is she mad?"

I'm like thistledown, thought Samuel. Swirl about and swirl again, on the toes now, shake those hips.

"Not so heavy, Sam. You're like a little Jumbo. When she went to school she used to post mice in the pillarbox and they ate up all the letters. And she used to do things to boys in the scullery. I can't tell you. You could hear them screaming all over the house."

But Samuel was not listening any more. He circled and stumbled to a rhythm of his own among the flying legs, dipped and retreated, hopped on one leg and spun, his hair falling over his eyes and his bottle swinging. He clung to George Ring's shoulder and zig-zagged away from him, then bounced up close again.

"Don't swing the bottle. Don't swing it. Look out. Sam. Sam."

Samuel's arm flew back and a small woman went down. She grabbed at his legs and he brought George Ring with him. Another man fell, catching fast to his partner's skirt. A long rip and she tumbled among them, her legs in the air, her head in a heave of bellies and arms.

Samuel lay still. His mouth pressed on the curls at the nape of the neck of the woman who had fallen first. He put out his tongue.

"Get off my head, you've got keys in your pocket."

"Oh, my leg!"

"That's right. Easy does it. Upsadaisy."

"Someone's licking me," cried the woman at the bottom.

Then the two girls from behind the bar were standing over them, slapping and kicking, pulling them up by the hair.

"It was that one's fault. He crowned her with a bottle. I saw him," said the bank manager's niece.

"Where'd he get the bottle from, Lola?"

The girl with the bow tie dragged Samuel up by the collar and pointed to his left hand. He tried to slip it in his pocket but a hand like a black boxing glove closed over the bottle. A large black face bent down and stared into his. He saw only the whites of the eyes and the teeth.

I don't want a cut on my face. Don't cut my lips open. They only use razors in stories. Don't let him have read any stories.

"Now, now," said Mrs. Dacey's voice. The black face jerked back as she thrust out her opened umbrella, and Samuel's hand was free.

"Throw him out, Monica."

"He was dancing like a monkey, throw him out."

"If you throw him out you can throw me out too," Mr. Allingham said from the bar. He raised his fists.

Two men walked over to him.

"Mind my glasses." He did not wear any.

They opened the door and threw him up the steps.

"Bloody nun," a voice shouted.

"Now you."

"And the old girl. Look out for her brolly, Dodie."

Samuel fell on the area step below Mr. Allingham, and

Mrs. Dacey came flying after with her umbrella held high.
It was still raining heavily.

4

"Just a passing call," said Mr. Allingham. As though he
were sitting indoors at a window, he put out his hand to
feel the rain. Shoes slopped past on the pavement above
his head. Wet trousers and stockings almost touched the
brim of his hat. "Just in and out," he said. "Where's
George?"

I've been bounced, Samuel thought.

"It reminds me of my old man." Mrs. Dacey's face was
hidden under the umbrella, as though in a private, accompanying thunder cloud. "In and out, in and out. Just one
look at him, and out he went like clockwork."

Oh, the Gayspot? Can't go there, old man. Samuel
winked seriously in the dark. Oh, carrying a cargo. Swinging a bottle around. One look at me, out I went.

"He used to carry a little book with all the places he
couldn't go to and he went to them every Saturday."

Fool, fool, fool, Samuel said to himself.

The steps were suddenly lit up as the door opened for
George Ring. He came out carefully and tidily, to a rush
of music and voices that faded at once with the vanishing
of the smoky light, and stood on Mrs. Dacey's step, his
mane of curls golden against the fanlight, a god or a half-
horse emerging from the underworld into the common rain.

"They're awfully cross," he said. "Mrs. Cavanagh ripped
her skirt and she didn't have anything on underneath. My
dear, it's like Ancient Rome down there and now she's
wearing a man's trousers and he's got legs exactly like a
spider's. All black and hairy. Why are you sitting in the
rain?"

"It's safe," Mr. Allingham said. "It's nice and safe in
the rain. It's nice and rational sitting on the steps in the
rain. You can't knock a woman down with a bottle here.
See the stars? That's Arcturus. That's the Great Bear.
That's Sirius, see, the green one. I won't show you where
Venus is. There's some people can't enjoy themselves unless they're knocking women down and licking them on the
floor. They think the evening's wasted unless they've done
that. I wish I was home. I wish I was lying in bed by
the ceiling. I wish I was lying under the chairs like Rosie."

"Who started to fight, anyway? Let's go round the corner to the Cheerioh."

"That was ethical."

They climbed up the street, George Ring first, then Mr. Allingham, then Samuel and Mrs. Dacey. She tucked his arm in hers.

"Don't you worry. You hold onto me. Cold? You're shivering."

"It'll be Cheerioh all right."

The Cheerioh was a bad blaze, an old hole of lights. In the dark, open a cupboard full of cast-off clothes moving in a wind from nowhere, the smell of mothballs and damp furs, and find a lamp lit, candles burning, a gramophone playing.

"No dancing for you," Mr. Allingham said. "You need space. You want the Crystal Palace."

Mrs. Dacey still held Samuel by the arm. "You're safe with me. I've taken a fancy," she said. "Once I take a fancy I never let go."

"And never trust a woman who can't get up." Mr. Allingham pointed to a woman sitting in a chair by the Speedboat pintable. "She's trying to get up all the time." The woman made a sudden movement of her shoulders. "No, no, legs first."

"This used to be the cowshed," George Ring said, "and there was real straw on the floor."

Mrs. Dacey never lets go. Samuel saw the fancy shining behind her glasses, and in her hard mousetrap mouth. Her cold hand hooked him. If he struggled and ran she would catch him in a corner and open her umbrella inside his nose.

"And real cows," Mr. Allingham said.

The men and women drinking and dancing looked like the older brothers and sisters of the drinkers and dancers in the club around the corner, but no one was black. There were deep green faces, dipped in a sea dye, with painted cockles for mouths and lichenous hair, sealed on the cheeks; red and purple, slate-gray, tide-marked, rat-brown and stickily white-washed, with violet-inked eyes or lips the colour of Stilton; pink chopped, pink lidded, pink as the belly of a newborn monkey, nicotine yellow with mustard flecked eyes, rust scraping through the bleach, black hairs axlegreased down among the peroxide; squashed fly stubbles, saltcellared necks thick with pepper powder; carrotheads, yolkheads, blackheads, heads bald as sweet-breads.

"All white people here," Samuel said.

"The salt of the earth," Mr. Allingham said. "The foul salt of the earth. Drunk as a pig. Ever seen a pig drunk? Ever see a monkey dancing like a man? Look at that king of the animals. See him? The one who's eaten his lips. That one smiling. That one having his honeymoon on her feet."

# After the Fair

The fair was over, the lights in the cocoanut stalls were put out, and the wooden horses stood still in the darkness, waiting for the music and the hum of the machines that would set them trotting forward. One by one, in every booth, the naphtha jets were turned down and the canvases pulled over the little gambling tables. The crowd went home, and there were lights in the windows of the caravans.

Nobody had noticed the girl. In her black clothes she stood against the side of the roundabouts, hearing the last feet tread upon the sawdust and the last voices die into the distance. Then, all alone on the deserted ground, surrounded by the shapes of wooden horses and cheap fairy boats, she looked for a place to sleep. Now here and now there, she raised the canvas that shrouded the cocoanut stalls and peered into the warm darkness. She was frightened to step inside, and as a mouse scampered across the littered shavings on the floor, or as the canvas creaked and a rush of wind set it dancing, she ran away and hid again near the roundabouts. Once she stepped on the boards; the bells round a horse's throat jingled and were still; she did not dare breathe until all was quiet again and the darkness had forgotten the noise of the bells. Then here and there she went peeping for a bed, into each gondola, under each tent. But there was nowhere, nowhere in all the fair for her to sleep. One place was too silent, and in another was the noise of mice. There was straw in the corner of the Astrologer's tent, but it moved as she touched it; she knelt by its side and put out her hand; she felt a baby's hand upon her own.

Now there was nowhere; so slowly she turned towards the caravans, and reaching them where they stood on the outskirts of the field, found all but two to be unlit. She stood, clutching her empty bag, and wondering which caravan she should disturb. At last she decided to knock upon the window of the little, shabby one near her, and standing on tiptoes, she looked in. The fattest man she had ever seen was sitting in front of the stove, toasting a piece of bread. She tapped three times on the glass, then hid in the shadows. She heard him come to the top of the steps and call out Who? Who? but she dared not answer. Who? Who? he called again; she laughed at his voice which was as thin as he was fat. He heard her laughter and turned to where the darkness concealed her. First you tap, he said. Then you hide, then, by jingo, you laugh. She stepped into the circle of light, knowing she need no longer hide herself. A girl, he said, Come in and wipe your feet. He did not wait but retreated into his caravan, and she could do nothing but follow him up the steps and into the crowded room. He was seated again, and toasting the same piece of bread. Have you come in? he said, for his back was towards her. Shall I close the door? she asked, and closed it before he replied.

She sat on the bed and watched him toasting the bread until it burnt. I can toast better than you, she said. I don't doubt it, said the Fat Man. She watched him put down the charred toast upon a plate by his side, take another round of bread and hold that, too, in front of the stove. It burnt very quickly. Let me toast it for you, she said. Ungraciously he handed her the fork and the loaf. Cut it, he said, Toast it, and eat it, by jingo. She sat on the chair. See the dent you've made on my bed, said the Fat Man. Who are you to come in and dent my bed? My name is Annie, she told him. Soon all the bread was toasted and buttered, so she put it in the centre of the table and arranged two chairs. I'll have mine on the bed, said the Fat Man. You'll have it here.

When they had finished their supper, he pushed back his chair and stared at her across the table. I am the Fat Man, he said. My home is Treorchy; the Fortune Teller next door is Aberdare. I am nothing to do with the fair— I am Cardiff, she said. There's a town, agreed the Fat Man. He asked her why she had come away. Money, said Annie. I have one and three, said the Fat Man. I have nothing, said Annie.

Then he told her about the fair and the places he had been to and the people he had met. He told her his age and his weight and the names of his brothers and what he would call his son. He showed her a picture of Boston Harbour and the photograph of his mother who lifted weights. He told her how summer looked in Ireland. I've always been a fat man, he said, And now I'm *the* Fat Man; there's nobody to touch me for fatness. He told her of a heat wave in Sicily and of the Mediterranean Sea and of the wonders of the South stars. She told him of the baby in the Astrologer's tent.

That's the stars again, by jingo; looking at the stars doesn't do anybody any good.

The baby'll die, said Annie. He opened the door and walked out into the darkness. She looked about her but did not move, wondering if he had gone to fetch a policeman. It would never do to be caught by the policeman again. She stared through the open door into the inhospitable night and drew her chair closer to the stove. Better to be caught in the warmth, she said. But she trembled at the sound of the Fat Man approaching, and pressed her hands upon her thin breast, as he climbed up the steps like a walking mountain. She could see him smile in the darkness. See what the stars have done, he said, and brought in the Astrologer's baby in his arms.

After she had nursed it against her and it had cried on the bosom of her dress, she told him how she had feared his going. What should I be doing with a policeman? She told him that the policeman wanted her. What have you done for a policeman to be wanting you? She did not answer but took the child nearer again to her wasted breast. If it was money, I could have given you one and three, he said. Then he understood her and begged her pardon. I'm not quick, he told her. I'm just fat; sometimes I think I'm almost too fat. She was feeding the child; he saw her thinness. You must eat, Cardiff, he said.

Then the child began to cry. From a little wail its crying rose into a tempest of despair. The girl rocked it to and fro on her lap, but nothing soothed it. All the woe of a child's world flooded its tiny voice. Stop it, stop it, said the Fat Man, and the tears increased. Annie smothered it in kisses, but its wild cry broke on her lips like water upon rocks. We must do something, she said. Sing it a lullabee. She sang, but the child did not like her singing.

There's only one thing, said Annie, we must take it on the roundabouts. With the child's arm around her neck, she stumbled down the steps and ran towards the deserted fair, the Fat Man panting behind her. She found her way through the tents and stalls into the centre of the ground where the wooden horses stood waiting, and clambered up on to a saddle. Start the engine, she called out. In the distance the Fat Man could be heard cranking up the antique machine that drove the horses all the day into a wooden gallop. She heard the sudden spasmodic humming of the engine; the boards rattled under the horses' feet. She saw the Fat Man clamber up by her side, pull the central lever and climb on to the saddle of the smallest horse of all. As the roundabout started, slowly at first and slowly gaining speed, the child at the girl's breast stopped crying, clutched its hands together, and crowed with joy. The night wind tore through its hair, the music jangled in its ears. Round and round the wooden horses sped, drowning the cries of the wind with the beating of their wooden hooves.

And so the men from the caravans found them, the Fat Man and the girl in black with a baby in her arms, racing round and round on their mechanical steeds to the ever-increasing music of the organ.

# The Enemies

It was morning in the green acres of the Jarvis valley, and
Mr. Owen was picking the weeds from the edges of his
garden path. A great wind pulled at his beard, the vegetable world roared under his feet. A rook had lost itself
in the sky, and was making a noise to its mate; but the
mate never came, and the rook flew into the west with a
woe in its beak. Mr. Owen, who had stood up to ease
his shoulders and look at the sky, observed how dark the
wings beat against the red sun. In her draughty kitchen
Mrs. Owen grieved over the soup. Once, in past days, the
valley had housed the cattle alone; the farmboys came
down from the hills to holla at the cattle and to drive them
to be milked; but no stranger set foot in the valley. Mr.
Owen, walking lonely through the country, had come
upon it at the end of a late summer evening when the
cattle were lying down still, and the stream that divided it
was speaking over the pebbles. Here, thought Mr. Owen,
I will build a small house with one storey, in the middle
of the valley, set around by a garden. And, remembering
clearly the way he had come along the winding hills, he
returned to his village and the questions of Mrs. Owen.
So it came about that a house with one storey was built
in the green fields; a garden was dug and planted, and
a low fence put up around the garden to keep the cows
from the vegetables.

That was early in the year. Now summer and autumn
had gone over; the garden had blossomed and died; there
was frost at the weeds. Mr. Owen bent down again, tidy-
ing the path, while the wind blew back the heads of the
nearby grasses and made an oracle of each green mouth.
Patiently he strangled the weeds; up came the roots, making war in the soil around them; insects were busy in the
holes where the weeds had sprouted, but, dying between

his fingers, they left no stain. He grew tired of their death, and tireder of the fall of the weeds. Up came the roots, down went the cheap, green heads.

Mrs. Owen, peering into the depths of her crystal, had left the soup to bubble on unaided. The ball grew dark, then lightened as a rainbow moved within it. Growing hot like a sun, and cooling again like an arctic star, it shone in the folds of her dress where she held it lovingly. The tea leaves in her cup at breakfast had told of a dark stranger. What would the crystal tell her? Mrs. Owen wondered.

Up came the roots, and a crooked worm, disturbed by the probing of the fingers, wriggled blind in the sun. Of a sudden the valley filled all its hollows with the wind, with the voice of the roots, with the breathing of the nether sky. Not only a mandrake screams; torn roots have their cries; each weed Mr. Owen pulled out of the ground screamed like a baby. In the village behind the hill the wind would be raging, the clothes on the garden lines would be set to strange dances. And women with shapes in their wombs would feel a new knocking as they bent over the steamy tubs. Life would go on in the veins, in the bones, the binding flesh, that had their seasons and their weathers even as the valley binding the house about with the flesh of the green grass.

The ball, like an open grave, gave up its dead to Mrs. Owen. She stared on the lips of women and the hairs of men that wound into a pattern on the face of the crystal world. But suddenly the patterns were swept away, and she could see nothing but the shapes of the Jarvis hills. A man with a black hat was walking down the paths into the invisible valley beneath. If he walked any nearer he would fall into her lap. There's a man with a black hat walking on the hills, she called through the window. Mr. Owen smiled and went on weeding.

It was at this time that the Reverend Mr. Davies lost his way; he had been losing it most of the morning, but now he had lost it altogether, and stood perturbed under a tree on the rim of the Jarvis hills. A great wind blew through the branches, and a great grey-green earth moved unsteadily beneath him. Wherever he looked the hills stormed up to the sky, and wherever he sought to hide from the wind he was frightened by the darkness. The farther he walked, the stranger was the scenery around him; it rose to undreamed-of heights, and then fell down again into a valley no bigger than the palm of his hand. And the trees walked like men. By a divine coincidence he reached the rim of the hills just as the sun reached the centre of the sky. With the wide world rocking from horizon to horizon, he stood under a tree and looked down into the valley. In the fields was a little house with a garden. The valley roared around it, the wind leapt at it like a boxer, but the house stood still. To Mr. Davies it seemed as though the house had been carried out of a village by a large bird and placed in the very middle of the tumultuous universe.

But as he climbed over the craggy edges and down the side of the hill, he lost his place in Mrs. Owen's crystal. A cloud displaced his black hat, and under the cloud walked a very old phantom, a shape of air with stars all frozen in its beard, and a half-moon for a smile. Mr. Davies knew nothing of this as the stones scratched his hands. He was old, he was drunk with the wine of the morning, but the stuff that came out of his cuts was a human blood.

Nor did Mr. Owen, with his face near the soil and his hands on the necks of the screaming weeds, know of the transformation in the crystal. He had heard Mrs. Owen prophesy the coming of the black hat, and had smiled as he always smiled at her faith in the powers of darkness. He had looked up when she called, and, smiling, had returned to the clearer call of the ground. Multiply, multiply, he had said to the worms disturbed in their channelling, and had cut the brown worms in half so that the halves might breed and spread their life over the garden and go out, contaminating, into the fields and the bellies of the cattle.

Of this Mr. Davies knew nothing. He saw a young man with a beard bent industriously over the garden soil; he saw that the house was a pretty picture, with the face of a pale young woman pressed up against the window. And, removing his black hat, he introduced himself as the rector of a village some ten miles away.

You are bleeding, said Mr. Owen.

Mr. Davies's hands, indeed, were covered in blood.

When Mrs. Owen had seen to the rector's cuts, she sat

him down in the armchair near the window, and made him a strong cup of tea.

I saw you on the hill, she said, and he asked her how she had seen him, for the hills are high and a long way off.

I have good eyes, she answered.

He did not doubt her. Her eyes were the strangest he had seen.

It is quiet here, said Mr. Davies.

We have no clock, she said, and laid the table for three.

You are very kind.

We are kind to those that come to us.

He wondered how many came to the lonely house in the valley, but did not question her for fear of what she would reply. He guessed she was an uncanny woman loving the dark because it was dark. He was too old to question the secrets of darkness, and now, with the black suit torn and wet and his thin hands bound with the bandages of the stranger woman, he felt older than ever. The winds of the morning might blow him down, and the sudden dropping of the dark be blind in his eyes. Rain might pass through him as it passes through the body of a ghost. A tired, white-haired old man, he sat under the window, almost invisible against the panes and the white cloth of the chair.

Soon the meal was ready, and Mr. Owen came in unwashed from the garden.

Shall I say grace? asked Mr. Davies when all three were seated around the table.

Mrs. Owen nodded.

O Lord God Almighty, bless this our meal, said Mr. Davies. Looking up as he continued his prayer, he saw that Mr. and Mrs. Owen had closed their eyes. We thank Thee for the bounties that Thou hast given us. And he saw that the lips of Mr. and Mrs. Owen were moving softly. He could not hear what they said, but he knew that the prayers they spoke were not his prayers.

Amen, said all three together.

Mr. Owen, proud in his eating, bent over the plate as he had bent over the complaining weeds. Outside the window was the brown body of the earth, the green skin of the grass, and the breasts of the Jarvis hills; there was a wind that chilled the animal earth, and a sun that had drunk up the dews on the fields; there was creation sweating out of the pores of the trees; and the grains of sand on faraway seashores would be multiplying as the sea rolled over them. He felt the coarse foods on his tongue; there was a meaning in the rind of the meat, and a purpose in the lifting of food to mouth. He saw, with a sudden satisfaction, that Mrs. Owen's throat was bare.

She, too, was bent over her plate, but was letting the teeth of her fork nibble at the corners of it. She did not eat, for the old powers were upon her, and she dared not lift up her head for the greenness of her eyes. She knew by the sound which way the wind blew in the valley; she knew the stage of the sun by the curve of the shadows on the cloth. Oh, that she could take her crystal, and see within it the stretches of darkness covering up this winter light. But there was a darkness gathering in her mind, drawing in the light around her. There was a ghost on her left; with all her strength she drew in the intangible light that moved around him, and mixed it in her dark brains.

Mr. Davies, like a man sucked by a bird, felt desolation in his veins, and, in a sweet delirium, told of his adventures on the hills, of how it had been cold and blowing, and how the hills went up and down. He had been lost, he said, and had found a dark retreat to shelter from the bullies in the wind; but the darkness had frightened him, and he had walked again on the hills where the morning tossed him about like a ship on the sea. Wherever he went he was blown in the open or frightened in the narrow shades. There was nowhere, he said pityingly, for an old man to go. Loving his parish, he had loved the surrounding lands, but the hills had given under his feet or plunged him into the air. And, loving his God, he had loved the darkness where men of old had worshipped the dark invisible. But now the hill caves were full of shapes and voices that mocked him because he was old.

He is frightened of the dark, thought Mrs. Owen, the lovely dark.

With a smile, Mr. Owen thought, He is frightened of the worm in the earth, of the copulation in the tree, of the living grease in the soil.

They looked at the old man, and saw that he was more ghostly than ever. The window behind him cast a ragged circle of light round his head.

Suddenly Mr. Davies knelt down to pray. He did not

understand the cold in his heart nor the fear that bewildered him as he knelt, but, speaking his prayers for deliverance, he stared up at the shadowed eyes of Mrs. Owen and at the smiling eyes of her husband. Kneeling on the carpet at the head of the table, he stared in bewilderment at the dark mind and the gross dark body. He stared and he prayed, like an old god beset by his enemies.

# The Tree

Rising from the house that faced the Jarvis hills in the long distance, there was a tower for the day-birds to build in and for the owls to fly around at night. From the village the light of the tower window shone like a glowworm through the panes; but the room under the sparrows' nests was rarely lit; webs were spun over its unwashed ceilings; it stared over twenty miles of the up-and-down county, and the corners kept their secrets where there were claw marks in the dust.

The child knew the house from roof to cellar; he knew the irregular lawns and the gardener's shed where flowers burst out of their jars; but he could not find the key that opened the door of the tower.

The house changed to his moods, and a lawn was the sea or the shore or the sky or whatever he wished it. When a lawn was a sad mile of water, and he was sailing on a broken flower down the waves, the gardener would come out of his shed near the island of bushes. He, too, would take a stalk, and sail. Straddling a garden broom, he would fly wherever the child wished. He knew every story from the beginning of the world.

In the beginning, he would say, there was a tree.

What kind of tree?

The tree where that blackbird's whistling.

A hawk, a hawk, cried the child.

The gardener would look up at the tree, seeing a monstrous hawk perched on a bough or an eagle swinging in the wind.

The gardener loved the Bible. When the sun sank and the garden was full of people, he would sit with a candle in his shed, reading of the first love and the legend of apples and serpents. But the death of Christ on a tree he loved most. Trees made a fence around him, and he knew of the changing of the seasons by the hues on the bark and the rushing of sap through the covered roots. His world moved and changed as spring moved along the branches, changing their nakedness; his God grew up like a tree from the apple-shaped earth, giving bud to His children and letting His children be blown from their places by the breezes of winter; winter and death moved in one wind. He would sit in his shed and read of the crucifixion, looking over the jars on his window-shelf into the winter nights. He would think that love fails on such nights, and that many of its children are cut down.

The child transfigured the blowsy lawns with his playing. The gardener called him by his mother's name, and seated him on his knee, and talked to him of the wonders of Jerusalem and the birth in the manger.

In the beginning was the village of Bethlehem, he whispered to the child before the bell rang for tea out of the growing darkness.

Where is Bethlehem?

Far away, said the gardener, in the East.

To the east stood the Jarvis hills, hiding the sun, their trees drawing up the moon out of the grass.

The child lay in bed. He watched the rocking horse and wished that it would grow wings so that he could mount it and ride into the Arabian sky. But the winds of Wales blew at the curtains, and crickets made a noise in the untidy plot under the window. His toys were dead. He started to cry and then stopped, knowing no reason for tears. The night was windy and cold, he was warm under the sheets; the night was as big as a hill, he was a boy in bed.

Closing his eyes, he stared into a spinning cavern deeper than the darkness of the garden where the first tree on which the unreal birds had fastened stood alone and bright as fire. The tears ran back under his lids as he thought of the first tree that was planted so near him, like a friend in the garden. He crept out of bed and tiptoed to the door. The rocking horse bounded forward on its springs, startling the child into a noiseless scamper back to bed. The child looked at the horse and the horse was quiet; he tiptoed again along the carpet, and reached the door, and turned the knob around, and ran on to the landing.

Feeling blindly in front of him, he made his way to the top of the stairs; he looked down the dark stairs into the hall, seeing a host of shadows curve in and out of the corners, hearing their sinuous voices, imagining the pits of their eyes and their lean arms. But they would be little and secret and bloodless, not cased in invisible armour but wound around with cloths as thin as a web; they would whisper as he walked, touch him on the shoulder, and say S in his ear. He went down the stairs; not a shadow moved in the hall, the corners were empty. He put out his hand and patted the darkness, thinking to feel some dry and velvet head creep under the fingers and edge, like a mist, into the nails. But there was nothing. He opened the front door, and the shadows swept into the garden.

Once on the path, his fears left him. The moon had lain down on the unweeded beds, and her frosts were spread on the grass. At last he came to the illuminated tree at the long gravel end, older even than the marvel of light, with the woodlice asleep under the bark, with the boughs standing out from the body like the frozen arms of a woman. The child touched the tree; it bent as to his touch. He saw a star, brighter than any in the sky, burn steadily above the first birds' tower, and shine on nowhere but on the leafless boughs and the trunk and the travelling roots.

The child had not doubted the tree. He said his prayers to it, with knees bent on the blackened twigs the night wind fetched to the ground. Then, trembling with love and cold, he ran back over the lawns towards the house.

There was an idiot to the east of the county who walked the land like a beggar. Now at a farmhouse and now at a widow's cottage he begged for his bread. A parson gave him a suit, and it lopped round his hungry ribs and shoulders and waved in the wind as he shambled over the fields. But his eyes were so wide and his neck so clear of the country dirt that no one refused him what he asked. And asking for water, he was given milk.

Where do you come from?

From the east, he said.

So they knew he was an idiot, and gave him a meal to clean the yards.

As he bent with a rake over the dung and the trodden grain, he heard a voice rise in his heart. He put his hand into the cattle's hay, caught a mouse, rubbed his hand over its muzzle, and let it go away.

All day the thought of the tree was with the child; all night it stood up in his dreams as the star stood above its plot. One morning towards the middle of December, when the wind from the farthest hills was rushing around the house, and the snow of the dark hours had not dissolved from lawns and roofs, he ran to the gardener's shed. The gardener was repairing a rake he had found broken. Without a word, the child sat on a seedbox at his feet, and watched him tie the teeth, and knew that the wire would not keep them together. He looked at the gardener's boots, wet with snow, at the patched knees of his trousers, at the undone buttons of his coat, and the folds of his belly under the patched flannel shirt. He looked at his hands as they busied themselves over the golden knots of wire; they were hard, brown hands, with the stains of the soil under the broken nails and the stains of tobacco on the tips of the fingers. Now the lines of the gardener's face were set in determination as time upon time he knotted the iron teeth only to feel them shake insecurely from the handle. The child was frightened of the strength and uncleanliness of the old man; but, looking at the long, thick beard, unstained and white as fleece, he soon became reassured. The beard was the beard of an apostle.

I prayed to the tree, said the child.

Always pray to a tree, said the gardener, thinking of Calvary and Eden.

I pray to the tree every night.

Pray to a tree.

The wire slid over the teeth.

I pray to that tree.

The wire snapped.

The child was pointing over the glasshouse flowers to the tree that, alone of all the trees in the garden, had no sign of snow.

An elder, said the gardener, but the child stood up from his box and shouted so loud that the unmended rake fell with a clatter on the floor.

The first tree. The first tree you told me of. In the beginning was the tree, you said. I heard you, the child shouted.

The elder is as good as another, said the gardener, lowering his voice to humour the child.

The first tree of all, said the child in a whisper.

Reassured again by the gardener's voice, he smiled through the window at the tree, and again the wire crept over the broken rake.

God grows in strange trees, said the old man. His trees come to rest in strange places.

As he unfolded the story of the twelve stages of the cross, the tree waved its boughs to the child. An apostle's voice rose out of the tarred lungs.

So they hoisted him up on a tree, and drove nails through his belly and his feet.

There was the blood of the noon sun on the trunk of the elder, staining the bark.

The idiot stood on the Jarvis hills, looking down into the immaculate valley from whose waters and grasses the mists of morning rose and were lost. He saw the dew dissolving, the cattle staring into the stream, and the dark clouds flying away at the rumour of the sun. The sun turned at the edges of the thin and watery sky like a sweet in a glass of water. He was hungry for light as the first and almost invisible rain fell on his lips; he plucked at the grass, and, tasting it, felt it lie green on his tongue. So there was light in his mouth, and light was a sound at his ears, and the whole dominion of light in the valley that had such a curious name. He had known of the Jarvis hills; their shapes rose over the slopes of the county to be seen for miles around, but no one had told him of the valley lying under the hills. Bethlehem, said the idiot to the valley, turning over the sounds of the word and giving it all the glory of the Welsh morning. He brothered the world around him, sipped at the air, as a child newly born sips and brothers the light. The life of the Jarvis valley, steaming up from the body of the grass and the trees and the long hand of the stream, lent him a new blood. Night had emptied the idiot's veins, and dawn in the valley filled them again.

Bethlehem, said the idiot to the valley.

The gardener had no present to give the child, so he took out a key from his pocket and said, This is the key to the tower. On Christmas Eve I will unlock the door for you.

Before it was dark, he and the child climbed the stairs to the tower, the key turned in the lock, and the door, like the lid of a secret box, opened and let them in. The room was empty. Where are the secrets? asked the child, staring up at the matted rafters and into the spiders' corners and along the leaden panes of the window.

It is enough that I have given you the key, said the gardener, who believed the key of the universe to be hidden in his pocket along with the feathers of birds and the seeds of flowers.

The child began to cry because there were no secrets. Over and over again he explored the empty room, kicking up the dust to look for a colourless trap-door, tapping the unpanelled walls for the hollow voice of a room beyond the tower. He brushed the webs from the window, and looked out through the dust into the snowing Christmas Eve. A world of hills stretched far away into the measured sky, and the tops of the hills he had never seen climbed up to meet the falling flakes. Woods and rocks, wide seas of barren land, and a new tide of mountain sky sweeping through the black beeches, lay before him. To the east were the outlines of nameless hill creatures and a den of trees.

Who are they? Who are they?

They are the Jarvis hills, said the gardener, which have been from the beginning.

He took the child by the hand and led him away from the window. The key turned in the lock.

That night the child slept well; there was power in snow and darkness; there was unalterable music in the silence of the stars; there was a silence in the hurrying wind. And Bethlehem had been nearer than he expected.

On Christmas morning the idiot walked into the garden. His hair was wet and his flaked and ragged shoes were thick with the dirt of the fields. Tired from the long journey from the Jarvis hills, and weak for the want of food, he sat down under the elder-tree where the gardener had rolled a log. Clasping his hands in front of him, he saw the desolation of the flower-beds and the weeds that grew in profusion on the edges of the paths. The tower stood up like a tree of stone and glass over the red eaves. He pulled his coat-collar round his neck as a fresh wind sprang up and struck the tree; he looked down at his hands and saw that they were praying. Then a fear of the garden came over him, the shrubs were his enemies, and the trees that made an avenue down to the gate lifted their arms in horror. The place was too high, peering down on to the tall hills; the place was too low, shivering up at the plumed shoulders of a new mountain. Here the wind was too wild, fuming about the silence, raising a Jewish voice out of the elder boughs; here the silence beat like a human heart. And as he sat under the cruel hills, he heard a voice that was in him cry out: Why did you bring me here?

He could not tell why he had come; they had told him to come and had guided him, but he did not know who they were. The voice of a people rose out of the garden beds, and rain swooped down from heaven.

Let me be, said the idiot, and made a little gesture against the sky. There is rain on my face, there is wind on my cheeks. He brothered the rain.

So the child found him under the shelter of the tree, bearing the torture of the weather with a divine patience, letting his long hair blow where it would, with his mouth set in a sad smile.

Who was the stranger? He had fires in his eyes, the flesh of his neck under the gathered coat was bare. Yet he smiled as he sat in his rags under a tree on Christmas Day.

Where do you come from? asked the child.

From the east, answered the idiot.

The gardener had not lied, and the secret of the tower was true; this dark and shabby tree, that glistened only in the night, was the first tree of all.

But he asked again:

Where do you come from?

From the Jarvis hills.

Stand up against the tree.

The idiot, still smiling, stood up with his back to the elder.

Put out your arms like this.

The idiot put out his arms.

The child ran as fast as he could to the gardener's shed, and, returning over the sodden lawns, saw that the idiot had not moved but stood, straight and smiling, with his back to the tree and his arms stretched out.

Let me tie your hands.

The idiot felt the wire that had not mended the rake close round his wrists. It cut into the flesh, and the blood from the cuts fell shining on to the tree.

Brother, he said. He saw that the child held silver nails in the palm of his hand.

# The Visitor

His hands were weary, though all night they had lain over the sheets of his bed and he had moved them only to his mouth and his wild heart. The veins ran, unhealthily blue streams, into the white sea. Milk at his side steamed out of a chipped cup. He smelt the morning, and knew that cocks in the yard were putting back their heads and crowing at the sun. What were the sheets around him if not the covering sheets of the dead? What was the busy-voiced clock, sounding between photographs of mother and dead wife, if not the voice of an old enemy? Time was merciful enough to let the sun shine on his bed, and merciless to chime the sun away when night came over and even more he needed the red light and the clear heat.

Rhianon was attendant on a dead man, and put the chipped edge of the cup to a dead lip. It could not be heart that beat under the ribs. Hearts do not beat in the dead. While he had lain ready for the inch-tape and the acid, Rhianon had cut open his chest with a book-knife, torn out the heart, put in the clock. He heard her say, for the third time, Drink the lovely milk. And, feeling it run sour over his tongue, and her hand caress his forehead, he knew he was not dead. He was a living man. For many miles the months flowed into the years, rounding the dry days.

Callaghan today would sit and talk with him. He heard in his brain the voices of Callaghan and Rhianon battle until he slept, and tasted the blood of words. His hands were weary. He brooded over his long, white body, marking the ribs stick through the sides. The hands had held other hands and thrown a ball high into the air. Now they were dead hands. He could wind them about his hair and let them rest untingling on his belly or lose them in the valley between Rhianon's breasts. It did not matter what

80

he did with them. They were as dead as the hands of the
clock, and moved to clockwork.

Shall I close the windows until the sun's warmer? said
Rhianon.

I'm not cold.

He would tell her that the dead feel neither cold nor
warmth, sun and wind could never penetrate his clothes.
But she would laugh in her kind way and kiss him on the
forehead and say to him, Peter, what's getting you down?
You'll be out and about one day. One day he would walk
on the Jarvis hills like a boy's ghost, and hear the people
say, There walks the ghost of Peter, a poet, who was dead
for years before they buried him.

Rhianon tucked the sheets around his shoulders, gave
him a morning kiss, and carried the chipped cup away.

A man with a brush had drawn a rib of colour under
the sun and painted many circles around the circle of the
sun. Death was a man with a scythe, but that summer day
no living stalk was to be cut down.

The invalid waited for his visitor. Peter waited for
Callaghan. His room was a world within a world. A world
in him went round and round, and a sun rose in him and
a moon fell. Callaghan was the west wind, and Rhianon
blew away the chills of the west wind like a wind from
Tahiti.

He let his hands rest on his head, stone on stone. Never
had the voice of Rhianon been so remote as when it told
him that the sour milk was lovely. What was she but a
sweetheart talking madly to her sweetheart under a coffin
of garments? Somebody in the night had turned him up
and emptied him of all but a false heart. That under the
ribs' armour was not his, not his the beating of a vein in
the foot. His arms could no longer make their movements
nor a circle around a girl to shield her from winds and
robbers. There was nothing more remote under the sun
than his own name, and poetry was a string of words
stringed on a beanstick. With his lips he rounded a little
ball of sound into some shape, and spoke a word.

There was no tomorrow for dead men. He could not
think that after the next night and its sleeping, life would
sprout up again like a flower through a coffin's cracks.

His room around him was a vast place. From their
frames the lying likenesses of women looked down on him.
That was the face of his mother, that nearly yellow oval

in its frame of old gold and thinning hair. And, next to her, dead Mary. Though Callaghan blew hard, the walls around Mary would never fall down. He thought of her as she had been, remembered her Peter, darling Peter, and her smiling eyes.

He remembered he had not smiled since that night, seven years ago, when his heart had trembled so violently within him that he had fallen to the ground. There had been strengthening in the unbelievable setting of the sun. Over the hills and the roof went the broad moons, and summer came after spring. How had he lived at all when Callaghan had not blown away the webs of the world with a great shout, and Millicent spread her loveliness about him? But the dead need no friends. He peered over the turned coffin-lid. Stiff and straight, a man of wax stared back. Taking away the pennies from those dead eyes, he looked on his own face.

Breed, cardboard on cardboard, he had cried, before I blow down your paste huts with one bellow out of my lungs. When Mary came, there was nothing between the changing of the days but the divinity he had built around her. His child killed Mary in her womb. He felt his body turn to vapour, and men who had been light as air walked, metal-hooved, through and beyond him.

He started to cry, Rhianon, Rhianon, someone has upped and kicked me in the side. Drip, drip, goes my blood in me. Rhianon, he cried.

She hurried upstairs, and time and time over again wiped away the tears from his cheeks with the sleeve of her dress.

He lay still as the morning matured and grew up into a noble noon. Rhianon passed in and out, her dress, he smelt as she bent over him, smelling of clover and milk. With a new surprise he followed her cool movements around the room, the sweep of her hands as she brushed the dead Mary in her frame. With such surprise, he thought, do the dead follow the movements of the quick, seeing the bloom under the living skin. She should be singing as she moved from mantelpiece to window, putting things right, or should be humming like a bee about her work. But if she had spoken, or laughed, or struck her nails against the thin metal of the candlesticks, drawing forth a bellnote, or if the room had been suddenly crowded with the noises of birds, he would have wept again. It pleased him to look upon the unmoving waves of the bedclothes, and think himself an island set somewhere in the south sea. Upon this island of rich and miraculous plants, the seeds grown fruits hung from the trees and, smaller than apples, dropped with the pacific winds on to the ground to lie there and be the harbourers of the summer slugs.

And thinking of the island set somewhere in the south caverns, he thought of water and longed for water. Rhianon's dress, rustling about her, made the soft noise of water. He called her over to him and touched the bosom of her dress, feeling the water on his hands. Water, he told her, and told her how, as a boy, he had lain on the rocks, his fingers tracing cool shapes on the surfaces of the pools. She brought him water in a glass, and held the glass up level with his eyes so that he could see the room through a wall of water. He did not drink, and she set the glass aside. He imagined the coolness under the sea. Now, on a summer day soon after noon, he wished again for water to close utterly around him, to be no island set above the water but a green place under, staring around a dizzy cavern. He thought of some cool words, and made a line about an olive-tree that grew under a lake. But the tree was a tree of words, and the lake rhymed with another word.

Sit and read to me, Rhianon.

After you have eaten, she said, and brought him food.

He could not think that she had gone down into the kitchen and, with her own hands, prepared his meal. She had gone and had returned with food, as simply as a maiden out of the Old Testament. Her name meant nothing. It was a cool sound. She had a strange name out of the Bible. Such a woman had washed the body after it had been taken off the tree, with cool and competent fingers that touched on the holes like ten blessings. He could cry out to her, Put a sweet herb under my arm. With your spittle make me fragrant.

What shall I read you? She asked when at last she sat by his side.

He shook his head, not caring what she read so long as he could hear her speak and think of nothing but the inflections of her voice.

*Ah! gentle may I lay me down, and gentle rest my head,*
*And gentle sleep the sleep of death, and gentle hear the voice*
*Of Him that walketh in the garden in the evening time.*

She read on until the Worm sat on the Lily's leaf.

Death lay over his limbs again, and he closed his eyes.

There was no ease from pain nor from the figures of death that went about their familiar business even in the darkness of the heavy lids.

Shall I kiss you awake? said Callaghan. His hand was cold on Peter's hand.

And all the lepers kissed, said Peter, and fell to wondering what he had meant.

Rhianon saw that he was no longer listening to her, and went on tiptoes away.

Callaghan, left alone, leant over the bed and spread the soft ends of his fingers on Peter's eyes. Now it is night, he said. Where shall we go tonight?

Peter opened his eyes again, saw the spreading fingers and the candles glowing like the heads of poppies. A fear and a blessing were on the room.

The candles must not be blown out, he thought. There must be light, light, light. Wick and wax must never be low. All day and all night the three candles, like three girls, must blush over my bed. These three girls must shelter me.

The first flame danced and then went out. Over the second and the third flame Callaghan pursed his grey mouth. The room was dark. Where shall we go tonight? he said, but waited for no answer, pulling the sheets back from the bed and lifting Peter in his arms. His coat was damp and sweet on Peter's face.

Oh, Callaghan, Callaghan, said Peter with his mouth pressed on the black cloth. He felt the movements of Callaghan's body, the tense, the relaxing muscles, the curving of the shoulders, the impact of the feet on the racing earth. A wind from under the clay and the limes of the earth swept up to his hidden face. Only when the boughs of trees scraped on his back did he know that he was naked. So that he might not cry aloud, he shut his lips firmly together over a damp fold of flesh. Callaghan, too, was naked as a baby.

Are we naked? We have our bones and our organs, our skin and our flesh. There is a ribbon of blood tied in your hair. Do not be frightened. You have a cloth of veins around your thighs. The world charged past them, the wind dropped to nothing, blowing the fruits of battle under the moon. Peter heard the songs of birds, but no such songs as he had heard the birds, on his bedroom sill, fetch out of their throats. The birds were blind.

Are they blind? said Callaghan. They have worlds in their eyes. There is white and black in their whistling. Do not be frightened. There are bright eyes under the shells of their eggs.

He came suddenly to a stop, Peter light as a feather in his arms, and set him gently down on a green globe of soil. Below there was a valley journeying far away with its burden of lame trees and grass into the distance where the moon hung on a navel-string from the dark. From the woods on either side came the sharp cracks of guns and the pheasants falling like a rain. But soon the night was silent, softening the triggers of the fallen twigs that had snapped out under Callaghan's feet.

Peter, conscious of his sick heart, put a hand to his side but felt none of the protecting flesh. The tips of his fingers tingled around the driving blood, but the veins were invisible. He was dead. Now he knew he was dead. The ghost of Peter, wound invisible about the ghost of the blood, stood on his globe and wondered at the corrupting night.

What is this valley? said Peter's voice.

The Jarvis valley, said Callaghan. Callaghan, too, was dead. Not a bone or a hair stood up under the steadily falling frost.

This is no Jarvis valley.

This is the naked valley.

The moon, doubling and redoubling the strength of her beams, lit up the barks and the roots and the branches of the Jarvis trees, the busy lice in the wood, the shapes of the stones and the black ants travelling under them, the pebbles in the streams, the secret grass, the untiring death-worms under the blades. From their holes in the flanks of the hills came the rats and weasels, hairs white in the moon, breeding and struggling as they rushed downward to set their teeth in the cattle's throats. No sooner did the cattle fall sucked on to the earth and the weasles race away, than all the flies, rising from the dung of the fields, came up like a fog and settled on the sides. There from the stripped valley rose the smell of death, widening the mountainous nostrils on the face of the moon. Now the sheep fell and the flies were at them. The rats and the weasels, fighting over the flesh, dropped one by one with a wound for the sheep's fleas staring out of their hair. It was to Peter but a little time before the dead, picked to the symmetrical bone, were huddled in under the soil by the wind that blew louder and harder as the fat flies dropped on to the grass. Now the worm and the death-beetle undid the fibres of the animal bones, worked at them brightly and minutely, and the weeds through the sockets and the flowers on the vanished breasts sprouted up with the colours of the dead life fresh on their leaves. And the blood that had flowed flowed over the ground, strengthening the blades of the grass, fulfilling the wind-planted seeds in its course, into the mouth of the spring. Suddenly all the streams were red with blood, a score of winding veins all over the twenty fields, thick with their clotted pebbles.

Peter, in his ghost, cried out with joy. There was life in the naked valley, life in his nakedness. He saw the streams and the beating water, how the flowers shot out of the dead, and the blades and roots were doubled in their power under the stride of the split blood.

And the streams stopped. Dust of the dead blew over the spring, and the mouth was choked. Dust lay over the waters like a dark ice. Light, that had been all-eyed and moving, froze in the beams of the moon.

Life in this nakedness, mocked Callaghan at his side, and Peter knew that he was pointing, with the ghost of a finger, down on to the dead streams. But as he spoke, and the shape that Peter's heart had taken in the time of the tangible flesh was aware of the knocks of terror, a life burst out of the pebbles like the thousand lives, wrapped in a boy's body, out of the womb. The streams again went on their way, and the light of the moon, in a new splendour, shone on the valley and magnified the shadows of the valley and pulled the moles and the badgers out of their winter into the deathless midnight season of the world.

Light breaks over the hill, said Callaghan, and lifted the invisible Peter in his arms. Dawn, indeed, was breaking far over the Jarvis wilderness still naked under the descending moon.

As Callaghan raced along the rim of the hills and into the woods and over an exultant country where the trees raced with him, Peter cried out joyfully.

He heard Callaghan's laughter like a rattle of thunder that the wind took up and doubled. There was a shouting in the wind, a commotion under the surface of the earth. Now under the roots and now on the tops of the wild trees, he and his stranger were racing against the cock. Over and under the falling fences of the light they climbed and shouted.

Listen to the cock, cried Peter, and the sheets of the bed rolled up to his chin.

A man with a brush had drawn a red rib down the east. The ghost of a circle around the circle of the moon spun through a cloud. He passed his tongue over his lips that had miraculously clothed themselves with skin and flesh. In his mouth was a strange taste, as if last night, three hundred nights ago, he had squeezed the head of a poppy and drunk and slept. There was the old rumour of Callaghan down his brain. From dawn to dark he had talked of death, had seen a moth caught in the candle, had heard the laughter that could not have been his ring in his ears. The cock cried again, and a bird whistled like a scythe through wheat.

Rhianon, with a sweet, naked throat, stepped into the room.

Rhianon, he said, hold my hand, Rhianon.

She did not hear him, but stood over his bed and fixed him with an unbreakable sorrow.

Hold my hand, he said. And then: Why are you putting the sheet over my face?

# The Lemon

Early one morning, under the arc of a lamp, carefully, silently, in smock and rubber gloves, old Doctor Manza grafted a cat's head on to a chicken's trunk. The cat-headed creature, in a house of glass, swayed on its legs; though it stared through the slits of its eyes, it saw nothing; there was the flutter of a strange pulse under its fur and feathers, and, lifting its foot to the right of the glass wall, it rocked again to the left. Change the sex of a dog: it cries like a bitch in a high heat, and sniffs, bewildered, over the blind litter. Such a strange dog, with a grafted ovary, howled in its cage. Old Doctor Manza put his ear to the glass, hoping for a new sound. The sun blew in through the laboratory windows, and the light of the wind was the colour of the sun. With music in his ears, old Doctor Manza moved among the phials and the bottles of his life; the mutilated were silent; the new born in the rabbits' cages drew down the hygienic air delightedly into their lungs. Tomorrow there were to be mastoids for the weasel by the window, but today it leapt in the sun.

The hill was as big as a mountain, and the house swelled like a hill on the topmost peak. Holding too many rooms, the house had a room for the wild owls, and a cellar for the vermin that multiplied on clean straw and grew fat as rabbits. The people in the house moved like too many ghosts among the white sheeted tables, met face to face in the corridors and covered their eyes for fear of a new stranger, or suddenly crowded together in the central hall, questioning one another as to the names of the new born. One by one the faces vanished, but there was always one to take their place, a woman with a child at her breast, or a blind man from the world. All had possession of the keys of the house. There was one boy among them who had the name of the house, and son of the house that was called a hill, he played with the shadows in the corridors and slept at

88

night in a high room shuttered from the stars. But the people of the house slept in sight of the moon; they heard the gulls from the sea, the noise of the waves, when the wind blew from the south, breaking on sand, and slept with their eyes open.

Doctor Manza woke up with the birds, seeing the sun rise each morning in a coloured water, and the day, like the growths in his jars, grow brighter and stronger as the growing hours let the rain or the shine and the particles of winter light fall from them. As was his custom, he turned, this one morning, from the window where the weasel leapt, to the life behind glass; he marked with an unmortal calm, with the never-ended beginning of a smile no mother bared with the mouth of her milk, how the young lapped at their mothers and his creatures, and the newly hatched fluttered, and the papped birds opened their beaks. He was God, he was power and the clay knife, he was the sound and the substance, for he made a hand of glass, a hand with a vein, and sewed it upon the flesh, and it straightened with the days and the heat of the false light, and the glass nails grew long; and who but God could trim his nails with the edge of a diamond? Life ran from his fingers, in the hues of his acids, on the surface of the boiling herbs; he had death in a thousand powders; he had frozen a crucifix of steam; all the great chemistries of the earth, the mystery of matter—See, he said aloud, A brand on a frog's forehead where there was neither—in his room at the top of the house had no mystery.

The house was one mystery. Everything happens in a blaze of light; the groping of the boy's blind hands along the walls of the corridor was a movement of light, though the last candle dimmed by the head of the stairs, and the lines of light at the feet of the locked doors were suddenly taken away. Nant, the boy, was not alone; he heard a frock rustle, a hand beneath his own scrape on the distemper. Whose hand? he said softly. Then, flying in a panic down the dark carpets, he cried more loudly, Never answer me. Your hand, said the dark, and Nant stopped still.

Death was too long for the Doctor, and eternity took too much time.

I was that boy in a dream, and I stood stock still, knowing myself to be alone, knowing that the voice was mine, and the dark not the death of the sun but the dark light thrown back by the walls of the windowless corridor, I put out my arm, and it turned into a tree.

Early, that one morning, under the arc of a lamp, old Doctor Manza made a new acid, turning it round and round with a spoon, seeing it have colour in its beaker and then, by a change of heat, be the colour of water. It was the strongest acid, burning the air, but it lapped around his fingers sweet as a syrup and did not burn at all. Carefully, silently he raised the beaker and opened the door of a cage. This was a new milk for the cat. He poured the acid into a saucer, and the cat-headed creature slipped down to drink. I was that cat-head in a dream; I drank the acid, and I slept; I woke up in death, but there I forgot the dream and moved on a different being in the image of the boy who was terrified of the dark. And, my arm no longer the branch of a tree, like a mole I hurried from light and to the light; for one blind moment I was a mole, with a child's hands, digging, up or down, I knew not which, in the Welsh earth. I knew that I was dreaming, but suddenly I awoke to the real, hard lack of light in the corridors of the house. There was nobody to guide me; Doctor Manza, the foreigner in a white coat making a new logic in his tower of birds, was my only friend. Nant raced for the doctor's tower. Up a spiral stairs and a broken ladder, seeing, by candle, a sign that said To London and the Sun, he climbed in my image, I in his, and we were two brothers climbing for the Doctor's tower. The key was on a chain ringed from my waist. Opening the door, I found the Doctor as I always found him, staring through the walls of a glass cage. He smiled but paid no heed to me who had lusted a hundred seconds for his smile and his white coat. I gave it my acid and it died, old Doctor Manza said. And, after ten minutes, the dead hen rose to its feet; it rubbed against glass like a cat, and I saw its cat's head. This was ten minutes' death.

A storm came up, black bodied, from the sea, bringing rain and twelve winds to drive the hill birds off the face of the sky; the storm, the black man, the whistler from the sea bottom and the fringes of the fish stones, the thunder, the lightning, the mighty pebbles, these came up; as a sickness, an afterbirth, coming up from the belly of weathers; the antichrist from a sea flame or a steam crucifix, coming up the putting on of rain; as the acid was stronger, the multiplying storm, the colour of temper, the whole, the unholy, rock handed, came up coming up.

This was the exterior world.

And the shadows, that were web and cloven footed in the house, with the beaks of birds, the shifted shadows that bore a woman in each hand, had no casting substances; and the foam horses of the exterior sea climbed like foxes on the hills. This that held Nant and Manza, the bone of a horse head, the ox and black man arising from the clay picture, was the interior world. This was the interior world where the acid grew stronger, and the death in the acid added ten days to the dead time.

Still Doctor Manza did not see me. I who was the doctor in a dream, the foreign logician, the maker of birds, engrossed in the acid strengthening and the search for oblivion, soon raised the beaker to my mouth as the storm came up. There was thunder as I drank; and as he fell, the lightning darted up the wind.

There is a dead man in the tower, a woman said to her companion as they stood by the door of the central hall. There is a dead man in the central tower, said the corner echoes, and their voices rose through the house. Suddenly the hall was crowded, and the people of the house moved among one another, questioning as to the name of the new dead.

Nant stood above the Doctor. Now the Doctor was dead. There was a corridor leading to the tower of ten days' death, and there a woman danced alone, with the hands of a man upon her shoulders. And soon the virgins joined her, bared to the waist, and made the movements of dancing; they danced towards the open doors of the corridor, stood lightly in the doorways; they danced four steps towards the doors, and then danced four steps away. In the long hall they danced in celebration of the dead. This was the dance of the halt, the blind and half dead, this the dance of the children, the grave girls bared to the waist, this the dance of the dreamers, the open eyed and the naked hopheads, sleeping as they moved. Doctor Manza was dead at my feet. I knelt down to count his ribs, to raise his jaw, to wrench the beaker of acid from his hand. But the dead hand stiffened.

Said a voice at my elbow, Unlock the hand. I moved to obey the voice, but a softer voice said at my ear, Let the hand stiffen. Strike the second voice. Strike the first voice. I struck at the two voices with my fist, and Nant's hand turned into a tree.

At noon the storm was stronger; all afternoon it shook the tower, pulling the slates from the roof; it came from the sea and the earth, from the sea beds and the roots of the forests. I could hear nothing but the voice of the thunder that drowned the two stricken voices; I saw the lightning stride up the hill, a bright, forked man blinding me through the tower windows. And still they danced, into the early evening, the storm increasing, and still the half-naked virgins danced to the doors. This was the dance of the celebration of death in the interior world.

I heard a voice say over the thunder, The dead shall be buried. This was not everlasting death, but a death of days; this was a sleep with no heart. We bury the dead, said the voice that heard my heart, The brief and the everlasting. The storm up the wind measured off the distances of the voice, but a lull in the rain let the two struggling voices at my side recall me to the hand and the acid. I dragged up the stiffening hand, unlocked the fingers, and raised the beaker to my mouth. As the glass burned me, there came a knocking at the door and a cry from the people of the house. They who were seeking the body of the new dead worried the door. Swiftly I glanced towards the table where a lemon lay on a plate. I punctured the skin of the lemon and poured in the acid. Then down came the storm of the dark voices and the knocks, and the tower door broke on its hinges. The dead was found. I fought between the shoulders of the entering strangers, and, leaving them to their picking, spiralled down, sped through the corridors, the lemon at my breast.

Nant and I were brothers in this wild world far from the border villages, from the sea that has England in its hand, from the spires of God and the uneaten graves beneath them. As one, one headed, two footed, we ran through the passages and halls, seeing no shadow, hearing none of the wicked intimacies of the house. We looked for a devil in the corners, but their secrets were ours. So we ran on, afraid of our footfalls, exulting in the knocking of the blood, for death was at our breast, a sharp fruit, a full and yellow tumour shaped to the skin.

Nant was a lonely runner in the house; I parted from him, leaving a half ache and a half terror, going my own way, the way of light breaking over Cathmarw hill and

the Black Valley. And, going his own way, he climbed alone
up a stone stairs to the last tower. He put his mouth to her
cheek and touched her nipple. The storm died as she
touched him.

He cut the lemon in half with the scissors dangling from
from the rope of her skirt.

And the storm came up again as they drank.

This was the coming of death in the interior world.

# The Burning Baby

They said that Rhys was burning his baby when a gorse bush broke into fire on the summit of the hill. The bush, burning merrily, assumed to them the sad white features and the rickety limbs of the vicar's burning baby. What the wind had not blown away of the baby's ashes, Rhys Rhys had sealed in a stone jar. With his own dust lay the baby's dust, and near him the dust of his daughter in a coffin of white wood.

They heard his son howl in the wind. They saw him walking over the hill, holding a dead animal up to the light of the stars. They saw him in the valley shadows as he moved, with the motion of a man cutting wheat, over the brows of the fields. In a sanatorium he coughed his lung into a basin, stirring his fingers delightedly in the blood. What moved with invisible scythe through the valley was a shadow and a handful of shadows cast by the grave sun.

The brush burned out, and the face of the baby fell away with the smoking leaves.

It was, they said, on a fine sabbath morning in the middle of the summer that Rhys Rhys fell in love with his daughter. The gorse that morning had burst into flames. Rhys Rhys, in clerical black, had seen the flames shoot up to the sky, and the bush on the edge of the hill burn red as God among the paler burning of the grass. He took his daughter's hand as she lay in the garden hammock, and told her that he loved her. He told her that she was more beautiful than her dead mother. Her hair smelt of mice, her teeth came over her lip, and the lids of her eyes were red and wet. He saw her beauty come out of her like a stream of sap. The folds of her dress could not hide from him the shabby nakedness of her body. It was not her bone, nor her flesh, nor her hair that he found suddenly beautiful. The poor soil shudders under the sun, he said. He moved his hand up and down her arm. Only the awkward and the

94

ugly, only the barren bring forth fruit. The flesh of her arm was red with the smoothing of his hand. He touched her breast. From the touch of her breast he knew each inch of flesh upon her. Why do you touch me there? she said.

In the church that morning he spoke of the beauty of the harvest, of the promise of the standing corn and the promise in the sharp edge of the scythe as it brings the corn low and whistles through the air before it cuts into the ripeness. Through the open windows at the end of the aisles, he saw the yellow fields upon the hillside and the smudge of heather on the meadow borders. The world was ripe.

The world is ripe for the second coming of the son of man, he said aloud.

But it was not the ripeness of God that glistened from the hill. It was the promise and the ripeness of the flesh, the good flesh, the mean flesh, flesh of his daughter, flesh, flesh, the flesh of the voice of thunder howling before the death of man.

That night he preached of the sins of the flesh. O God in the image of our flesh, he prayed.

His daughter sat in the front pew, and stroked her arm. She would have touched her breast where he had touched it, but the eyes of the congregation were upon her.

Flesh, flesh, flesh, said the vicar.

His son, scouting in the fields for a mole's hill or the signs of a red fox, whistling to the birds and patting the calves as they stood at their mother's sides, came upon a dead rabbit sprawling on a stone. The rabbit's head was riddled with pellets, the dogs had torn open its belly, and the marks of a ferret's teeth were upon its throat. He lifted it gently up, tickling it behind the ears. The blood from its head dropped on his hand. Through the rip in the belly, its intestines had dropped out and coiled on the stone. He held the little body close to his jacket, and ran home through the fields, the rabbit dancing against his waistcoat. As he reached the gate of the vicarage, the worshippers dribbled out of church. They shook hands and raised their hats, smiling at the poor boy with his long green hair, his ass's ears, and death buttoned under his jacket. He was always the poor boy to them.

Rhys Rhys sat in his study, the stem of his pipe stuck between his flybuttons, the bible unopened upon his knees. The day of God was over, and the sun, like another sabbath, went down behind the hills. He lit the lamp, but his own oil burned brighter. He drew the curtains, shutting out the unwelcome night. But he opened his own heart up, and the bald pulse that beat there was a welcome stranger. He had not felt love like this since the woman who scratched him, seeing the woman witch in his male eyes, had fallen into his arms and kissed him, and whispered Welsh words as he took her. She had been the mother of his daughter and had died in her pains, stealing, when she was dead, the son of his second love, and leaving the greenhaired changeling in its place. Merry with desire, Rhys Rhys cast the bible on the floor. He reached for another book, and read, in the lamplit darkness, of the old woman who had deceived the devil. The devil is poor flesh, said Rhys Rhys.

His son came in, bearing the rabbit in his arms. The lank, redcoated boy was a flesh out of the past. The skin of the unburied dead patched to his bones, the smile of the changeling on his mouth, and the hair of the sea rising from his scalp, he stood before Rhys Rhys. A ghost of his mother, he held the rabbit gently to his breast, rocking it to and fro. Cunningly, from under halfclosed lids, he saw his father shrink away from the vision of death. Be off with you, said Rhys Rhys. Who was this green stranger to carry in death and rock it, like a baby under a warm shawl of fur, before him? For a minute the flesh of the world lay still; the old terror set in; the waters of the breast dried up; the nipples grew through the sand. Then he drew his hand over his eyes, and only the rabbit remained, a little sack of flesh, half empty, swaying in the arms of his son. Be off, he said. The boy held the rabbit close, and rocked it, and tickled it again.

Changeling, said Rhys Rhys. He is mine, said the boy, I'll peel him and keep the skull. His room in the attic was crowded with skulls and dried pelts, and little bones in bottles.

Give it to me.

He is mine.

Rhys Rhys tore the rabbit away, and stuffed it deep in the pockets of his smoking coat. When his daughter came in, dressed and ready for bed, with a candle in her hand, Rhys Rhys had death in his pocket.

She was timid, for his touch still ached on her arm and breast but she bent unblushing over him. Saying good-night, she kissed him, and he blew her candle out. She was smiling as he lowered the wick of the lamp.

Step out of your shift, said he. Shiftless, she stepped towards his arms.

I want the little skull, said a voice in the dark.

From his room at the top of the house, through the webs on the windows, and over the furs and the bottles, the boy saw a mile of green hill running away into the darkness of the first dawn. Summer storm in the heat of the rain, flooring the grassy mile, had left some new morning brightness, out of the dead night, in each reaching root.

Death took hold of his sister's legs as she walked through the calf-deep heather up the hill. He saw the high grass at her thighs. And the blades of the upgrowing wind, out of the four windsmells of the manuring dead, might drive through the soles of her feet, up the veins of the legs and stomach, into her womb and her pulsing heart. He watched her climb. She stood, gasping for breath, on a hill of the wider hill, tapping the wall of her bladder, fondling her matted chest (for the hair grew on her as on a grown man), feeling the heart in her wrist, loving her coveted thinness. She was to him as ugly as the sowfaced woman of Llareggub who had taught him the terrors of the flesh. He remembered the advances of that unlovely woman. She blew out his candle as he stepped towards her on the night the great hail had fallen and he had hidden in her rotting house from the cruelty of the weather. Now half a mile off his sister stood in the morning, and the vermin of the hill might spring upon her as she stood, uncaring, rounding the angles of her ugliness. He smiled at the thought of the devouring rats, and looked around the room for a bottle to hold her heart. Her skull, fixed by a socket to the nail above his bed, would be a smiling welcome to the first pains of waking.

But he saw Rhys Rhys stride up the hill, and the bowl of his sister's head, fixed invisibly above his sheets, crumbled away. Standing straight by the side of a dewy tree, his sister beckoned. Up went Rhys Rhys through the calf-deep heather, the death in the grass, over the boulders and up through the reaching ferns, to where she stood. He took her hand. The two shadows linked hands, and climbed together to the top of the hill. The boy saw them go, and turned his face to the wall as they vanished, in one dull shadow, over the edge, and down to the dingle at the west foot of the lovers' alley.

Later, he remembered the rabbit. He ran downstairs and found it in the pocket of the smoking coat. He held death against him, tasting a cough of blood upon his tongue as he climbed, contented, back to the bright bottles and the wall of heads.

In the first dew of light he saw his father clamber for her white hand. She who was his sister walked with a swollen belly over the hill. She touched him between the legs, and he sighed and sprang at her. But the nerves of her face mixed with the quiver in his thighs, and she shot from him. Rhys Rhys, over the bouldered rim, led her to terror. He sighed and sprang at her. She mixed with him in the fourth and the fifth terrors of the flesh. Said Rhys Rhys, Your mother's eyes. It was not her eyes that saw him proud before her, nor the eyes in her thumb. The lashes of her fingers lifted. He saw the ball under the nail.

It was, they said, on a fine sabbath morning in the early spring that she bore him a male child. Brought to bed of her father, she screamed for an anaesthetic as the knocking head burst through. In her gown of blood she slept until twilight, and a star burst bloody through each ear. With a scissors and rag, Rhys Rhys attended her, and, gazing on the shrivelled features and the hands like the hands of a mole, he gently took the child away, and his daughter's breast cried out and ran into the mouth of the surrounding shadows. The shadow pouted for the milk and the binding cottons. The child spat in his arms, the noise of the running air was blind in its ears, and the deaf light died from its eyes.

Rhys Rhys, with the dead child held against him, stepped into the night, hearing the mother moan in her sleep and the deadly shadow, filled sick with milk, flowing around the house. He turned his face towards the hills. A shadow walked close to him and, silent in the shadow of a full tree, the changeling waited. He made an image for the moon, and the flesh of the moon fell away, leaving a star-eyed skull. Then with a smile he ran back over the lawns and into the crying house. Halfway up the stairs, he heard his sister die. Rhys Rhys climbed on.

On the top of the hill he laid the baby down, and propped it against the heather. Death propped the dark flowers. The baby stiffened in the rigor of the moon. Poor flesh, said Rhys Rhys as he pulled at the dead heather and furze. Poor angel, he said to the listening mouth of the baby. The fruit of the flesh falls with the worm from the tree. Conceiving the worm, the bark crumbles. There lay the poor star of flesh that had dropped, like the bead of a woman's milk, through the nipples of a wormy tree.

He stacked the torn heathers in a circle. On the head of the purple stack, he piled the dead grass. A stack of death, the heather grew as tall as he, and loomed at last over his windy hair.

Behind a boulder moved the accompanying shadow, and the shadow of the boy was printed under the fiery flank of a tree. The shadow marked the boy, and the boy marked the bones of the naked baby under their chilly cover, and how the grass scraped on the bald skull, and where his father picked out a path in the cancerous growths of the silent circle. He saw Rhys Rhys pick up the baby and place it on the top of the stack, saw the head of a burning match, and heard the crackle of the bush, breaking like a baby's arm.

The stack burst into flame. Rhys Rhys, before the red eye of the creeping fire, stretched out his arms and beckoned the shadow from the stones. Surrounded by shadows, he prayed before the flaming stack, and the sparks of the heather blew past his smile. Burn, child, poor flesh, mean flesh, flesh, flesh, sick sorry flesh, flesh of the foul womb, burn back to dust, he prayed.

And the baby caught fire. The flames curled round its mouth and blew upon the shrinking gums. Flames round its red cord lapped its little belly till the raw flesh fell upon the heather.

A flame touched its tongue. Eeeeeh, cried the burning baby, and the illuminated hill replied.

# The Orchards

He had dreamed that a hundred orchards on the road to
the sea village had broken into flame; and all the windless
afternoon tongues of fire shot through the blossom. The
birds had flown up as a small red cloud grew suddenly
from each branch; but as night came down with the rising
of the moon and the swinging-in of the mile-away sea, a
wind blew out the fires and the birds returned. He was
an apple-farmer in a dream that ended as it began: with
the flesh-and-ghost hand of a woman pointing to the trees.
She twined the fair and dark tails of her hair together,
smiled over the apple fields to a sister figure who stood in
a circular shadow by the walls of the vegetable garden;
but the birds flew down on to her sister's shoulders, un-
afraid of the scarecrow face and the cross-wood nakedness under the rags. He gave the woman a kiss, and she
kissed him back. Then the crows came down to her arms
as she held him close; the beautiful scarecrow kissed him,
pointing to the trees as the fires died.

Marlais awoke that summer morning with his lips still
wet from her kiss. This was a story more terrible than the
stories of the reverend madmen in the Black Book of
Llareggub, for the woman near the orchards, and her
sister-stick by the wall, were his scarecrow lovers for ever
and ever. What were the sea-village burning orchards and
the clouds at the ends of the branches to his love for
these bird-provoking women? All the trees of the world
might blaze suddenly from the roots to the highest leaves,
but he would not sprinkle water on the shortest fiery field.
She was his lover, and her sister with birds on her shoulders held him closer than the women of LlanAsia.

Through the top-storey window he saw the pale blue,
cloudless sky over the tangle of roofs and chimneys, and
the promise of a lovely day in the rivers of the sun. There,
in a chimney's shape, stood his bare, stone boy and the

three blind gossips, blowing fire through their skulls, who huddled for warmth in all weathers. What man on a roof had turned hs weathercock's head to stare at the red-and-black girls over the town and, by his turning, made them stone pillars? A wind from the world's end had frozen the roof-walkers when the town was a handful of houses; now a circle of coal table-hills, where the children played Indians, cast its shadow on the black lots and the hundred streets; and the stone-blind gossips cramped together by his bare boy and the brick virgins under the towering crane-hills.

The sea ran to the left, a dozen valleys away, past the range of volcanoes and the great stack forests and ten towns in a hole. It met the Glamorgan shores where a half-mountain fell westward out of the clump of villages in a wild wood, and shook the base of Wales. But now, thought Marlais, the sea is slow and cool, full of dolphins; it flows in all directions from a green centre, lapping the land stones; it makes the shells speak on the blazing half-mountain sand, and the lines of time even shall not join the blue sea surface and the bottomless bed.

He thought of the sea running; when the sun sank, a fire went in under the liquid caverns. He remembered, while he dressed, the hundred fires around the blossoms of the apple-trees, and the uneasy salt rising of the wind that died with the last pointing of the beautiful scarecrow's hand. Water and fire, sea and apple-tree, two sisters and a crowd of birds, blossomed, pointed, and flew down all that midsummer morning in a top-storey room in the house on a slope over the black-housed town.

He sharpened his pencil and shut the sky out, shook back his untidy hair, arranged the papers of a devilish story on his desk, and broke the pencil-point with a too-hard scribble of "sea" and "fire" on a clean page. Fire would not set the ruled lines alight, adventure, burning, through the heartless characters, nor water close over the bogy heads and the unwritten words. The story was dead from the devil up; there was a white-hot tree with apples where a frozen tower with owls should have rocked in a wind from Antarctica; there were naked girls, with nipples like berries, on the sand in the sun, where a cold and un-holy woman should be wailing by the Kara Sea or the Sea of Azov. The morning was against him. He struggled with his words like a man with the sun, and the sun stood victoriously at high noon over the dead story.

Put a two-coloured ring of two women's hair round the blue world, white and coal-black against the summer-coloured boundaries of sky and grass, four-breasted stems at the poles of the summer sea-ends, eyes in the sea-shells, two fruit-trees out of a coal hill: poor Marlais's morning, turning to evening, spins before you. Under the eyelids, where the inward night drove backwards, through the skull's base, into the wide, first world on the far-away eye, two love-trees smouldered like sisters. Have an orchard sprout in the night, an enchanted woman with a spine like a railing burn her hand in the leaves, man-on-fire a mile from a sea have a wind put out your heart: Marlais's death in life in the circular going down of the day that had taken no time blows again in the wind for you.

The world was the saddest in the turning world, and the stars in the north, where the shadow of a mock moon spun until a wind put out the shadow, were the ravaged south faces. Only the fork-tree breast of the woman's scarecrow could bear his head like an apple on the white wood where no worm would enter, and her barbed breast alone pierce the worm in the dream under her sweetheart's eyelid. The real round moon shone on the women of LlanAsia and the love-torn virgins of This street.

The word is too much with us. He raised his pencil so that its shadow fell, a tower of wood and lead, on the clean paper; he fingered the pencil tower, the half-moon of his thumb-nail rising and setting behind the leaden spire. The tower fell, down fell the city of words, the walls of a poem, the symmetrical letters. He marked the disintegration of the ciphers as the light failed, the sun drove down into a foreign morning, and the word of the sea rolled over the sun. Image, all image, he cried to the fallen tower as the night came on, whose harp is the sea? whose burning candle is the sun? An image of man, he rose to his feet and drew the curtains open. Peace, like a simile, lay over the roofs of the town. Image, all image, cried Marlais, stepping through the window on to the level roofs.

The slates shone around him, in the smoke of the magnified stacks and through the vapours of the hill. Below him, in a world of words, men on their errands moved to no purpose but the escape of time. Brave in his desolation, he scrambled to the edge of the slates, there to stand

perilously above the tiny traffic and the lights of the street
signals. The toy of the town was at his feet. On went the
marzipan cars, changing gear, applying brake, over the
nursery carpets into a child's hands. But soon height had
him and he swayed, feeling his legs grow weak beneath him
and his skull swell like a bladder in the wind. It was the
image of an infant city that threw his pulses into confusion.
There was dust in his eyes; there were eyes in the grains of
dust ascending from the street. Once on the leveller roofs,
he touched his left breast. Death was the bright magnets
of the streets; the wind pulled off the drag of death and the
falling visions. Now he was stripped of fear, strong, night-
muscled. Over the housetops he ran towards the moon.
There the moon came, in a colder glory than before, attended by stars, drawing the tides of the sea. By a parapet
he watched her, finding a word for each stage of her journey in the directed sky, calling her same-faced, wondering
at her many masks. Death mask and dance mask over her
mountainous features transformed the sky; she struggled
behind a cloud, and came with a new smile over the wall
of wind. Image, and all was image, from Marlais, ragged
in the wind, to the appalling town, he on the roofs invisible
to the street, the street beneath him blind to his walking
word. His hand before him was five-fingered life.

A baby cried, but the cry grew fainter. It is all one, the
loud voice and the still voice striking a common silence,
the dowdy lady flattening her nose against the panes, and
the well-mourned lady. The word is too much with us, and
the dead word. Cloud, the last muslin's rhyme, shapes
above tenements and bursts in cold rain on the suburban
drives. Hail falls on cinder track and the angelled stone.
It is all one, the rain and the macadam; it is all one, the
hail and cinder, the flesh and the rough dust. High above
the hum of the houses, far from the skyland and the frozen
fence, he questioned each shadow; man among ghosts, and
ghost in clover, he moved for the last answer.

The bare boy's voice through a stone mouth, no longer
smoking at this hour, rose up unanswerably: Who walks,
mad among us, on the roofs, by my cold, brick-red side
and the weathercock-frozen women, walks over This street,
under the image of the Welsh summer heavens walks all
night loverless, has two sister lovers ten towns away. Past
the great stack forests to the left and the sea his lovers
burn for him endlessly by a hundred orchards. The gossips'

voices rose up unanswerably: Who walks by the stone virgins is our virgin Marlais, wind and fire, and the coward on the burning roofs.

He stepped through the open window.

Red sap in the trees bubbled from the cauldron roots to the last spray of blossom, and the boughs, that night after the hollow walk, fell like candles from the trunks but could not die for the heat of the sulphurous head of the grass burned yellow by the dead sun. And flying there, he rounded, half mist, half man, all apple circles on the sea-village road in the high heat of noon as the dawn broke; and as the sun rose like a river over the hills so the sun sank behind a tree. The woman pointed to the hundred orchards and the black birds who flocked around her sister, but a wind put the trees out and he woke again. This was the intolerable, second waking out of a life too beautiful to break, but the dream was broken. Who had walked by the virgins near the orchards was a virgin, wind and fire, and a coward in the destroying coming of the morning. But after he had dressed and taken breakfast, he walked up This street to the hilltop and turned his face towards the invisible sea.

Good morning, Marlais, said an old man sitting with six greyhounds in the blackened grass.

Good morning, Mr. David Davies.

You are up very early, said David Two Times.

I am walking towards the sea.

The wine-coloured sea, said Dai Twice.

Marlais strode over the hill to the greener left, and down behind the circle of the town to the rim of Whippet valley where the trees, for ever twisted between smoke and slag, tore at the sky and the black ground. The dead boughs prayed that the roots might shoulder up the soil, leaving a dozen channels empty for the leaves and the spirit of the cracking wood, a hole in the valley for the mole-handed sap, a long grave for the last spring's skeleton that once had leapt, when the blunt and forked hills were sharp and straight, through the once-green land. But Whippet's trees were the long dead of the stacked south of the country; who had vanished under the hacked land pointed, thumb-to-hill, these black leaf-nailed and warning fingers. Death in Wales had twisted the Welsh dead into those valley cripples.

The day was a passing of days. High noon, the story-killer and the fire bug (the legends of the Russian seas died as the trees awoke to their burning), passed in all the high noons since the fall of man from the sun and the first sun's pinnacling of the half-made heavens. And all the valley summers, the once monumental red and the now headstone-featured, all that midsummer afternoon were glistening in the seaward walk. Through the ancestral valley where his fathers, out of their wooden dust and full of sparrows, wagged at a hill, he walked steadily; on the brink of the hole that held LlanAsia as a grave holds a town, he was caught in the smoke of the forests and, like a ghost from the clear-cut quarters under the stack roots, climbed down on to the climbing streets.

Where are you walking, Marlais? said a one-legged man by a black flower-bed.

Towards the sea, Mr. William Williams.

The mermaid-crowded sea, said Will Peg.

Marlais passed out of the tubercular valley on to a waste mountain, through a seedy wood to a shagged field; a crow, on a molehill, in Prince Price's skull cawed of the breadth of hell in the packed globe; the afternoon broke down, the stumped land heaving, and, like a tree or lightning, a wind, roots up, forked between smoke and slag as the dusk dropped; surrounded by echoes, the red-hot travellers of voices, and the devils from the horned acres, he shuddered on his enemies' territory as a new night came on in the nightmare of an evening. Let the trees collapse, the dusty journeymen said, the boulders flake away and the gorse rot and vanish, earth and grass be swallowed down on to a hill's v balancing on the grave that proceeds to Eden. Winds on fire, through vault and coffin and fossil we'll blow a manfull of dust into the garden. Where the serpent sets the tree alight, and the apple falls like a spark out of its skin, a tree leaps up; a scarecrow shines on the cross-boughs, and, by one in the sun, the new trees arise, making an orchard round the crucifix. By midnight two more valleys lay beneath him, dark with their two towns in the palms of the mined mountains; a valley, by one in the morning, held Aberbabel in its fist beneath him. He was a young man no longer but a legendary walker, a folk-man walking, with a cricket for a heart; he walked by Aberbabel's chapel, cut through the graveyard over the unstill headstones, spied a red-cheeked man in a night-shirt two foot above ground.

The valleys passed; out of the water-dipping hills, the moments of mountains, the eleventh valley came up like an hour. And coming out timelessly through the dwarf's eye of the telescope, through the ring of light like a circle's wedding on the last hill before the sea, the shape of the hundred orchards magnified with the immaculate diminishing of the moon. This was the spectacle that met the telescope, and the world Marlais saw in the morning following upon the first of the eleven untold adventures: to his both sides the unbroken walls, taller than the beanstalks that married a story on the roof of the world, of stone and earth and beetle and tree; a graveyard before him the ground came to a stop, shot down and down, was lost with the devil in bed, rose shakily to the sea-village road where the blossoms of the orchards hung over the wooden walls and sister-roads ran off into the four white country points; a rock line thus, straight to the hilltop, and the turning graph scored with trees; dip down the county, deep as the history of the final fire burning through the chamber one story over Eden, the first green structure after the red downfall; down, down, like a stone stuck with towns, like the river out of a glass of places, fell his footholding hill. He was a folkman no longer but Marlais the poet walking, over the brink into ruin, up the side of doom, over hell in bed to the red left, till he reached the first of the fields where the unhatched apples were soon to cry fire in a wind from a half-mountain falling westward to the sea. A man-in-a-picture Marlais, by noon's blow to the centre, stood by a circle of apple-trees and counted the circles that travelled over the shady miles into a clump of villages. He laid himself down in the grass, and noon fell back bruised to the sun; and he slept till a handbell rang over the fields. It was a windless afternoon in the sisters' orchards, and the fair-headed sister was ringing the bell for tea.

He had come very near to the end of the indescribable journey. The fair girl, in a field sloping seaward three fields and a stile from Peter, laid out a white cloth on a flat stone. Into one of a number of cups she poured milk and tea, and cut the bread so thin she could see London through the white pieces. She stared hard at the stile and the pruned, transparent hedge, and as Marlais climbed over, ragged and unshaven, his stripped breast burned by the sun, she rose from the grass and smiled and poured tea for him.

This was the end to the untold adventures. They sat in the grass by the stone table like lovers at a picnic, too loved to speak, desireless familiars in the shade of the hedge corner. She had shaken a handbell for her sister, and called a lover over eleven valleys to her side. Her many lovers' cups were empty on the flat stone.

And he who had dreamed that a hundred orchards had broken into flame saw suddenly then in the windless afternoon tongues of fire shoot through the blossom. The trees all around them kindled and crackled in the sun, the birds flew up as a small red cloud grew from each branch, the bark caught like gorse, the unborn, blazing apples whirled down devoured in a flash. The trees were fireworks and torches, smouldered out of the furnace of the fields into a burning arc, cast down their branded fruit like cinders on the charred roads and fields.

Who had dreamed a boy's dream of her flesh-and-ghost hand in the windless afternoon saw then, at the red height, when the wooden step-roots splintered at the orchard entrance and the armed towers came to grief, that she raised her hand heavily and pointed to the trees and birds. There was a flurry in the sky, of wing and fire and near-to-evening wind in the going below of the burned day. As the new night was built, she smiled as she had done in the short dream eleven valleys old; lame like Pisa, the night leaned on the west walls; no trumpet shall knock the Welsh walls down before the last crack of music; she pointed to her sister in a shadow by the disappearing garden, and the dark-headed figure with crows on her shoulders appeared at Marlais's side.

This was the end of a story more terrible than the stories of the quick and the undead in mountainous houses on Jarvis hills, and the unnatural valley that Idris waters is a children's territory to this eleventh valley in the seaward travel. A dream that was no dream skulked there; the real world's wind came up to kill the fires; a scarecrow pointed to the extinguished trees.

This he had dreamed before the blossom's burning and the putting-out, before the rising and the salt swinging-in, was a dream no longer near these orchards. He kissed the two secret sisters, and a scarecrow kissed him back. He heard the birds fly down on to his lovers' shoulders. He saw the fork-tree breast, the barbed eye, and the dry, twig hand.

# The Mouse and the Woman

## 1

In the eaves of the lunatic asylum were birds who whistled the coming in of spring. A madman, howling like a dog from the top room, could not disturb them, and their tunes did not stop when he thrust his hands through the bars of the window near their nests and clawed the sky. A fresh smell blew with the winds around the whte building and its grounds. The asylum trees waved green hands over the wall to the world outside.

In the gardens the patients sat and looked up at the sun or upon the flowers or upon nothing, or walked sedately along the paths, hearing the gravel crunch beneath their feet with a hard, sensible sound. Children in print dresses might be expected to play, not noisily, upon the lawn. The building, too, had a sweet expression, as though it knew only the kind things of life and the polite emotions. In a middle room sat a child who had cut off his double thumb with a scissors.

A little way off the main path leading from house to gate, a girl, lifting her arms, beckoned to the birds. She enticed the sparrows with little movements of her fingers, but to no avail. It must be spring, she said. The sparrows sang exultantly, and then stopped.

The howling in the top room began again. The madman's face was pressed close to the bars of the window. Opening his mouth wide, he bayed up at the sun, listening to the inflections of his voice with a remorseless concentration. With his unseeing eyes fixed on the green garden, he heard the revolution of the years as they moved softly back. Now there was no garden. Under the sun the iron bars melted. Like a flower, a new room pulsed and opened.

## 2

Waking up when it was still dark, he turned the dream over and over on the tip of his brain until each little symbol became heavy with a separate meaning. But there were symbols he could not remember, they came and went so quickly among the rattle of leaves, the gestures of women's hands spelling on the sky, the falling of rain and the humming wind. He remembered the oval of her face and the colour of her eyes. He remembered the pitch of her voice, though not what she said. She moved again wearily up and down the same ruler of turf. What she said fell with the leaves, and spoke in the wind whose brother rattled the panes like an old man.

There had been seven women, in a mad play by a Greek, each with the same face, crowned by the same hoop of mad, black hair. One by one they trod the ruler of turf, then vanished. They turned the same face to him, intolerably weary with the same suffering.

The dream had changed. Where the women were was an avenue of trees. And the trees leant forward and interlaced their hands, turning into a black forest. He had seen himself, absurd in his nakedness, walk into the depths. Stepping on a dead twig, he was bitten.

Then there was her face again. There was nothing in his dream but her tired face. And the changes of the details of the dream and the celestial changes, the levers of the trees and the toothed twigs, these were the mechanisms of her delirium. It was not the sickness of sin that was upon her face. Rather it was the sickness of never having sinned and of never having done well.

He lit the candle on the little deal table by his bedside. Candle light threw the shadows of the room into confusion, and raised up the warped men of shadow out of the corners. For the first time he heard the clock. He had been deaf until then to everything except the wind outside the window and the clean winter sounds of the night-world. But now the steady tick tock tick sounded like the heart of someone hidden in his room. He could not hear the night birds now. The loud clock drowned their crying, or the wind was too cold for them and made commotion among their feathers. He remembered the dark hair of the woman in the trees and of the seven women treading the ruler of turf.

He could no longer listen to the speaking of reason. The pulse of a new heart beat at his side. Contentedly he let the dream dictate its rhythm. Often he would rise when the sun had dropped down, and, in the lunatic blackness under the stars, walk on the hill, feeling the wind finger his hair and at his nostrils. The rats and the rabbits on his towering hill came out in the dark, and the shadows consoled them for the night of the harsh sun. The dark woman, too, had risen out of darkness, pulling down the stars in their hundreds and showing him a mystery that hung and shone higher in the night of the sky than all the planets crowding beyond the curtains.

He fell to sleep again and woke in the sun. As he dressed, the dog scratched at the door. He let it in and felt its wet muzzle in his hand. The weather was hot for a midwinter day. The little wind there was could not relieve the sharpness of the heat. With the opening of the bedroom window, the uneven beams of the sun twisted his images into the hard lines of light.

He tried not to think of the woman as he ate. She had risen out of the depths of darkness. Now she was lost again. She is drowned, dead, dead. In the clean glittering of the kitchen, among the white boards, the oleographs of old women, the brass candlesticks, the plates on the shelves, and the sounds of kettle and clock, he was caught between believing in her and denying her. Now he insisted on the lines of her neck. The wilderness of her hair rose over the dark surface. He saw her flesh in the cut bread; her blood, still flowing through the channels of her mysterious body, in the spring water.

But another voice told him that she was dead. She was a woman in a mad story. He forced himself to hear the voice telling that she was dead. Dead, alive, drowned, raised up. The two voices shouted across his brain. He could not bear to think that the last spark in her had been put out. She is alive, alive, cried the two voices together.

As he tidied the sheets on his bed, he saw a block of paper, and sat down at the table with a pencil poised in his hand. A hawk flew over the hill. Seagulls, on spread, unmoving wings, cried past the window. A mother rat, in a hole in the hillside near the holes of rabbits, suckled its young as the sun climbed higher in the clouds.

He put the pencil down.

3

One winter morning, after the last crowing of the cock, in the walks of his garden, had died to nothing, she who for so long had dwelt with him appeared in all the wonder of her youth. She had cried to be set free, and to walk in his dreams no longer. Had she not been in the beginning, there would have been no beginning. She had moved in his belly when he was a boy, and stirred in his boy's loins. He at last gave birth to her who had been with him from the beginning. And with him dwelt a dog, a mouse, and a dark woman.

4

It is not a little thing, he thought, this writing that lies before me. It is the telling of a creation. It is the story of birth. Out of him had come another. A being had been born, not out of the womb, but out of the soul and the spinning head. He had come to the cottage on the hill that the being within him might ripen and be born away from the eyes of men. He understood what the wind that took up the woman's cry had cried in his last dream. Let me be born, it had cried. He had given a woman being. His flesh would be upon her, and the life that he had given her would make her walk, talk, and sing. And he knew, too, that it was upon the block of paper she was made absolute. There was an oracle in the lead of the pencil.

In the kitchen he cleaned up after his meal. When the last plate had been washed, he looked around the room. In the corner near the door was a hole no bigger than a half-crown. He found a tiny square of tin and nailed it over the hole, making sure that nothing could go in or come out. Then he donned his coat and walked out on to the hill and down towards the sea.

Broken water leapt up from the inrushing tide and fell into the crevices of the rocks, making innumerable pools. He climbed down to the half-circle of beach, and the clusters of shells did not break when his foot fell on them. Feeling his heart knock at his side, he turned to where the greater rocks climbed perilously up to the grass. There, at the foot, the oval of her face towards him, she stood and smiled. The spray brushed her naked body, and the creams of the sea ran unheeded over her feet. She lifted her hand. He crossed to her.

## 5

In the cool of the evening they walked in the garden behind the cottage. She had lost none of her beauty with the covering up of her nakedness. With slippers on her feet she stepped as gracefully as when her feet were bare. There was a dignity in the poise of her head, and her voice was clear as a bell. Walking by her side along the narrow path, he heard no discord in the crying together of the gulls. She pointed out bird and bush with her finger, illuminating a new loveliness in the wings and leaves, in the sour churning of water over pebbles, and a new life along the dead branches of the trees.

It is quiet here, she said as they stood looking out to sea and the dark coming over the land. Is it always as quiet?

Not when the storms come in with the tide, he said. Boys play behind the hill, lovers go down to the shore.

Late evening turned to night so suddenly that, where she stood, stood a shadow under the moon. He took its hand, and they ran together to the cottage.

It was lonely for you before I came, she said.

As a cinder hissed into the grate, he moved back in his chair, making a startled gesture with his hand.

How quickly you become frightened, she said, I am frightened of nothing.

But she thought over her words and spoke again, this time in a low voice.

One day I may have no limbs to walk with, no hands to touch with. No heart under my breast.

Look at the million stars, he said. They make some pattern on the sky. It is a pattern of letters spelling a word. One night I shall look up and read the word.

But she kissed him and calmed his fear.

## 6

The madman remembered the inflections of her voice, heard, again, her frock rustling, and saw the terrible curve of her breast. His own breathing thundered in his ears. The girl on the bench beckoned to the sparrows. Somewhere a child purred, stroking the black columns of a wooden horse that neighed and then lay down.

## 7

They slept together on the first night, side by side in the dark, their arms around one another. The shadows in the corner were trimmed and shapely in her presence, losing their old deformity. And the stars looked in upon them and shone in their eyes.

Tomorrow you must tell me what you dream, he said.

It will be what I have always dreamed, she said. Walking on a little length of grass, up and down, up and down, till my feet bleed. Seven images of me walking up and down.

It is what I dream. Seven is a number in magic.

Magic? she said.

A woman makes a wax man, puts a pin in its chest; and the man dies. Someone has a little devil, tells it what to do. A girl dies, you see her walk. A woman turns into a hill.

She let her head rest on his shoulder, and fell to sleep.

He kissed her mouth, and passed his hand through her hair.

She was asleep, but he did not sleep. Wide awake, he stared into darkness. Now he was drowned in terror, and the sucking waters closed over his skull.

I, I have a devil, he said.

She stirred at the noise of his voice, and then again her head was motionless and her body straight along the curves of the cool bed.

I have a devil, but I do not tell it what to do. It lifts my hand. I write. The words spring into life. She, then, is a woman of the devil.

She made a contented sound, nestled ever nearer to him. Her breath was warm on his neck, and her foot lay on his like a mouse. He saw that she was beautiful in her sleep. Her beauty could not have sprouted out of evil. God, whom he had searched for in his loneliness, had formed her for his mate as Eve for Adam out of Adam's rib.

He kissed her again, and saw her smile as she slept.

God at my side, he said.

He had not slept with Rachel and woken with Leah. There was the pallor of dawn on her cheeks. He touched them lightly with a finger-nail. She did not stir.

But there had been no woman in his dreams. Not even

a thread of woman's hair had dangled from the sky. God had come down in a cloud and the cloud had changed to a snakes' nest. Foul hissing of snakes had suggested the sound of water, and he had been drowned. Down and down he had fallen, under green shiftings and the bubbles that fishes blew from their mouths, down and down on to the bony floors of the sea.

Then against a white curtain of people had moved and moved to no purpose but to speak mad things.

What did you find under the tree?

I found an airman.

No, no, under the other tree?

I found a bottle of foetus.

No, no, under the other tree?

I found a mouse-trap.

He had been invisible. There had been nothing but his voice. He had flown across back gardens, and his voice, caught in a tangle of wireless aerials, had bled as though it were a thing of substance. Men in deck-chairs were listening to the loud-speakers speaking:

What did you find under the tree?

I found a wax man.

No, no, under the other tree?

He could remember little else except the odds and ends of sentences, the movement of a turning shoulder, the sudden flight or drop of syllables. But slowly the whole meaning edged into his brain. He could translate every symbol of his dreams, and he lifted the pencil so that they might stand hard and clear upon the paper. But the words would not come. He thought he heard the scratching of velvet paws behind a panel. But when he sat still and listened close, there was no sound.

She opened her eyes.

What are you doing? she said.

He put down the paper, and kissed her before they rose to dress.

What did you dream last night? he asked her, when they had eaten.

Nothing. I slept, that is all. What did you dream?

Nothing, he said.

## 8

There was creation screaming in the steam of the kettle, in the light making mouths on the china and the floor she swept as a child sweeps the floor of a doll's house. There was nothing to see in her but the ebb and flood of creation, only the transcendent sweep of being and living in the careless fold of flesh from shoulder-bone to elbow. He could not tell, after the horror he had found in the translating symbols, why the sea should point to the fruitful and unfailing stars with the edge of each wave, and an image of fruition disturb the moon in its dead course.

She moulded his images that evening. She lent light, and the lamp was dim beside her who had the oil of life glistening in every pore of her hand.

And now in the garden they remembered how they had walked in the garden for the first time.

You were lonely before I came.

How quickly you become frightened.

She had lost none of her beauty with the covering up of her nakedness. Though he had slept at her side, he had been content to know the surface of her. Now he stripped her of her clothes and laid her on a bed of grass.

9

The mouse had waited for this consummation. Wrinkling its eyes, it crept stealthily along the tunnel, littered with scraps of half-eaten paper, behind the kitchen wall. Stealthily, on tiny, padded paws, it felt its way through darkness, its nails scraping on the wood. Stealthily, it worked its way between the walls, screamed at the blind light through the chinks, and filed through the square of tin. Moonlight dropped slowly into the space where the mouse, working its destruction, inched into light. The last barrier fell away. And on the clean stones of the kitchen floor the mouse stood still.

10

That night he told of the love in the garden of Eden.

A garden was planted eastward, and Adam lived in it. Eve was made for him, out of him, bone of his bones, flesh of his flesh. They were as naked as you upon the sea-shore, but Eve could not have been as beautiful. They ate with the devil, and saw that they were naked, and covered up their nakedness. In their good bodies they saw evil for the first time.

Then you saw evil in me, she said, when I was naked. I would as soon be naked as be clothed. Why did you cover up my nakedness?

It was not good to look upon, he said.

But it was beautiful. You yourself said that it was beautiful, she said.

It was not good to look upon.

You said the body of Eve was good. And yet you say I was not good to look upon. Why did you cover up my nakedness?

It was not good to look upon.

## 11

Welcome, said the devil to the madman. Cast your eyes upon me. I grow and grow. See how I multiply. See my sad, Grecian stare. And the longing to be born in my dark eyes. Oh, that was the best joke of all.

I am an asylum boy tearing the wings of birds. Remember the lions that were crucified. Who knows that it was not I who opened the door of the tomb for Christ to struggle out?

But the madman had heard that welcome time after time. Ever since the evening of the second day after their love in the garden, when he had told her that her nakedness was not good to look upon, he had heard the welcome ring out in the sliding rain, and seen the welcome words burnt into the sea. He had known at the ringing of the first syllable in his ears that nothing on the earth could save him, and that the mouse would come out.

But the mouse had come out already.

The madman cried down at the beckoning girl to whom, now, a host of birds edged closer on a bough.

## 12

Why did you cover up my nakedness?
It was not good to look upon.
Why, then, No, no, under the other tree?
It was not good, I found a wax cross.

As she had questioned him, not harshly, but with bewilderment, that he whom she loved should find her nakedness unclean, he heard the broken pieces of the old dirge break into her questioning.

Why, then, she said, No, no, under the other tree?

He heard himself reply, It was not good, I found a talking thorn.

Real things kept changing place with unreal, and, as a bird burst into song, he heard the springs rattle far back in its throat.

She left him with a smile that still poised over a question, and, crossing the strip of hill, vanished into the half-dark where the cottage stood like another woman. But she returned ten times, in ten different shapes. She breathed at his ear, passed the back of her hand over his dry mouth, and lit the lamp in the cottage room more than a mile away.

It grew darker as he stared at the stars. Wind cut through the new night. Very suddenly a bird screamed over the trees, and an owl, hungry for mice, hooted in the mile-away wood.

There was contradiction in heartbeat and green Sirius, an eye in the east. He put his hand to his eyes, hiding the star, and walked slowly towards the lamp burning far away in the cottage. And all the elements come together, of wind and sea and fire, of love and the passing of love, closed in a circle around him.

She was not sitting by the fire, as he had expected her to be, smiling upon the folds of her dress. He called her name at the foot of the stairs. He looked into the empty bedroom, and called her name in the garden. But she had gone, and all the mystery of her presence had left the cottage. And the shadows that he thought had departed when she had come crowded the corners, muttering in women's voices among themselves. He turned down the wick in the lamp. As he climbed upstairs, he heard the corner voices become louder and louder until the whole cottage reverberated with them, and the wind could not be heard.

## 13

With tears in his cheeks and with a hard pain in his heart, he fell to sleep, coming at last to where his father sat in an alcove carved in a cloud.

Father, he said, I have been walking over the world, looking for a thing worthy of love, but I drove it away and go now from place to place, moaning my hideousness, hearing my own voice in the voices of the corncrakes and the frogs, seeing my own face in the riddled faces of the beasts.

He held out his arms, waiting for words to fall from that old mouth hidden under a white beard frozen with tears. He implored the old man to speak.

Speak to me, your son. Remember how we read the classic books together on the terraces. Or on an Irish harp you would pluck tunes until the geese, like the seven geese of the Wandering Jew, rose squawking into the air. Father, speak to me, your only son, a prodigal out of the herbaceous spaces of small towns, out of the smells and sounds of the city, out of the thorny desert and the deep sea. You are a wise old man.

He implored the old man to speak, but, coming closer to him and staring into his face, he saw the stains of death upon mouth and eyes and a nest of mice in the tangle of the frozen beard.

It was weak to fly, but he flew. And it was a weakness of the blood to be invisible, but he was invisible. He reasoned and dreamed unreasonably at the same time, knowing his weakness and the lunacy of flying but having no strength to conquer it. He flew like a bird over the fields, but soon the bird's body vanished, and he was a flying voice. An open window beckoned him by the waving of its blinds, as a scarecrow beckons a wise bird by its ragged waving, and into the open window he flew, alighting on a bed near a sleeping girl.

Awake, girl, he said. I am your lover come in the night.

She awoke at his voice.

Who called me?

I called you.

Where are you?

I am upon the pillow by your head, speaking into your ear.

Who are you?

I am a voice.

Stop calling into my ear, then, and hop into my hand so that I may touch you and tickle you. Hop into my hand, voice.

He lay still and warm in her palm.

Where are you?

I am in your hand.

Which hand?

The hand on your breast, left hand. Do not make a fist or you will crush me. Can you not feel me warm in your hand? I am close to the roots of your fingers.

Talk to me.

I had a body, but was always a voice. As I truly am, I come to you in the night, a voice on your pillow.

I know what you are. You are the still, small voice I must not listen to. I have been told not to listen to that still, small voice that speaks in the night. It is wicked to listen. You must not come here again. You must go away.

But I am your lover.

I must not listen, said the girl, and suddenly clenched her hand.

## 14

He could go into the garden, regardless of rain, and bury his face in the wet earth. With his ears pressed close to the earth, he would hear the great heart, under soil and grass, strain before breaking. In dreams he would say to some figure, Lift me up. I am only ten pounds now. I am lighter. Six pounds. Two pounds. My spine shows through my breast. The secret of that alchemy that had turned a little revolution of the unsteady senses into a golden moment was lost as a key is lost in undergrowth. A secret was confused among the night, and the confusion of the last madness before the grave would come down like an animal on the brain.

He wrote upon the block of paper, not knowing what he wrote, and dreading the words that looked up at him at last and could not be forgotten.

## 15

And this is all there was to it: a woman had been born, not out of the womb, but out of the soul and the spinning head. And he who had borne her out of darkness loved his creation, and she loved him. But this is all there was to it: a miracle befell a man. He fell in love with it, but could not keep it, and the miracle passed. And with him dwelt a dog, a mouse, and a dark woman. The woman went away, and the dog died.

## 16

He buried the dog at the end of the garden. Rest in peace, he told the dead dog. But the grave was not deep enough and there were rats in the underhanging of the bank who bit through the sack shroud.

## 17

Upon town pavements he saw the woman step loose, her breasts firm under a coat on which the single hairs from old men's heads lay white on black. Her life, he knew, was only a life of days. Her spring had passed with him. After the summer and the autumn, unhallowed time between full life and death, there would be winter corrugating charm. He who knew the subtleties of every reason, and sensed the four together in every symbol of the earth, would disturb the chronology of the seasons. Winter must not appear.

## 18

Consider now the old effigy of time, his long beard whitened by an Egyptian sun, his bare feet watered by the Sargasso sea. Watch me belabour the old fellow. I have stopped his heart. It split like a chamber pot. No, this is no rain falling. This is the wet out of the cracked heart.

Parhelion and sun shine in the same sky with the broken moon. Dizzy with the chasing of moon by sun, and by the twinkling of so many stars, I run upstairs to read again of the love of some man for a woman. I tumble down to see the half-crown hole in the kitchen wall stabbed open, and the prints of a mouse's pads on the floor.

Consider now the old effigies of the seasons. Break up the rhythm of the old figures' moving, the spring trot, summer canter, sad stride of autumn, and winter shuffle. Break, piece by piece, the continuous changing of motion into a spindle-shanked walking.

Consider the sun for whom I know no image but the old image of a shot eye, and the broken moon.

### 19

Gradually the chaos became less, and the things of the surrounding world were no longer wrought out of their own substance into the shapes of his thoughts. Some peace fell about him, and again the music of creation was to be heard trembling out of crystal water, out of the holy sweep of the sky down to the wet edge of the earth where a sea flowed over. Night came slowly, and the hill rose to the unrisen stars. He turned over the block of paper and upon the last page wrote in a clear hand:

### 20

The woman died.

### 21

There was dignity in such a murder. And the hero in him rose up in all his holiness and strength. It was just that he who had brought her forth from darkness should pack her away again. And it was just that she should die not knowing what hand out of the sky struck upon her and laid her low.

He walked down the hill, his steps slow as in procession, and his lips smiling at the dark sea. He climbed on to the shore, and, feeling his heart knock at his side, turned to where the greater rocks climbed perilously to the grass. There at the foot, her face towards him, she lay and smiled. Sea-water ran unheeded over her nakedness. He crossed to her, and touched her cold cheek with his nails.

### 22

Acquainted with the last grief, he stood at the open window of his room. And the night was an island in a sea of mystery and meaning. And the voice out of the night was a voice of acceptance. And the face of the moon was the face of humility.

He knew the last wonder before the grave and the mystery that bewilders and incorporates the heavens and the earth. He knew that he had failed before the eye of God and the eye of Sirius to hold his miracle. The woman had shown him that it was wonderful to live. And now, when at last he knew how wonderful, and how pleasant the blood in the trees, and how deep the well of the clouds, he must close his eyes and die. He opened his eyes, and looked up at the stars. There were a million stars spelling the same word. And the word of the stars was written clearly upon the sky.

## 23

Alone in the kitchen, among the broken chairs and china, stood the mouse that had come out of the hole. Its paws rested lightly upon the floor painted all over with the grotesque figures of birds and girls. Stealthily, it crept back into the hole. Stealthily, it worked its way between the walls. There was no sound in the kitchen but the sound of the mouse's nails scraping upon wood.

## 24

In the eaves of the lunatic asylum the birds still whistled, and the madman, pressed close to the bars of the window near their nests, bayed up at the sun.

Upon the bench some distance from the main path, the girl was beckoning to the birds, while on a square of lawn danced three old women, hand in hand, simpering in the wind, to the music of an Italian organ from the world outside.

Spring is come, said the warders.

# The Horse's Ha

He saw the plague enter the village on a white horse. It was a cancerous horseman, with a furuncle for a hat, that galloped the beast over grass and cobble and the coloured hill. Plague, plague, cried Tom Twp as the horse on the horizon, scenting the stars, lifted a white head. Out came the grocer with an egg in his hand, and the butcher in a bloody coat. They followed the line of the lifted finger, but the horse had gone, the trees were no speakers, and the birds who flew crisscross on the sky said no word of warning to the parson's rookery or the chained starlings in the parlour of ApLlewelyn. As white, said Tom Twp, as the egg in your hand. He remembered the raw head of the horseman, and whispered slyly, As red as mother's rump in your window. The clouds darkened, the sun went in, the suddenly ferocious wind broke down three fences, and the cows, blue-eyed with plague, nibbled at the centres of the marrow beds. The egg fell, and the red yolk struggled between the spaces of the cobbles, the white mixed with the rain that dripped from the scarlet coat. In went the grocer with a stained hand, and the butcher among the hands of veal. Tom Twp, following his finger towards the horizon where the horse of plague had stamped and vanished, reached the dark church as the rain grew sick of the soil and drew back to heaven. He ran between the graves where the worm rubbed in the tradesmen's hands. Mrs. ApLlewelyn raised a stone breast above the grass. Softly opening the door, he came upon the parson praying for disarmament in the central aisle. Disarm the forces of the army and the navy, he heard the parson murmur to the Christ of the stained glass who smiled like a nannygoat above him, hearing the cries from Cardiff and the smoking West. Disarm the territorial forces, the parson prayed. In anger, God smote him. There is plague, said Tom Twp. ApLlewelyn in the organ loft reached for the bass stops.

The white plague drifted through the church to the music of the savage voluntary. Parson and sinner stood beneath the reflections of the Holy Family, marking in each ginger halo the hair of blood. There was to one the voice of an arming God in the echo of each chord, and, to the other, the horse's ha.

One by one the starlings died; the last remaining bird, with a pain in its crop, whistled at the late afternoon. ApLlewelyn, returning from music and marvelling at the sky, heard the last starling's voice as he walked up the drive. Why is there no welcome, wondered the keeper, from my starling charges. Every day of the year they had lost their tempers, tore at the sashes of the window watching on the flying world; they had scraped on the glass, and fetched up their wings from the limed bar, signalling before him. On the rug at his feet lay six starlings, cold and stiff, the seventh mourning. Death in his absence had laid six singers low. He who marks the sparrow's fall has no time for my birds, said ApLlewelyn. He smote big, bloody death, and death, relenting, pulled a last fart from the bodies of the dead birds.

Plague, plague, cried Tom Twp, standing in a new rain. Where the undertaker's house had died in the trees, he holla'd, like ApLlewelyn, of big, bloody death; he heard the rooks cawing in the trees, and saw a galloping shadow. The trees smelt of opium and mice, to Tom two sorts of the hell-headed animal who ran in the skirtings of the grave. There were, on the branches of the trees and hanging upright from the earth, the owls that ate the mice and the mouths of the rosy flowers that fed on opium. To the chimneys of Last House and the one illuminated window he called the plague. Out came the undertaker in a frock coat; distrusting the light of the moon, he carried a candle in his gloved hand, the candle casting three shadows. To the middle shadow Tom Twp addressed his words of the white coming. Shall I measure, said the shadow on the left, the undead of Wales? Plague on a horse, said Tom Twp to the left shadow, and heard the darker shadow on the right reply.

No drug of man works on the dead. The parson, at his pipe, sucked down a dead smoke from the nostrils of the travelling horse, who now, on a far-off mountain, neighed down at Africa. Smitten by God, the parson, as the dark rose grew deepest where the moon rose in a blaze of light, counted his blessings, the blazing fire, the light in the tobacco, and the shape of the deep bowl. Hell was this fire, the dark denial burning like a weed, and the poppy out of the smoking earth. The lines of the bowl, that patterned his grave, were the lines of the weedy world; the light in the tobacco faded; the weed was at the parson's legs, worrying him into a longer fall than the fall from heaven, and, heavier than the poppy, into a long sleep.

Butcher and baker fell asleep that night, their women sleeping at their sides. Butcher and baker took their women in no image; their women broke again for them the accustomed maidenheads, their erected saviours crossing, in my language, the hill of hairs. Over the shops, the cold eggs that had life, the box where the rats worked all night on the high meat, the shopkeepers gave no thought to death. They felt, in the crowded space between hip and belly, the action of a third lover. Death, in the last gristle, broke on the minutes, and, by twelve beneath Cathmarw steeple, the towers fell.

Shall I measure the undead? This, said the undertaker in his parlour, pointing through the uncurtained window to the shape of the night, is the grave for the walking and the breathing. Here lay the sleepy body, the smoking body, the flesh that burned a candle, and the lessening manwax. Go home and die, he had told Tom Twp, and, telling it again to the made moon, he remembered the story of the resurrection-men who had snatched a talking body out of the Cathmarw yards. He heard the dead die around him, and a live man, in his grafted suit, break up the gravel on the drive of Last House. Cathmarw, in a bath of blood, slept still for the light day, Tom twisted in the hedge, butcher and baker stiff by their loves, and parson with a burnt-out pipe loose in his jaws. ApLlewelyn skinned the six starlings; he dropped to the ground at last, holding two handfuls of red and broken feathers; the seventh bird, naked as its dead mates, still shivered and sang on the limed bar. Plague is upon us, said Mr. Montgomery, the undertaker, for the wind was resounding with the noise of departure, and the smell of the departing flesh crept up the wind. In the skin of this Western Wales, through the veins of the county, the rub of the plague transformed into a circle of sick and invisible promise the globes of seeds; swollen in the tubers of the trees, death poisoned the green buds, and coloured the birthmarks of the forest with a fresh stain. Mr. Montgomery threw his glass of vinegar in the plague's face; the glass broke on the window, and the vinegar ran down the broken panes. He cardboarded each slit and crack, smelling the running acid as he nailed up a cloth to shield night from him; he bolted and barred the doors of his wooden house and stuffed the holes in the parlour corners, until, buried at last in a coffin with chimneys, he took down his mother's book. Cures for the sickness of the body and the sickness of the mind, ingredients for a saucer for resurrection, calls to the dead, said Bronwen Montgomery. The hand that wrote squarely to the crowded planet held a worm, and rain beat down the letters of her living name, and of Cathmarw's plague she said, in a translated tongue, that the horse was a white beast ridden over the hill by a raw-headed horseman. Take, said Bronwen, the blood of a bird, and mix it with the stuff of man. Take, of a dead man and bird, a bowl of death, and pour the bird's blood and the mortal sap through the sockets of the bowl. Stir with a finger, and, if a dead finger, drink my brew by me. He cast her aside. There was a bird and man in the unbolted darkness, plague in the loin and feather tickling the flesh and bone, uplifted fingers in the trees, and an eye in the air. These were his common visions; plague could not cloud the eye, nor the wind in the trees split the fingernail. Unbolting, unbarring the coffin with chimneys, he walked into the single vision of the night; the night was one bird's blood, one pocket of man, one finger lifted in the many and the upward world. He walked through the woods and onto the dusty road that led to Wales all ways, to the left, to the right, to the north, to the south, down through the vegetations, and up through the eye of the air. Looking at the still trees in the darkness, he came at last to the house of ApLlewelyn. He opened the gate and walked up the drive. There in the parlour, lay ApLlewelyn, six featherless starlings at his side, the seventh mourning. Take, take, said Bronwen out of the Cathmarw yards, the blood of a bird. He gathered a dead bird up, tore at his throat, and caught the cold blood in his hands. Drink my brew by me, said Bronwen at his ear. He found a cup on the dresser, and half-filled it with the blood of the shrunken starling. Though he rot he must wait, said Mr. Montgomery to the organist, till I drink her brew by her. Take, take, said his mother, the stuff of man. He hurried out and on, hearing the last starling mourn for the new departure.

Tom Twp was twisted in the hedge. He did not feel the jackknife at his finger, and the going of the grassy wedding ring around it did not trouble him at all.

Parson, dead in his chair, did not cry aloud as his trousers slid down to his boots, and promise filled the bladder of a fountain pen.

The cup was full. Mr. Montgomery stirred it with a wedding finger, and drank from it in the Cathmarw yards by the grave of his mother. Down went the red brew. The graves spun around him, the angels shifted on their stones, and the lids, invisible to the silent drinker, creaked on their hinges. Poison stirred him, and he spun, one foot in his mother's grave. Dead Cathmarw made a movement out of the wooden hamlet towards the hill of hairs. The hair rose on his scalp. Blood in his blood, and the cold ounce of the parson's seed edging to creation, he counted the diminishings of the moon; the stationary sun slipped down, and the system he could not take to the ground broke in half and in a hundred stars. Three days went by in a wind, the fourth rising cloudless and sinking again to too many strokes from the out-counted steeple. The fourth night got up like a man; the vision altering, a woman in the moon lit up the yards. He counted the diminishings of the sun. Too many days, he said, sick of his mother's brew and of the poisoned hours that passed and repassed him, leaving on the gravel path a rag and a bone in a faded frock coat.

But as the days passed, so the dead grew tired of waiting. Tom, uneasy in the hedge, raised a four-fingered hand to stifle the yawn that broke up the last remaining skins upon his face. Butcher and baker ached in too long a love, and cursed the beds that bore them. The six naked starlings rose on their wings, the seventh singing, and ApLlewelyn, out of a deep sleep, drifted into a reawakened world where the birds danced about him. So, tired of waiting, the dead rose and sought their undertaker, for the rot had set in, and their flesh fell as they walked, in a strange procession, along the dusty road that led all ways to the graves of Cathmarw.

Mr. Montgomery saw them come, and, as a new sunshine descended on the yards, offered them his cup of brew. But the dead refused his hand. Tom Twp hunched, the sterile parson, butcher and baker ungainly in their loves, and

ApLlewelyn with his hands around the feathers, clawed at the earth, making a common grave. Far, far above them, the seven naked starlings scratched on the sky.

A darkness descended on the yards, but lifted again as Mr. Montgomery questioned the parson as to the God of death. What is God's death? Lifting his head from the soil, the parson said: God took my promise. And he smote the earth. I am your tombmaker, said Mr. Montgomery, as the unshrouded parson climbed into the grave. I took your promise, he said, as the soil closed over.

What is death's music? One note or many? The chord of contagion? Thus questioned the undertaker, the cup three-quarters empty in his gloved hand. He who marks the sparrow's fall has no time for my birds, said ApLlewelyn. What music is death? What should I know of the music of death who am no longer the keeper of birds? ApLlewelyn vanished into the second quarter of the grave. I, I slew your birds, said the undertaker to the vanishing man.

The butcher was dead meat. Let me answer your platitudes, said the butcher's wife, scrubbing the surface of the double hole in the earth. I was love, I am dead, and my man still walks in me.

What is death's love? said the undertaker to the woman. Let me answer your platitudes, said the grocer's wife. I was dead, I am love, and my man still treads in me. They who filled and were filled, in a two-backed death, filled the third quarter.

And Tom Twp, counting his fingers at the edge of their acre, found a tenth miraculous finger, with a nail red as blood and a clear half-moon. Death is my last finger, said Tom Twp, and dived into the closing grave.

So Mr. Montgomery was left alone, by the desolate church, under a disappearing moon. One by one the stars went out, leaving a hole in heaven. He looked upon the grave, and slowly removed his coat.

# A Prospect of the Sea

It was high summer, and the boy was lying in the corn. He was happy because he had no work to do and the weather was hot. He heard the corn sway from side to side above him, and the noise of the birds who whistled from the branches of the trees that hid the house. Lying flat on his back, he stared up into the unbrokenly blue sky falling over the edge of the corn. The wind, after the warm rain before noon, smelt of rabbits and cattle. He stretched himself like a cat, and put his arms behind his head. Now he was riding on the sea, swimming through the golden corn waves, gliding along the heavens like a bird; in seven-league boots he was springing over the fields; he was building a nest in the sixth of the seven trees that waved their hands from a bright, green hill. Now he was a boy with tousled hair, rising lazily to his feet, wandering out of the corn to the strip of river by the hillside. He put his fingers in the water, making a mock sea-wave to roll the stones over and shake the weeds; his fingers stood up like ten tower pillars in the magnifying water, and a fish with a wise head and a lashing tail swam in and out of the tower gates. He made up a story as the fish swam through the gates into the pebbles and the moving bed. There was a drowned princess from a Christmas book, with her shoulders broken and her two red pigtails stretched like the strings of a fiddle over her broken throat; she was caught in a fisherman's net, and the fish plucked her hair. He forgot how the story ended, if ever there were an end to a story that had no beginning. Did the princess live again, rising like a mermaid from the net, or did a prince from another story tauten the tails of her hair and bend her shoulder-bone into a harp and pluck the dead, black tunes for ever in the courts of the royal country? The boy sent a stone skidding over the green water. He saw a rabbit scuttle, and threw a stone at its tail. A fish leaped at the gnats, and a lark darted out of the green earth. This was the best summer since the first seasons of the world. He did not believe in God, but God had made this summer full of blue winds and heat and pigeons in the house wood. There were no chimneys on the hills with no name in the distance, only the trees which stood like women and men enjoying the sun; there were no cranes or coal-tips, only the nameless distance and the hill with seven trees. He could think of no words to say how wonderful the summer was, or the noise of the wood-pigeons, or the lazy corn blowing in the half-wind from the sea at the river's end. There were no words for the sky and the sun and the summer country: the birds were nice, and the corn was nice.

He crossed the nice field and climbed the hill. Under the innocent green of the trees, as black birds flew out towards the sun, the story of the princess died. That afternoon there was no drowning sea to pull her pigtails; the sea had flowed and vanished, leaving a hill, a cornfield, and a hidden house; tall as the first short tree, she clambered down from the seventh, and stood in front of him in a torn cotton frock. Her bare brown legs were scratched all over, there were berry stains round her mouth, her nails were black and broken, and her toes poked through her rubber shoes. She stood on a hill no bigger than a house, but the field below and the shining strip of river were as little as though the hill were a mountain rising over a single blade and a drop of water; the trees round the farmhouse were firesticks; and the Jarvis peaks, and Cader peak beyond it to the edge of England, were molehills and stones' shadows in the still, single yard of the distance. From the first shade, the boy stared down at the river disappearing, the corn blowing back into the soil, the hundred house trees dwindling to a stalk, and the four corners of the yellow field meeting in a square that he could cover with his hand. He saw the many-coloured county shrink like a coat in the wash. Then a new wind sprang from the pennyworth of water at the river-drop's end, blowing the hill field to its full size, and the corn stood up as before, and the one stalk that hid the house was split into a hundred trees. It happened in half a second.

Black birds again flew out from the topmost boughs in a cloud like a cone; there was no end to the black, triangular flight of birds towards the sun; from hill to sun the winged bridge mounted silently; and then again a wind blew up, and this time from the vast and proper sea, and snapped the bridge's back. Like partridges the common birds fell down in a shower.

All of it happened in half a second. The girl in the torn cotton frock sat down on the grass and crossed her legs; a real wind from nowhere lifted her frock, and up to her waist she was brown as an acorn. The boy, still standing timidly in the first shade, saw the broken, holiday princess die for the second time, and a country girl take her place on the live hill. Who had been frightened of a few birds flying out of the trees, and a sudden daze of the sun that made river and field and distance look so little under the hill? Who had told him the girl was as tall as a tree? She was no taller or stranger than the flowery girls on Sundays who picnicked in Whippet valley.

What were you doing up the tree? he asked her, ashamed of his silence in front of her smiling, and suddenly shy as she moved so that the grass beneath her rose bent and green between her brown legs. Were you after nests? he said, and sat down beside her. But on the bent grass in the seventh shade, his first terror of her sprang up again like a sun returning from the sea that sank it, and burned his eyes to the skull and raised his hair. The stain on her lips was blood, not berries; and her nails were not broken but sharpened sideways, ten black scissorblades ready to snip off his tongue. If he cried aloud to his uncle in the hidden house, she would make new animals, beckon Carmarthen tigers out of the mile-away wood to jump around him and bite his hands; she would make new, noisy birds in the air to whistle and chatter away his cries. He sat very still by her left side, and heard the heart in her breast drown every summer sound; every leaf of the tree that shaded them grew to man-size then, the ribs of the bark were channels and rivers wide as a great ship; and the moss on the tree, and the sharp grass ring round the base, were all the velvet covering of a green county's meadows blown hedge to hedge. Now on the world-sized hill, with the trees like heavens holding up the weathers, in the magnified summer weather she leaned towards him so that he could not see the cornfield nor his uncle's house for her thick, red hair; and sky and far ridge were points of light in the pupils of her eyes. This is death, said the boy to himself, consumption and whooping-cough and the stones inside you and the death from playing with yourself and the way your face stays if you make too many faces in the looking-glass. Her mouth was an inch from his. Her long forefingers touched his eyelids. This is a story, he said to himself, about a boy on a holiday kissed by a broom-rider; she flew from a tree on to a hill that changes its size like a frog that loses its temper; she stroked his eyes and put her chest against him; and when she had loved him until he died she carried him off inside her to a den in a wood. But the story, like all stories, was killed as she kissed him; now he was a boy in a girl's arms, and the hill stood above a true river, and the peaks and their trees towards England were as Jarvis had known them when he walked there with his lovers and horses for half a century, a century ago.

Who had been frightened of a wind out of the light swelling the small country? The piece of a wind in the sun was like the wind in an empty house; it made the corners mountains, and crowded the attics with shadows which broke through the roof; through the country corridors it raced in a hundred voices, each voice larger than the last, until the last voice tumbled down and the house was full of whispers. Where do you come from? she whispered in his ear. She took her arms away but still sat close, one knee between his legs, one hand on his hands. Who had been frightened of a sunburned girl no taller or stranger than the pale girls at home who had babies before they were married? I come from Amman valley, said the boy. I have a sister in Egypt, she said, who lives in a pyramid. She pressed down her knee, and laughed when he drew in his breath. You mustn't, he said. She mimicked his Mustn't, you mustn't, and drew him closer. They're calling me in for tea, he said. She lifted her frock to her waist. If she loves me until I die, said the boy to himself under the seventh tree on the hill that was never the same for three minutes, she will carry me away inside her, run with me rattling inside to a den in a wood, to a hole in a tree where my uncle will never find me. This is the story of a boy being stolen. She has put a knife in my belly and turned my stomach round.

She whispered in his ear: I'll have a baby on every hill; what's your name, Amman? The afternoon was dying; lazily, namelessly drifting westward through the insects in the shade; over hill and tree and river and corn and grass to the evening shaping in the sea; blowing away; being blown from Wales in a wind, in the slow, blue grains, like a wind full of dreams and medicines; down the tide of the sun on to the grey and chanting shore where the birds from Noah's ark glide by with bushes in their mouths, and tomorrow and tomorrow tower over the cracked sand-castles.

So she stroked her clothes into place and patted back her hair as the day began to die; she rolled over on to her left side, careless of the low sun and the darkening miles. The boy awoke cautiously into a more curious dream, a summer vision broader than the one black cloud poised in the unbroken centre on a tower shaft of light; he came out of love through a wind full of turning knives and a cave full of flesh-white birds on to a new summit, standing like a stone that faces the stars blowing and stands no ceremony from the sea wind, a hard boy angry on a mound in the middle of a country evening; he put out his chest and said hard words to the world. Out of love he came marching, head on high, through a cave between two doors to a vantage hall room with an iron view over the earth. He walked to the last rail before pitch space; though the earth bowed round quickly, he saw every plough crease and beast's print, man track and water drop, comb, crest, and plume mark, dust and death groove and signature and time-cast shade, from ice field to ice field, sea rims to sea centres, all over the apple-shaped ball under the metal rails beyond the living doors. He saw through the black thumbprint of a man's city to the fossil thumb of a once-lively man of meadows; through the grass and clover fossil of the country print to the whole hand of a forgotten city drowned under Europe; through the handprint to the arm of an empire broken like Venus; through the arm to the breast, from history to the thigh, through the thigh in the dark to the first and West print between the dark and the green Eden; and the garden was undrowned, to this next minute and for ever, under Asia in the earth that rolled on to its music in the beginning evening. When God was sleeping, he had climbed a ladder, and the room three jumps above the final rung was roofed and floored with the live pages of the book of days; the pages were gardens, the built words were trees, and Eden grew above him into Eden, and Eden grew down to Eden through the lower earth, an endless corridor of boughs and birds and leaves. He stood on a slope no wider than the loving room of the world, and the two poles kissed behind his shoulders; the boy stumbled forward like Atlas, loped over the iron view through the cave of knives and the capsized overgrowths of time to the hill in the field that had been a short mark under the platform in the clouds over the multiplying gardens.

Wake up, she said into his ear; the iron characters were broken in her smile, and Eden shrank into the seventh shade. She told him to look in her eyes. He had thought that her eyes were brown or green, but they were sea-blue with black lashes, and her thick hair was black. She rumpled his hair, and put his hand deep in her breast so that he knew the nipple of her heart was red. He looked in her eyes, but they made a round glass of the sun, and as he moved sharply away he saw through the transparent trees; she could make a long crystal of each tree, and turn the house wood into gauze. She told him her name, but he had forgotten it as she spoke; she told him her age, and it was a new number. Look in my eyes, she said. It was only an hour to the proper night, the stars were coming out and the moon was ready. She took his hand and led him racing between trees over the ridge of the dewy hill, over the flowering nettles and the shut grass-flowers, over the silence into sunlight and the noise of a sea breaking on sand and stone.

The hill in a screen of trees: between the incountry fields and the incoming sea, night on the wood and the stained beach yellow in the sun, the vanishing corn through the ten dry miles of farmland and the golden wastes where the split sand lapped over rocks, it stood between time over a secret root. The hill in two searchlights: the black moon shone on seven trees, and the sun of a strange day moved above water in the spluttering foreground. The hill between an owl and a seagull: the boy heard two birds' voices as brown wings climbed through the branches and the white wings before him fluttered on the sea waves. Tu wit tu woo, do not adventure any more. Now the gulls that swam in the sky told him to race on along the warm sand until the water hugged him to its waves and the spindrift tore around him like a wind and a chain. The girl had her hand in his, and she rubbed her cheek on his shoulder. He was glad of her near him, for the princess was broken, and the monstrous girl was turned into a tree, and the frightening girl who threw the country into a daze of sizes, and drove him out of love into the cloudy house, was left alone in the moon's circle and the seven shades behind the screen.

It was hot that morning in the unexpected sunshine. A girl dressed in cotton put her mouth to his ear. I'll run you to the sea, she said, and her breasts jumped up and down as she raced in front of him, with her hair flying wild, to the edge of the sea that was not made of water and the small, thundering pebbles that broke in a million pieces as the dry sea moved in. Along the bright wrackline, from the horizon where the vast birds sailed like boats, from the four compass corners, bellying up through the weed-beds, melting from orient and tropic, surging through the ice hills and the whale grounds, through sunset and sunrise corridors, the salt gardens and the herring fields, whirlpool and rock pool, out of the trickle in the mountain, down the waterfalls, a white-faced sea of people, the terrible mortal number of the waves, all the centuries' sea drenched in the hail before Christ, who suffered tomorrow's storm wind, came in with the whole world's voices on the endless beach. Come back, come back, the boy cried to the girl. She ran on unheeding over the sand and was lost among the sea. Now her face was a white drop of water in the horizontal rainfall, and her limbs were white as snow and lost in the white, walking tide. Now the heart in her breast was a small red ball that rang in a wave, her colourless hair fringed the spray, and her voice lapped over the flesh-and-bone water. He cried again, but she had mingled with the people moving in and out. Their tides were drawn by a grave moon that never lost an arc. Their long, sea gestures were deliberate, the flat hands beckoning, the heads uplifted, the eyes in the mask faces set in one direction. Oh where was she now in the sea? Among the white, walking, and the coral-eyed. Come back, come back. Darling, run out of the sea. Among the processional waves. The bell in her breast was ringing over the sand. He ran to the yellow foot of the dunes, calling over his shoulder. Run out of the sea. In the once-green water where the fishes swam, where the gulls rested, where the luminous stones were rubbed and rocked on the scales of the green bed, when ships puffed over the tradeways, and the mad, nameless animals came down to drink the salt. Among the measuring people. Oh where was she now? The sea was lost behind the dunes. He stumbled on over sand and sandflowers like a blind boy in the sun. The sun dodged round his shoulders.

There was a story once upon a time whispered in the water voice; it blew out the echo from the trees behind the beach in the golden hollows, scraped on the wood until the musical birds and beasts came jumping into sunshine. A raven flew by him, out of a window in the Flood to the blind, wind tower shaking in tomorrow's anger like a scarecrow made out of weathers.

> Once upon a time, said the water voice.
> Do not adventure any more, said the echo.
> She is ringing a bell for you in the sea.
> I am the owl and the echo; you shall never go back.

On a hill to the horizon stood an old man building a boat, and the light that slanted from the sea cast the holy mountain of a shadow over the three-storied decks and the Eastern timber. And through the sky, out of the beds and gardens, down the white precipice built of feathers, the loud combs and mounds, from the caves in the hill, the cloudy shapes of birds and beasts and insects drifted into the hewn door. A dove with a green petal followed in the raven's flight. Cool rain began to fall.

# The Holy Six

The Holy Six of Wales sat in silence. The day was drawing to a close, and the heat of the first discussion grew cooler with the falling sun. All through the afternoon they had talked of nothing but the disappearance of the rector of Llareggub, and now, as the first lack of light moved in a visible shape and colour through the room, and their tongues were tired, and they heard the voices in their nerves, they waited only for the first darkness to set in. At the first signs of night they would step from the table, adjust their hats and smiles, and walk into the wicked streets. Where the women smiled under the lamps, and the promise of the old sickness stirred in the fingertips of the girls in the dark doorways, the Six would pass dreaming, to the scrape of their boots on the pavement, of the women throughout the town smiling and doctoring love. To Mr. Stul the women drifted in a maze of hair, and touched him in a raw place. The women drifted around Mr. Edger. He caught them close to him, holding their misty limbs to his with no love or fire. The women moved again, with the grace of cats, edging down the darker alleys where Mr. Vyne, envious of their slant-eyed beauty, would scrape and bow. To Mr. Rafe, their beauties, washed in blood, were enemies of the fluttering eyes, and moved, in what image they would, full-breasted, fur-footed, to a massacre of the flesh. He saw the red nails, and trembled. There was no purpose in the shaping wombs but the death of the flesh they shaped, and he shrank from the contact of death, and the male nerve was pulled alone. Tugging and tweaking, putting salt on the old love-cuts, Mr. Lucytre conducted an imaginary attack upon the maiden-heads. Now here and now there he ripped the women, and kissing them, he bit into their lips. Spitefully, Mr. Stipe watched him. Down fell the women on the sharp blade, and his heart smiled within him as they rose to dress their wounds.

The holy life was a constant erection to these six gentlemen. Miss Myfanwy came in with a letter.

Mr. Edger opened the envelope. It contained a square piece of paper that might be a banknote. It was a letter from Mrs. Amabel Owen and was written in a backward hand.

She put malignity in the curves and tails of the characters, a cloven foot, a fork, and a snake's sting coming out from the words in a separate life as the words lay back giddy from her revolving pen along the lines.

She, like Peter the poet, wrote of the Jarvis valley. But while she saw by each bare tree a barer ghost and the ghost of the last spring and summer, he saw the statue of the tree and no ghost but his own that whistled out of the sick bed and raced among seaward fields.

Here in the valley, wrote Mrs. Owen, my husband and I live quiet as two mice.

As she writes, thought Mr. Stul, she feels the weight of her breasts on her ink-black arm.

Do the holy gentlemen believe in ghosts?

With the chains of cloud and iron suspended from their limbs, thought Mr. Rafe, they would drip the deadly nightshade into my ear.

May she bear a vampire's baby, said Mr. Stipe.

The Reverend Mr. Davies of Llareggub is staying with us for an indefinite period, she wrote in her secret hand.

Over the more level roadway on the lower hills, drawn in a jogcart by a sweating pony, the Holy Six journeyed in search of Mrs. Owen. Miss Myfanwy, seated uncomfortably between Mr. Stul and Mr. Lucytre, conscious of the exposure of her calf and the pressure of Mr. Lucytre's hand in the small of her back, prayed that the moon might not go in. There in the crowded cart the darkness would conceal the roving of the holy hands, and better Mr. Stul's delight.

The wheels of the cart bumped on a boulder.

Over we go, said Mr. Rafe, too frightened to brood upon the dissolution of his delicate body tumbling down the slope.

Over we go, said Mr. Vyne, thinking how hard it was that death should come alone, the common flesh of Miss Myfanwy seated so near him.

As the cart balanced on one wheel, and the pony, with the entire weight on one back leg, pawed at the air with its hanging hooves. Mr. Stul thrust his hand high up under Miss Myfanwy's skirt, and Mr. Lucytre, smiling at destruction, drove his fingers into her back until the knuckles tingled and the invisible flesh reddened with pain. Mr. Edger clasped everything within reach, holding tight to his phallic hat. Mr. Stipe leant suddenly to one side. The pony slipped on the wet turf, whinnied, and fell. God is good, said old Vole the carter, and down he went, gathering speed, a white-haired boulder plunging into the craggy meadow fifty feet below. In one tight, black ball, the rest of the company rolled over the side. Is it blood? is it blood? cried Miss Myfanwy as they fell. Mr. Stul smiled, and fixed his arm more tightly round her.

On the grass below, old Vole lay quietly on his back. He looked at the winter moon, that had not slipped, and the peace in the field. As six clergical hats and a draggled bonnet dropped near his feet, he turned on one side and saw the bodies of his passengers tumbling down upon him like a bony manna.

Darkness came for the second time. Now, with the hiding of the moon, the Holy Six arrived at the foot of the hills that separated the Jarvis valley from the fields of the wild land. The trees on those ridges were taller than any they had seen in their journey from the fatal meadow, greener and straighter than the trees in the town parks. There was a madman in each tree. This they did not know, seeing only the sanity of the trees on the broad back of the upper grasses. The hills, that had curved all day in the circle of light, now straightened out against the sky, in a hundred straight lines ascended to the clouds, and in one stark shadow blocked out the moon. Shifting along the properties of the soil, man's chemic blood, pulled from him by the warring wind, mixed with the dust that the holy gentlemen, like six old horses, stamped into a cloud. The dust lay thick on their black boots; on old Vole's beard it scraped, grey as water, between the ginger and the white; it drifted over Miss Myfanwy's patent boots and was lost in the cracks of her feet. For a minute they stood, trembling at the height of the hills. Then they adjusted their hats.

One behind the other they clambered upward, very far from the stars. The roots beneath their feet cried in the voices of the springing trees. It was to each member of

the expedition a strange and a different voice that sounded
along the branches. They reached the top of the hill, and
the Jarvis valley lay before them. Miss Myfanwy smelt
the cloves in the grass, but Mr. Lucytre smelt only the
dead birds. There were six vowels in the language of the
branches. Old Vole heard the leaves. Their sentimental
voice, as they clung together, spoke of the season of the
storks and the children under the bushes. The Holy Six
went down the hill, and the carter followed on the dark
heels.

But, before they knew where they were and before the
tenth Jarvis field had groaned beneath them, and before
Mrs. Owen spelt out their flesh and bone in the big ball on
her table, morning suddenly came down; the meadows
were oaksided, standing greener than a sea as a lull came
to the early light, lying under the wind as the south-west
opened; the ancient boughs had all the birds of Wales
upon them, and, from the farms among the trees and the
fields on the unseen hillside, the cocks crew and the sheep
cried. The wood before them, glowing from a bloody
centre, burned like cantharides, a tuft of half-parting
blooms and branches erect on the land that spouted up
to the summits of the hills, angelically down, through
ribbed throats of flowers and rising poisons, to the county's
heart. The grass that was heavy with dew, though the
crystals on each blade broke lightly, lay still as they
walked, a woman's stillness under the thrust of man lying
in the waking furze and the back of the bedded ribs of
the hill's half heather, the halves of gold and green by
the slope quarries staining a rich shire and a common soil.
And it was early morning, and the world was moist, when
the crystal-gazer's husband, a freak in knickerbockers with
an open coppish and a sabbath gamp, came over the stones
outside his house to meet the holy travellers.

His beard was wagging as he bowed. Your holiness,
said Mr. Owen to the Six. Battered and bruised, the soles
of their boots dragging like black and muddy wings along
the ground, piously the Six responded. Mr. Owen bowed
to Miss Myfanwy who, as his shirt wagged like a beard
from his open trousers, curtsied low and blushed.

In the parlour, where Mrs. Owen had read out the
bloody coming, the Six gathered coldly round the fire, and
two kettles sang. An old and ragged man dragged in a

tub. Where is the mustard, Mr. Davies? questioned the crystal-gazer from her chair in the darkest corner. Aware of her presence for the first time, the Holy Six spun round, seeing the big ball move inwardly, the unendurable head of evil, green as the woman's eyes and blacker than the shadows pouched under the lower lids, wriggle over the wet hint of hills at the globe's edges. She was a tidy little body, with plump hands and feet, and a love-curl glistened on her forehead; dressed, like a Sunday, in cold and shining black, with a brooch of mother's ivory and a bone-white bangle, she saw the Holy Six reflected as six solid stumps, the amputated limbs of the deadly man who rotted in her as she swayed before his eyes, before his twelve bright eyes and the power of the staring Six.

Her womb and her throat and her hair.

Her green witch's eyes.

Her costly bangle.

The moles on her cheek.

Her young complexion.

The bones of her legs, her nails, her thumb.

The Six stood in front of her and touched her craftily, like the old men with Susannah, and stared upon her where the unborn baby stirred manfully in the eighth month.

The old man returned with mustard.

This is the Reverend Mr. Davies of Llareggub, said Mrs. Owen.

The Holy Six rubbed their hands.

These are the Holy Six of Wales.

Mr. Davies bowed, took off the kettles, half filled the tin tub, and poured the mustard on to the boiling water. Mr. Owen, appearing suddenly at his shoulder, gave him a yellow sponge. Bewildered by the yellow water that sucked at the spoon, by the dripping sponge in his fingers, and by the silence in the parlour, Mr. Davies turned trembling to the holy gentlemen. A timeless voice spoke in his ear, and a hand on his shrouded shoulder sank through the collar-bone; a hand was on his heart, and the intolerable bloodbeat struck on a strong shadow. He knelt down in the wilderness of the tiny parlour, and off came the holy socks and boots. I, Davies, bathed their feet, muttered the grey minister. So that he might remember, the old, mad man said to himself, I, Davies, the poor ghost, washed the six sins in mustard and water.

Light was in the room, the world of light, and the holy

Jewish word. On clock and black fire, light brought the
inner world to pass, and the shape in his image that
changed with the silent changes of the shape of light
twisted his last man's-word. The word grew like light.
He loved and coveted the last, dark light, turning from
his memories to the yellow sea and the prowed beak of the
spoon. In the world of love, through the drowning memories, he shifted one lover's smile to the mouth of a naughty
lover cruel to the slept-with dead who died before dressing,
and slowly turned to the illuminated face and the firer of
the dead. Touching Mr. Stul on the ankle, his ghost who
laboured—now he was three parts ghost, and his manhood
withered like the sap in a stick under a scarecrow's tatters—leapt out to marry Mary; all-sexed and nothing,
intangible hermaphrodite riding the neuter dead, the
minister of God in a grey image mounted dead Mary. Mrs.
Owen, wise to the impious systems, saw through the inner
eye that the round but unbounded earth rotted as she
ripened; a circle, not of her witch's making, grew around
her; the immaculate circle broadened, taking a generation's
shape. Mr. Davies touched the generation's edges; up rose
the man-stalking seed; and the circle broke. It was Mr.
Stul, the horny man, the father of Aberystwyth's bastards,
who bounded over the broken circle, and, hand in hand
with the grey ghost, kissed on divinity until the heavens
melted.

The Holy five were not aware of this.

The lank-shanked Mr. Edger put out his right foot, and
Mr. Davies washed it; careful of the temperature of the
water rippling round the glassy skin, the minister of God
washed the left foot; he remembered poor Davies, poor
ghostly Davies, the man of bone and collar, howling, from
a religious hill, of the infinite curve of matter and the
sound of the unspoken word; and, remembering Llareggub, the village with a rotting house, he grasped at the
fat memories, the relics of the flesh that hung shabbily
from him, and the undeniable desires; he grasped at the
last senile hair on the skull as windily the world broke
Davies up, and the ghost, having no greed or desire, came
undead out of the particles.

Neither were the Holy four aware of this.

It was the fox-whiskered Mr. Vyne who said out of the
darkness to the ghost Davies: Beautiful is Mrs. Amabel
Owen, the near-mother, the generation-bellied, from her

teeth to her ten toes. My smile is a red hole, and my toes are like fingers. He sighed behind Mary and caught his breath at the seedy rim of the circle, seeing how beautiful she was as she shifted about him in the mothering middle of the earth. And out of the roots of the earth, lean as trees and whiter than the spring froth, rose her tall attendants. As the crystal-gazer and the virgin walked in one magic over their double grave, dead Davies and dead Vyne cried enviously: Beautiful is Amabel Mary, the ravished maiden, from her skull to her grave-walking feet.

Where but an hour earlier a far sea wind had blown the sun about, black night dropped down. Time on the clock denied the black coming.

Mr. Rafe was more frightened of the dark than anything else in the world. He watched, with wide, white eyes, the lighting of the parlour lamp. What would the red lamp disclose? A mouse in a corner playing with an ivory tooth, a little vampire winking at his shoulder, a bed of spiders with a long woman in it.

Suddenly would the beautiful Mrs. Owen be a skeleton with a worm inside her? Oh, oh, God's wrath on such small deer, and the dogs as big as your thumb. Mr. Owen turned up the wick.

And secretly holding hands in the hour between the seconds, in the life that has no time for time, outside under the dark walked Mr. Rafe and the ghost Davies. Was the grass dead under the night, and did the spirit of the grass, greener than Niagara's devil, sprout through the black weather like the flowers through a coffin's cracks? Nothing that was not half the figure of a ghost moved up the miles. And, as the minister had seen his buried squires spin from the system of the dead and, ruddier-cheeked than ever, dance on the orbit of a flower in the last, long acre of Llareggub, so now he saw the buried grass shoot through the new night and move on the hill wind. Were the faces of the west stars the backs of the east? he questioned his dead parishioners. God's wrath, cried Mr. Rafe, in the shadow of a voice, nothing that was not half the substance of a man writhing in his shadow as it fell aslant on the hill, on the double-thumbed piskies about me. Down, down—he slashed at the blades—down, you bald girls from Merthyr. He slashed at a walking echo, Ah, ah, oh, ah, cried the voice of Jerusalem, and Mary, from the moon's arc over the hill, ran like a wolf at the wailing ministers.

Midnight, guessed Mrs. Owen. The hours had gone by in a wind.

Mr. Stipe put out his right foot, and nagged at the water with his left. He crept with ghost Davies through a narrow world; in his hair were the droppings of birds from the boughs of the mean trees; leading the ghost through dark dingles, he sprung the spiked bushes back, and pissed against the wind. He hissed at the thirsty dead who bit their lips, and gave them a dry cherry; he whistled through his fingers, and up rose Lazarus like a weazel. And when the virgin came on a white ass by his grave, he raised a ragged hand and tickled the ass's belly till it brayed and threw Mary among the corpse-eaters and the quarreling crows.

Mr. Lucytre was not aware of this.

The world, for him, rocked on a snapped foot; the shattered and the razor-bedded sea, the green skewered hulk with a stuffing of eyes, the red sea socket itself and the dead ships crawling around the rim, ached through the gristles and the bone, the bitten patch, the scaled and bubbling menses, the elastic tissues of the deep, the barbed, stained and scissored, the clotted-with-mucus, sawn and thorny flesh, ached on a never-ending ache. As on a crucifix, and turning on her nails, the skinny earth, each country pricked to the bladder, each racked sea torn in the tide, hung despairing in a limp space. What should the cruel Lucytre, who drags ghost Davies over a timeless agony, smooth on her wounds? Rust and salt and vinegar and alcohol, the juice of the upas tree, the scorpion's ointment and a sponge soaked in dropsy.

The Holy Six stood up.

They took the six glasses of milk from Mr. Owen's tray.

And will the holy gentlemen honour us for the night?

A life in Mrs. Owen was stirring behind the comfortable little wall. She smiled at Mr. Davies, this time with an intimate wrinkling of the corners of her mouth; Mr. Owen smiled over his shoulder; and, caught between two smiles and understanding neither, he felt his own lips curl. They shared a mysterious smile, and the Six stood silently behind them.

My child, said Mrs. Owen from her corner, shall be greater than all great men.

Your child is my child, said Mr. Owen.

And Mr. Davies, as suddenly as in the first bewilderment he had gone down upon his knees to pray, leant forward and patted the woman's hand. He would have laid his hands upon the fold of her frock from hip to hip, blessing the unborn under the cotton shroud, but the fear of the power of her eyes held his hand.

Your child is my child, said Mr. Davies.

The ghost in him had coupled with the virgin, the virgin ghost that all the great stirrings of her husband's love had left as whole as a flower in a cup of milk.

But Mr. Owen burst out laughing; he threw back his head, and laughed at the mating shadows, at the oil in the clear, glass bag of the lamp. That there could be seed, shuffling to the spring of heat, in the old man's glands. That there could be life in the ancient loins. Father of the jawbones of asses and the hair-thighed camel's fleas, Mr. Davies swayed before him in a mist of laughter. He could blow the old man up the sky with a puff of his lungs.

He is your child, said Mrs. Owen.

She smiled at the shadow between them, the eunuch shadow of a man that fitted between the curving of their shoulders.

So Mr. Davies smiled again, knowing the shadow to be his. And Mr. Owen, caring for no shadow but that cast on his veins by the rising and setting of the blood, smiled at them both.

The holy gentlemen would honour them that night.

And the Six circled the three.

# Prologue to an Adventure

As I walked through the wilderness of this world, as I walked through the wilderness, as I walked through the city with the loud electric faces and the crowded petrols of the wind dazzling and drowning me that winter night before the West died, I remembered the winds of the high, white world that bore me and the faces of a noiseless million in the busyhood of heaven staring on the afterbirth. They who nudged through the literate light of the city, shouldered and elbowed me, catching my trilby with the spokes of their umbrellas, who offered me matches and music, made me out of their men's eyes into a manshape walking. But take away, I told them silently, the flannel and cotton, the cheap felt and leather. I am the nakedest and baldest nothing between the pinnacle and the base, an alderman of ghosts holding to watch-chain and wallet on the wet pavement, the narrator of echoes moving in man's time. I have Old Moore by the beard, and the news of the world is no world's news, the gossips of heaven and the fallen rumours are enough and too much for a shadow that casts no shadow, I said to the blind beggars and the paperboys who shouted into the rain. They were hurrying by me on the narrow errands of the world, time bound to their wrists or blinded in their pockets, who consulted the time strapped to a holy tower, and dodged between bonnets and wheels, heard in my fellow's footsteps the timeless accents of another walking. On the brilliant pavements under a smoky moon, their man's world turning to the bass roll of the traffic, they saw in the shape of my fellow another staring under the pale lids, and heard the spheres turn as he spoke. This is a strange city, gentlemen on your own, gentlemen arm-in-arm making a rehearsed salute, gentlemen with ladies, ladies this is a strange city. For them in the friendless houses in the streets of pennies and pleasures a million ladies and gentlemen moved up in bed, time moved with the practised moon over a million roofs that night, and grim policemen stood at each corner in the black wind.

O mister lonely, said the ladies on their own, we shall be naked as newborn mice, loving you long in the short sparks of the night. We are not the ladies with feathers between their breasts, who lay eggs on the quilt. As I walked through the skyscraping centre, where the lamps walked at my side like volted men or the trees of a new scripture, I jostled the devil at my elbow, but lust in his city shadows dogged me under the arches, down the black blind streets. Now in the shape of a bald girl smiling, a wailing wanton with handcuffs for earrings, or the lean girls that lived on pickings, now in ragged woman with a muckrake curtseying in the slime, the tempter of angels whispered over my shoulder. We shall be naked but for garters and black stockings, loving you long on a bed of strawberries and cream, and the nakeder for a ribbon that hides the nipples. We are not the ladies that eat into the brain behind the ear, or feed on the fat of the heart. I remembered the sexless shining women in the first hours of the world that bore me, and the golden sexless men that cried All Praise in the sounds of shape. Taking strength from a sudden shining, I have Old Scratch by the beard, I cried aloud. But the short-time shapes still followed, and the counsellor of an unholy nakedness nagged at my heels. No, not for nothing did the packed thoroughfares confront me at each cross and pavement's turning with these figures in the shapes of sounds, the lamp-chalked silhouettes and the walking frames of dreams, out of a darker allegory than the fictions of the earth could turn in twelve suns' time.

There was more than man's meaning to the man-skulled bogies thumbing the skeletons of their noses, to the marrow-merry andrews scratching their armpits in a tavern light, and to the dead man, smiling through his bandages, who laid hand on my sleeve, saying in no man's voice, There is more than man's meaning in a stuffed man talking, split from navel to arsehole, and more in the horned ladies at your heels than a pinch of the cloven delights and the tang of sulphur. Heaven and Hell shift up and down the city. I have the God of Israel in the image of a painted boy, and Lucifer, in a woman's shirt, pisses from a window in Damaroid Alley. See now, you shining ones, how the tuner of harps has fallen, and the painter of winds like a bag of henna into the gutter. The high hopes lie broken with

broken bottles and suspenderbelts, the white mud falls
like feathers, there out of Pessary Court comes the Bishop
of Bumdom, dressed like a ratcatcher, a holy sister in
Gamarouche Mews sharpens her index tooth on a blood-
stone, two weazels couple on All Paul's altar. It was an
ungodly meaning, or the purpose of the fallen gods whose
haloes magnified the wrong-cross-steepled horns on the
pointed heads, that windily informed me of man's lower
walking, and, as I thrust the dead-and-bandaged and a
split-like-cabbage enemy to my right side, up sidled my no-
bigger-than-a-thimble friends to the naked left. He who
played the sorcerer, appearing all at one time in a dozen
sulphurous beckonings, saying, out of a dozen mouths, We
shall be naked as the slant-thighed queens of Asia in your
dreams, was a symbol in the story of man's journey through
the symboled city. And that which shifted with the greased
lightning of a serpent from the nest holes in the bases of
the cathedral's pillars, tracking round the margins of the
four cindery winds, was, too, a symbol in that city journey.
In a mouse-tailed woman and a holy snake, the symbols of
the city writhed before me. But by one red horn I had that
double image, tore off the furry stays and leather jacket.
We shall be naked, said Old Scratch variously emerging, as
a Jewgirl crucified to the bedposts. We are all metaphors
of the sound of shape of the shape of sound, break us we
take another shape. Sideways the snake and the woman
stroked a cross in the air. I saw the starfall that broke a
cloud up, and dodged between bonnets and wheels to the
iller-lit streets where I saw Daniel Dom lurching after a
painted shadow.

We walked into the Seven Sins. Two little girls danced
barefoot in the sawdust, and a bottle splintered on their
legs. A Negress loosened the straps of her yellow frock and
bared a breast, holding a plate under the black flesh. Buy a
pound, she said, and thrust her breast in Daniel's face. He
faced the woman as they moved, a yellow, noisy sea
towards us, and caught the half-naked Negress by the
wrist. Like a woman confronted by a tower, You are so
strong, my love, she said, and kissed him full on the mouth.
But before the sea could circle us, we were out through
the swing-doors into the street and the mid-winter night
where the moonlight, salt white no longer, hung windlessly
over the city. They were night's enemies who made a lamp
out of the devil's eye, but we followed a midnight radiance

around the corners, like two weird brothers trod in the glittering webprints. In their damp hats and raincoats, in the blaze of shopwindows, the people jostled against us on the pavements, and a gutter-boy caught me by the sleeve. Buy an almanac, he said. It was the bitter end of the year. Now the starfall had ended, the sky was a hole in space. How long, how long, lord of the hail, shall my city rock on, and the seven deadly seas wait tidelessly for the moon, the bitter end, and the last tide-spinning of the full circle. Daniel lamented, trailing the midnight radiance to the door of the Deadly Virtue where the light went out and the seven webprints faded. We were forever climbing the steps of a sea-tower, crying aloud from the turret that we might warn us, as we clambered, of the rusty rack and the spiked maiden in the turret corners. Make way for Mister Dom and friend. Walking into the Deadly Virtue, we heard our names announced through the loudspeaker trumpet of the wooden image over the central mirror, and, staring in the glass as the oracle continued, we saw two distorted faces grinning through the smoke. Make way, said the loud-speaker, for Daniel, ace of Destruction, Old Dom the toper of Doom's kitchen, and for the alderman of ghosts. Is the translator of man's manuscript, his walking chapters, said the trumpet-faced, a member of my Deadly Virtue? What is the colour of the narrator's blood? Put a leech on his forearm. Make way, the image cried, for bald and naked Mister Dreamer of the bluest veins this side of the blood-coloured sea. As the sea of faces parted, the bare-backed ladies scraped back from the counter, and the matchstick-waisted men, the trussed and corsetted stilt-walkers with the tits of ladies, sought out the darker recesses of the saloon, we stumbled forward to the fiery bottles. Brandy for the dreamer and the pilgrim, said the wooden voice. Gentle-men, it is my call, said the live loudspeaker, death on my house. It was then, in the tangled hours of a new morning, surrounded by the dead faces of the drinkers, the wail of lost voices, and the words of the one electric image, that Daniel, hair-on-end, lamented first to me of the death on the city and the lost hero of the heart. There can be no armistice for the sexless, golden singers and the sulphurous hermaphrodites, the flying beast and the walking bird that war about us, for the horn and the wing. I could light the voices of the fiery virgins winking in my glass, catch the brandy-brown beast and bird as they fumed before my eyes, and kiss the two-antlered angel. No, not for nothing were these two intangible brandymaids neighboring Daniel who cried, syringe in hand, Open your coke-white legs, you ladies of needles, Dom thunder Daniel is the lightning drug and the doctor.

Now a wind sprang through the room from the dead street; from the racked tower where two men lay in chains and a hole broke in the wall, we heard our own cries travel through the fumes of brandy and the loudspeaker's music; we pawed, in our tower agony, at the club shapes dancing, at the black girls tattooed from shoulder to nipple with a white dancing shape, frocked with snail-headed rushes and capped like antlers. But they slipped from us into the rubber corners where their black lovers waited invisibly; and the music grew louder until the tower cry was lost among it; and again Daniel lurched after a painted shadow that led him, threading through smoke and dancers, to the stained window.

Beneath him lay the city sleeping, curled in its streets and houses, lamped by its own red-waxed and iron stars, with a built moon above it, and the spires crossed over the bed. I stared down, rocking at his side, on to the unsmoking roofs and the burned-out candles. Destruction slept. Slowly the room behind us flowed, like four waters, down the seven gutters of the city into a black sea. A wave, catching the live loudspeaker in its mouth, sucked up the wood and music; for the last time a mountainous wave circled the drinkers and dragged them down, out of the world of light, to a crawling sea-bed; we saw a wave jumping and the last bright eyes go under, the last raw head, cut like a straw, fall crying through the destroying water. Daniel and I stood alone in the city. The sea of destruction lapped around our feet. We saw the starfall that broke the night up. The glass lights on iron went out, and the waves grew down into the pavements.

# The Map of Love

Here dwell, said Sam Rib, the two-backed beasts. He pointed to his map of Love, a square of seas and islands and strange continents with a forest of darkness at each extremity. The two-backed island, on the line of the equator, went in like the skin of lupus to his touch, and the blood sea surrounding found a new motion in its waters. Here seed, up the tide, broke on the boiling coasts; the sand grains multiplied; the seasons passed; summer, in a father's heat, went down to the autumn and the first pricks of winter, leaving the island shaping the four contrary winds out of its hollows.

Here, said Sam Rib, digging his fingers in the hills of a little island, dwell the first beasts of love. And here the get of the first loves mixed, as he knew, with the grasses that oiled their green upgoings, with their own wind and sap nurtured the first rasp of love that never, until spring came, found the nerves' answer in the fellowing blades.

Beth Rib and Reuben marked the green sea around the island. It ran through the landcracks like a boy through his first caves. Under the sea they marked the channels, painted in skeleton, that linked the first beasts' island with the boggy lands. For shame of the half-liquid plants sprouting from the bog, the pen-drawn poisons seething in the grass, and the copulation in the second mud, the children blushed.

Here, said Sam Rib, two weathers move. He traced with his finger the lightly drawn triangles of two winds, and the mouths of two cornered cherubs. The weathers moved in one direction. Singly they crawled over the abominations of the swamp, content in the shadow of their own rains and snowings, in the noise of their own sighs, and the pleasures of their own green achings. The weathers, like a girl and a boy, moved through the tossing world, the sea storm

151

dragging under them, the clouds divided in many rages of movement as they stared on the raw wall of wind.

Return, synthetic prodigals, to thy father's laboratory, declaimed Sam Rib, and the fatted calf in a test-tube. He indicated the shift of locations, the pen lines of the separate weathers travelling over the deep sea and the second split between the lovers' worlds. The cherubs blew harder; wind of the two tossing weathers and the sprays of the cohering sea drove on and on; on the single strand of two coupled countries, the weathers stood. Two naked towers on the two-loves-in-a-grain of the million sands, they mixed, so the map arrows said, into a single strength. But the arrows of ink shot them back; two weakened towers, wet with love, they trembled at the terror of their first mixing, and two pale shadows blew over the land.

Beth and Reuben scaled the hill that cast an eye of stone on the striped valley; hand-in-hand they ran down the hill, singing as they went, and took off their gaiters at the wet grass of the first of the twenty fields. There was a spirit in the valley that would roll on when all the hills and trees, all the rocks and streams, had been buried under the West death. Here was the first field wherein mad Jarvis, a hundred years before, had sown his seed in the belly of a bald-headed girl who had wandered out of a distant county and lain with him in the pains of love.

Here was the fourth field, a place of wonder, where the dead might spin all drunken-legged out of the dry graves, or the fallen angels battle upon the waters of the streams. Planted deeper in the soil of the valley than the blind roots could burrow after their mates, the spirit of the fourth field rose out of darkness, drawing the deep and the dark from the hearts of all who trod the valley a score or more miles from the borders of the mountainous county.

In the tenth and the central field Beth Rib and Reuben knocked at the doors of the bungalows, asking the location of the first island surrounded by loving hills. They knocked at the back door and received a ghostly admonishment.

Barefooted and hand-in-hand, they ran through the ten remaining fields to the edge of the Idris water where the wind smelt of seaweed and the valley spirit was wet with sea rain. But night came down, hand on thigh, and shapes in the further stretches of the now misty river drew a new shape close to them. An island shape walled round with darkness a half-mile up river. Stealthily Beth Rib and

Reuben tiptoed to the lapping water. They saw the shape grow, unlocked their fingers, took off their summer clothes, and, naked, raced into the river.

Up river, up river, she whispered.

Up river, he said.

They floated down river as a current tugged at their legs, but they fought off the current and swam towards the still growing island. Then mud rose from the bed of the river and sucked at Beth's feet.

Down river, down river, she called, struggling from the mud.

Reuben, weed-bound, fought with the grey heads that fought his hands, and followed her back to the brink of the sea-going valley.

But, as Beth swam, the water tickled her; the water pressed on her side.

My love, cried Reuben, excited by the tickling water and the hands of the weeds.

And, as they stood naked on the twentieth field, My love, she whispered.

First fear shot them back. Wet as they were, they pulled their clothes on them.

Over the fields, she said.

Over the fields, in the direction of the hills and the hill-home of Sam Rib, like weakened towers the children ran, no longer linked, bewildered by the mud and blushing at the first tickle of the misty island water.

Here dwell, said Sam Rib, the first beasts of love. In the cool of a new morning the children listened, too frightened to touch hands. He touched again the sagging hill above the island, and pointed the progression of the skeleton channels linking mud with mud, green sea with darker, and all love-hills and islands into one territory. Here the grass mates, the green mates, the grains, said Sam Rib, and the dividing waters mate and are mated. The sun with the grass and the green, sand with water, and water with the green grass, these mate and are mated for the bearing and fostering of the globe. Sam Rib had mated with a green woman, as Great-Uncle Jarvis with his bald girl; he had mated with a womanly water for the bearing and fostering of the child who blushed by him. He marked how the boggy lands lay so near the first beast doubling a back, the round of doubled beasts under as high a hill as Great-Uncle's hill that had frowned last night and wrapped itself in stones. Great-Uncle's hill had cut the children's feet, for the daps and the gaiters were lost forever in the grass of the first field.

Thinking of the hill, Beth Rib and Reuben sat quiet. They heard Sam say that the hill of the first island grew soft as wool for the descent, or smooth as ice for tobogganing. They remembered the tame descent last night.

Tame hill, said Sam Rib, grows wild for the ascending. Lining the adolescents' hill was a white route of stone and ice marked with the sliding foot or sledge of the children going down; another route, at the foot, climbed upwards in a line of red stone and blood marked with the cracking prints of the ascending children. The descent was soft as wool. Fail on the first island, and the ascending hill wraps itself in a sharp thing of stones.

Beth Rib and Reuben, never forgetful of the humpbacked boulders and the flints in the grass, turned to each other for the first time that day. Sam Rib had made her and would mould him, would make and mould the boy and girl together into a double climber that sought the island and melted there into a single strength. He told them again of the mud, but did not frighten them. And the grey heads of the weeds were broken, never to swell again in the hands of the swimmer. The day of ascending was over; the first descent remained, a hill on the map of love, two branches of stone and olive in the children's hands.

Synthetic prodigals returned that night to the room of the hill, through caves and chambers running to the roof, discerning the roof of stars, and happy in their locked hands. There lay the striped valley before them, and the grass of the twenty fields fed the cattle; the night cattle moved by the hedges or lapped at warm Idris water. Beth Rib and Reuben ran down the hill, and the tender stones lay still under their feet; faster, they ran down the Jarvis flank, the wind at their hair, smells of the sea blown to their quivering nostrils from the north and the south where there was no sea; and, slowing their speed, they reached the first field and the rim of the valley to find their gaiters placed neatly in a cow-cloven spot in the grass.

They buttoned on their gaiters, and ran through the falling blades.

Here is the first field, said Beth Rib to Reuben.

The children stopped, the moonlight night went on, a voice spoke from the hedge darkness.

Said the voice, You are the children of love.

Where are you?

I am Jarvis.

Who are you?

Here, my dears, here in the hedge with a wise woman.

But the children ran away from the voice in the hedge.

Here in the second field.

They stopped for breath, and a weasel, making his noise, ran over their feet.

Hold harder.

I'll hold you harder.

Said a voice, Hold hard, the children of love.

Where are you?

I am Jarvis.

Who are you?

Here, here, lying with a virgin from Dolgelley.

In the third field the man of Jarvis lay loving a green girl, and, as he called them the children of love, lay loving her ghost and the smell of buttermilk on her breath. He loved a cripple in the fourth field, for the twist in her limbs made loving longer, and he cursed the straight children who found him with a straight-limbed lover in the fifth field marking the quarter.

A girl from Tiger Bay held Jarvis close, and her lips marked a red, cracked heart upon his throat; this was the sixth and the weather-tracked field where, turning from the maul of her hands, he saw their innocence, two flowers wagging in a sow's ear. My rose, said Jarvis, but the seventh love smelt in his hands, his fingering hands that held Glamorgan's canker under the eighth hedge. From the Convent of Bethel's Heart, a holy woman served him the ninth time.

And the children in the central field cried as ten voices came up, came up, came down from the ten spaces of the half-night and the hedging world.

It was full night when they answered, when the voices of one voice compassionately answered the two-voiced question ringing on the strokes of the upward, upward, and the downward air.

We, said they, are Jarvis, Jarvis under the hedge, in the arms of a woman, a green woman, a woman bald as a badger, on a nun's thigh.

They counted the numbers of their loves before the children's ears. Beth Rib and Reuben heard the ten oracles, and shyly they surrendered. Over the remaining fields, to the whispers of the last ten lovers, to the voice of ageing Jarvis, grey-haired in the final shadows, they sped to Idris. The island shone, the water babbled, there was a gesture of the limbs in each wind's stroke denting the flat river. He took off her summer clothes, and she shaped her arms like a swan. The bare boy stood at her shoulder; and she turned and saw him dive into the ripples in her wake. Behind them her fathers' voices slipped out of sound.

Up river, called Beth, up river.

Up river, he answered.

Only the warm, mapped waters ran that night over the edges of the first beasts' island white in a new moon.

# In the Direction of the Beginning

In the light tent in the swinging field in the great spring
evening, near the sea and the shingled boat with a mast
of cedarwood, the hinderwood decked with beaks and shells,
a folded, salmon sail, and two finned oars; with gulls in
one flight high over, stork, pelican, and sparrow, flying to
the ocean's end and the first grain of a timeless land that
spins on the head of a sandglass, a hoop of feathers down
the dark of the spring in a topsy-turvy year; as the rocks
in history, by every feature and scrawled limb, eye of a
needle, shadow of a nerve, cut in the heart, by rifted fibre
and clay thread, recorded for the rant of odyssey the dropping of the bayleaf toppling of the oaktree splintering of
the moonstone against assassin avatar undead and num-
bered waves, a man was born in the direction of the beginning. And out of sleep, where the moon had raised him
through the mountains in her eyes and by the strong, eyed
arms that fall behind her, full of tides and fingers, to the
blown sea, he wrestled over the edge of the evening, took
to the beginning as a goose to the sky, and called his furies
by their names from the wind-drawn index of the grave
and waters. Who was this stranger who came like a hail-
stone, cut in ice, a snowleafed seabush for her hair, and
taller than a cedarmast, the north white rain descending
and the whale-driven sea cast up to the caves of the eye,
from a fishermen's city on the floating island? She was salt
and white and travelling as the field, on one blade, swung
with its birds around her, evening centered in the neverstill
heart, he heard her hands among the treetops—a feather
dived, her fingers flowed over the voices—and the world
went drowning down through a siren stranger's vision of
grass and waterbeasts and snow. The world was sucked
to the last lake's drop; the cataract of the last particle worried in a lather to the ground, as if the rain from heaven
had let its clouds fall turtle-turning like a manna made of

the soft-bellied seasons, and the hard hail, falling, spread and flustered in a cloud half flower half ash or the comb-footed scavenger's wind through a pyramid raised high with mud or the soft slow drift of mingling steam and leaves. In the exact centre of enchantment he was a shore-man in deep sea, lashed by his hair to the eye in the cyclop breast, with his swept thighs strung among her voice; white bears swarm and sailors drowned to the music she scaled and drew with hands and fables from his up-right hair; she plucked his terror by the ears, and bore him singing into light through the forest of the serpent-haired and the stone-turning voice. Revelation stared back over its transfixed shoulder. Which was her genesis, the last spark of judgment or the first whale's spout from the waterland? The conflagration at the end, a burial fire jump-ing, a spent rocket hot on its tail, or, where the first spring and its folly climbed the seabarriers and the garden locks were bruised, capped and douting water over the moun-tain candlehead? Whose was the image in the wind, the print on the cliff, the echo knocking to be answered? She was orioled and serpent-haired. She moved in the swal-lowing, salty field, the chronicle and the rocks, the dark anatomies, the anchored sea itself. She raged in the mule's womb. She faltered in the galloping dynasty. She was loud in the old grave, kept a still, quick tongue in the sun. He marked her outcast image, mapped with a nightmare's foot in poison and framed against the wind, print of her thumb that buckled on its hand with a webbed shadow, interro-gation of the familiar echo: which is my genesis, the granite fountain extinguishing where the first flame is cast in the sculptured world, or the bonfire maned like a lion in the threshold of the last vault? One voice then in that evening travelled the light and water waves, one lineament took on the sliding moods, from where the gold green sea cantharis dyes the trail of the octopus one venom crawled through foam, and from the four map corners one cherub in an island shape puffed the clouds to sea.

# An Adventure from a Work in Progress

The boat tugged its anchor, and the anchor flew up from the seabed like an iron arrow and hung poised in a new wind and pointed over the corkscrew channels of the sea to the dark holes and caves in the horizon. He saw birds soaring out of the pitted distance blind by his anchor as he swam with a seal at his side to the boat that stamped the water. He gripped on the bows like a mane, the arrowing anchor shot north, and the boat sped beneath it with winds and invisible fire puffing and licking. His animal boat split the water into a thousand boat-sized seas, bit deep into the flying shoals, halved and multiplied the flying fishes, it dived under waves like a wooden dolphin and wagged the fingering wrack off its stern, it swerved past a black and gold buoy with cathedral chimes and kept cold north. Spray turned to ice as it whipped through his hair, and pierced his cheeks and eyelids, and the running blood froze hard. He saw through a coat of red ice that the sea was transparent; under his boat the drowned dead burned in a pale-green, grass-high fire; the sea rained on the flames. But on through the north, between glass hills on which she-bears climbed and saw themselves reflected, eating the sea between the paddling floes, a shell of lightning fibres skimming and darting under an anchorbolt, tossed and magnified among the frozen window weeds, through a slow snowstorm whose flakes fell like hills one at a time down the white air, lost in a round sudden house of the six-year night and slipping through an arch of sleeping birds each roosted on an icicle, the boat came into blue water. Birds with blue feathers set alight by the sun, with live flames for their crests, flew by the hovering anchor to the trees and bushes on the rims of the soft sand round the sea that brushed his boat slowly and whispered it like a name in letters of parting water towards a harbour grove and a slowly spinning island with lizards in its lap. The salmon of the still sail turned to the blue of the birds' eggs in the tips of the fringing forest of each wave. The feathers crackled from the birds and drifted down and fell upon bare rods and stalks that fenced the island entrance, the rods and stalks grew into trees with musical leaves still burning. The history of the boat was spelt in knocking water on the hanging harbour bank; each syllable of his adventure struck on grass and stone and rang out in the passages of the disturbed rock plants and was chattered from flame to tree. The anchor dived to rest. He strode through the blazing fence. The print of the ice was melting. The island spun. He saw between trees a tall woman standing on the opposite bank. He ran directly towards her but the green thighs closed. He ran on the rim towards her but she was still the same distance from him on the roundabout island. Time was about to fall; it had slept without sound under and over the blaze and spinning; now it was raised ready. Flowers in the centre of the island caught its tears in a cup. It hardened and shouted and shone in dead echoes and pearls. It fell as he ran on the outer rim, and oaks were felled in the acorn and lizards laid in the shell. He held the woman drowning in his arms, her driftwood limbs, her winking ballast head of glass; he fought with her blood like a man with a waterfall turning to fishdust with ash, and her salvaged seaweed hair twisted blindly about his eyes. The boat with anchor hovering and finned oars trembling for water after land, the beaks at the stern gabbling and the shells alive, was blown alongside him, by a wind that took a corner on one breath, from the harbour bank where roots of trees drove up the sky and foliage in cinders smouldered down, the lopped leg of a bird scratched against rock, a thundering cave sat upright and bolted mouthdown into the sea; he dipped the gills of the oars, the cedarmast shook like a cloth, warm north the boat sped off again from an island no longer spinning but split into vanishing caves and contrary trees. Time that had fallen rested in the edges of its knives and the hammock of its fires, the memory of the woman was strong on his hands, her claws and anemones, weedwrack and urchin hair, the sea was deserted and colourless, direction was dead as the island and north was a circle, a bird above the anchor spurted through a stationary cloud to catch its cry, the boat with gilled oars swimming ploughed through the foam in the wake, her pale brow glistened in the new moon of his nails and the drenched thread of her nerves sprang up and down behind them, the stern beaks quacked and yawned, crabs clacked from the shells, a mist rose up that dressed and unshaped the sky and the sea flowed in secret. Through the mist, dragging a black weather with it, a spade-shaped shoal of clouds tacked to its peak, a broken moon, a wind with trumpets, came a mountain in a moment. The boat struck rock. The beaks were still. The shells snapped shut. He leaped into mud as the wind cried his name to the flapping shoals; his name rolled about the mountain, echoed through caves and crevices, ducked in venomous pools, slap on black walls, translated into the voice of dying stone, growling through slime into silence. He gazed at the mountain peak; a cloud obscured it, cords of light from the moon were looped around the tentacles of the crags. Lightning with a horn and bone on, with gristle white as a spine hardening and halving the forked sides, struck through the tacked cloud cap, lit the stone head, scorched the mist-curled fringe, cut through the cords until the moon sailed upwards like a kite. With the turning out of the lightning, the jackknife doubling up of the limp spine, the weather in tow rocked to work and flight in a sealed air, the mountain vanished leaving a hole in space to keep the shape of his horror as he sank, as the monuments of the dark mud toppled and his raised arms were cemented against rock with the wet maggot sacks and the mixed, crawling breasts of statues and creatures who once stood on the ledges of the mountain foot or blocked the crying mouths of caves. The wind, blowing matter with a noise, stuck to his cheek. The sea climbed his limbs like a sailor. Bound and drowning in that dismembered masonry, his eyes on a level with the shuffled circle of headpieces floating, he saw the lightning dart to strike again, and the horned bone stiffen among the forks; hope, like another muscle, broke the embraces of the nuzzling bodies, thrust off the face that deathmasked his, for the mountain appeared on the strike of light and the hollow shape of his horror was filled with crags and turrets, rock webs and dens, spinning black balconies, the loud packed smashing of separate seas, and the abominable substances of a new colour. The world happened at once. There was the

furnished mountain built in a flash and thunderclap col-
liding. The shapes of rain falling made a new noise and
number. And the lightning stayed striking; its charted
shaft of sawteeth struck and bit in continual light; one
blind flash was a year of mornings. The mummyfolds, the
mudpots, the wet masks, the quick casts, the closing
sheathes, melted under the frostbite heat of that unwink-
ing lightning. He boxed free from the statues and the
caved and toppling watchers. From a man-sized dent in
a melting thigh he came up strung with shells and mussed
with weed like a child from the roots of the original sea
into a dazzling bed. Once on hard land, with shells that
swung from his hair ringing from the tail of a weed, and
shells repeating the sea, he shook away calamity, bounced
the weeds off his bare breast, threw back his head until the
pealing shells took in their echo the voices of all miscel-
laneous water, and grappled with the mountainside. His
shadow led and beckoned; he turned curves of the eel-
backed paths, his shadow pointed to the footprints that
appeared before his feet; he followed where his footprints
led, saw the smudged outline of his hand on a wet stone
as he quarreled with stones and trees towards it up an
attacking valley; animals closed their lips round the shout
of a wind walking by and scooped his name to welcome it
up hollow trunks and walls. He followed the flight of his
name: it slipped to a stop at the peak; there a tall woman
caught the flying name to her lips. He flourished in the
middle of the pain of the mountain and joy sped with his
shadow, the strong memory of the driftwrack woman was
dead on his hands digging deep in the soil towards this
stranger tall as a pulled tree and whiter at that great and
shortening distance than the lightning-coloured sea a hundred dangers below. The thighs smooth as groundstone and
sensual cleft, limpet eye and musselmouth, the white boulders bent, blue shadows and pricked berries, the torrential
flowers and blacks of the bush on the skull and the muffed
pits, the draped cellars, the lashed stones, the creased face
on the knees, all for a moment while he stood in love were
still and near. Then slowly her peak in a cloud's alcove
—carved animals on an abbey, wind in an amice, arching
accusing her—rose with his lovely dashing from stillness.
Slowly her peak got up the cloudy arches, the stones he
stumbled on followed her at the same speed. Though he
hugged like a bear and climbed fast, she kept her distance

from him. The mountain in the intervals of his breathing grew many times its size until time fell and cut and burned it down. The peak collapsed, the mountain folded, he clasped the woman diminishing in his arms; the downpours of her hair were short falls, her limbs stunted, her hands blunt, her teeth were small and square as dice and the rot marked them. A haloe cracked like china, wings were spoked. Blood flapped behind all the windows of the world. And with the wasting of her limbs suddenly she grew young. Holding her small body, he cried in the nightmare of a naked child kissing and blaspheming close, breasts small as pears with milk foaming from them, the innocent holes of the open eyes, the thin, rouged mussel-mouth, when the head falls, the eyes loll, the small throat snaps, and the headless child lies loving in the dark. The mad bug trotted in at the ear with the whole earth on a feeler. With his cries she caved in younger. He held her hard. The marrow in her bones was soft as syrup. From a scar in the peak came a shadow with black gamp and scarlet basin. She dangled there with bald and monstrous skull, bunched monkey face, and soaked abdominal tail. Out of the webbed sea-pig and water-nudging fish a white pool spat in his palm. Reeling to run seaweed and away, he trod the flats of waves. The splintered claw of a crab struck from the killed hindershells. And, after the anchor burrowing through blind cloud, he rowed and sailed, that the world might happen to him once, past the events of revolving islands and elastic hills, on the common sea.

# The School for Witches

On Cader Peak there was a school for witches where the doctor's daughter, teaching the unholy cradle and the devil's pin, had seven country girls. On Cader Peak, half ruined in an enemy weather, the house with a story held the seven girls, the cellar echoing, and a cross reversed above the entrance to the inner rooms. Here the doctor, dreaming of illness, in the centre of the tubercular hill, heard his daughter cry to the power swarming under the West roots. She invoked a particular devil, but the gehenna did not yawn under the hill, and the day and the night continued with their two departures; the cocks crew and the corn fell in the villages and yellow fields as she taught the seven girls how the lust of man, like a dead horse, stood up to her injected mixtures. She was short and fat-thighed; her cheeks were red; she had red lips and innocent eyes. But her body grew hard as she called to the black flowers under the tide of roots; when she fetched the curdlers out of the trees to bore through the cow's udders, the seven staring stared at the veins hardening in her breast; she stood uncovered, calling the devil, and the seven uncovered closed round her in a ring.

Teaching them the intricate devil, she raised her arms to let him enter. Three years and a day had vanished since she first bowed to the moon, and, maddened by the mid light, dripped her hair seven times in the salt sea, and a mouse in honey. She stood, still untaken, loving the lost man; her fingers hardened on light as on the breastbone of the unentering devil.

Mrs. Price climbed up the hill, and the seven saw her. It was the first evening of the new year, the wind was motionless on Cader Peak, and a half red, promising dusk floated over the rocks. Behind the midwife the sun sank as a stone sinks in a marsh, the dark bubbled over it, and the mud sucked it down into the bubble of the bottomless fields.

In Bethlehem there is a prison for mad women, and in Cathmarw by the parsonage trees a black girl screamed as she laboured. She was afraid to die like a cow on the straw, and to the noises of the rooks. She screamed for the doctor on Cader Peak as the tumultuous West moved in its grave. The midwife heard her. A black girl rocked in her bed. Her eyes were stones. Mrs. Price climbed up the hill, and the seven saw her.

Midwife, midwife, called the seven girls. Mrs. Price crossed herself. A chain of garlic hung at her throat. Carefully, she touched it. The seven cried aloud, and ran from the window to the inner rooms where the doctor's daughter, bent on uncovered knees, counselled the black toad, her familiar, and the divining cat slept by the wall. The familiar moved its head. The seven danced, rubbing the white wall with their thighs until the blood striped the thin symbols of fertility upon them. Hand in hand they danced among symbols, under the charts that marked the rise and fall of the satanic seasons, and their white dresses swung around them. The owls commenced to sing, striking against the music of the suddenly awaking winter. Hand in hand the dancers spun around the black toad and the doctor's daughter, seven stags dancing, their antlers shaking, in the confusion of the unholy room.

She is a very black woman, said Mrs. Price, and curtsied to the doctor.

He woke to the midwife's story out of a dream of illness, remembering the broken quicked, the black patch and echo, the mutilated shadows of the seventh sense.

She lay with a black scissor-man.

He wounded her deep, said the doctor, and wiped a lancet on his sleeve.

Together they stumbled down the rocky hill.

A terror met them at the foot, the terror of the blind tapping their white sticks and the stumps of the arms on the solid darkness; two worms in the foil of a tree, bellies on the rubber sap and the glues of a wrong-grained forest, they, holding tight to hats and bags, crawled now up the path that led to the black birth. From right, from left, the cries of labour came in under the branches, piercing the dead wood, from the earth where a mole sneezed, and from the sky, out of the worms' sight.

They were not the only ones caught that night in the torrential blindness; to them, as they stumbled, the land was empty of men, and the prophets of bad weather alone walked in their neighbourhoods. Three tinkers appeared out of silence by the chapel wall. Capel Cader, said the panman. Parson is down on tinkers, said John Bucket. Cader Peak, said the scissorman, and up they went. They passed the midwife close; she heard the scissors clacking, and the branch of a tree drum on the buckets. One, two, three, they were gone, invisibly shuffling as she hugged her skirts. Mrs. Price crossed herself for the second time that day, and touched the garlic at her throat. A vampire with a scissors was a Pembroke devil. And the black girl screamed like a pig.

Sister, raise your right hand. The seventh girl raised her right hand. Now say, said the doctor's daughter, rise up out of the bearded barley. Rise out of the green grass asleep in Mr. Griffith's dingle. Big man, black man, all eye, one tooth, rise up out of Cader marshes. Say the devil kisses me. The devil kisses me, said the girl cold in the centre of the kitchen. Kiss me out of the bearded barley. Kiss me out of the bearded barley. The girls giggled in a circle. Swive me out of the green grass. Swive me out of the green grass. Can I put on my clothes now? said the young witch, after encountering the invisible evil.

Throughout the hours of the early night, in the smoke of the seven candles, the doctor's daughter spoke of the sacrament of darkness. In her familiar's eyes she read the news of a great and an unholy coming; divining the future in the green and sleepy eyes, she saw, as clearly as the tinkers saw the spire, the towering coming of a beast in stag's skin, the antlered animal whose name read backwards, and the black, black, black wanderer climbing a hill for the seven wise girls of Cader. She woke the cat. Poor Bell, she said, smoothing his fur the wrong way. And, Ding dong, Bell, she said, and swung the spitting cat.

Sister, raise your left hand. The first girl raised her left hand. Now with your right hand put a needle in your left hand. Where is a needle? Here, said the doctor's daughter, is a needle, here in your hair. She made a gesture over the black hair, and drew a needle out from the coil at her ear. Say I cross you. I cross you, said the girl, and, with the needle in her hand, struck at the black cat racked on the daughter's lap.

For love takes many shapes, cat, dog, pig, or goat; there was a lover, spellbound in the time of mass, now formed and featured in the image of the darting cat; his belly bleeding, he sped past the seven girls, past parlour and dispensary, into the night, on to the hill; the wind got at his wound, and swiftly he darted down the rocks, in the direction of the cooling streams.

He passed the three tinkers like lightning. Black cat is luck, said the panman. Bloody cat is bad luck, said John Bucket. The scissorman said nothing. They appeared out of silence by the wall of the Peak house, and heard a hellish music through the open door. They peered through the stained-glass window, and the seven girls danced before them. They have beaks, said the panman. Web feet, said John Bucket. The tinkers walked in.

At midnight the black girl bore her baby, a black beast with the eyes of a kitten and a stain at the corner of its mouth. The midwife remembering birthmarks, whispered to the doctor of the gooseberry on his daughter's arm. Is it ripe yet? said Mrs. Price. The doctor's hand trembled, and his lancet cut the baby under the chin. Scream you, said Mrs. Price, who loved all babies.

The wind howled over Cader, waking the sleepy rooks who cawed from the trees and, louder than owls, disturbed the midwife's meditations. It was wrong for the rooks, those sleepy birds over the zinc roofs, to caw at night. Who put a spell on the rooks? The sun might rise at ten past one in the morning.

Scream you, said Mrs. Price, the baby in her arms, this is a wicked world. The wicked world, with a voice out of the wind, spoke to the baby half smothering under the folds of the midwife's overcoat. Mrs. Price wore a man's cap, and her great breasts heaved under the black blouse. Scream you, said the wicked world, I am an old man blinding you, a wicked little woman tickling you, a dry death parching you. The baby screamed, as though a flea were on its tongue.

The tinkers were lost in the house, and could not find the inner room where the girls still danced with the beaks of birds upon them and their web feet bare on the cobblestones. The panman opened the dispensary door, but the bottles and the tray of knives alarmed him. The passages were too dark for John Bucket, and the scissorman surprised him at a corner. Christ defend me, he cried. The girls stopped dancing, for the name of Christ rang in the outer halls. Enter, and, Enter, cried the doctor's daughter to the welcome devil. It was the scissorman who found the door and turned the handle, walking into candlelight. He stood before Gladwys on the threshold, a giant black as ink with a three days' beard. She lifted her face to his, and her sackcloth fell away.

Up the hill, the midwife, cooing as she came, held the newborn baby in her arms, and the doctor toiled behind her with his black bag rattling. The birds of the night flew by them, but the night was empty, and the restless wings and voices, hindering emptiness forever were the feathers of shadows and the accents of an invisible flying. What purpose there was in the shape of Cader Peak, in the bouldered breast of the hill and the craters poxing the green-black flesh, was no more than the wind's purpose that willy nilly blew from all corners the odd turfs and stones of an unmoulded world. The grassy rags and bones of the steep hill were, so the doctor pondered as he climbed behind the baby rocking into memory on a strange breast, whirled together out of the bins of chaos by a winter wind. But the doctor's conceits came to nothing, for the black child let out a scream so high and loud that Mr. Griffiths heard it in his temple in the dingle. The worshipper of vegetables, standing beneath his holy marrow nailed in four places to the wall, heard the cry come down from the heights. A mandrake cried on Cader. Mr. Griffiths hastened in the direction of the stars.

John Bucket and the panman stepped into candlelight, seeing a strange company. Now in the centre circle of the room, surrounded by the unsteady lights, stood the scissorman and a naked girl; she smiled at him, he smiled at her, his hands groped for her body, she stiffened and slackened, he drew her close, smiling she stiffened again, and he licked his lips.

John Bucket had not seen him as a power for evil baring the breasts and the immaculate thighs of the gentlewomen, a magnetic blackman with the doom of women in his smile, forcing open the gates of love. He remembered a black companion on the roads, sharpening the village scissors, and, in the shadows, when the tinkers took the night, a coal-black shadow, silent as the travelling hedges.

Was this tall man, the panman murmured, who takes the doctor's daughter with no how-d'you-do, was he Tom the scissorman? I remember him on the highways in the heat of the sun, a black, three-coated tinker.

And, like a god, the scissorman bent over Gladwys, he healed her wound, she took his ointment and his fire, she burned at the tower altar, and the black sacrifice was done. Stepping out of his arms, her offering cut and broken, the gut of a lamb, she smiled and cried manfully: Dance, dance, my seven. And the seven danced, their antlers shaking, in the confusion of the unholy room. A coven, a coven, cried the seven as they danced. They beckoned the panman from the door. He edged towards them, and they caught his hands. Dance, dance, my strange man, the seven cried. John Bucket joined them, his buckets drumming, and swiftly they dragged him into the rising fury of the dance. The scissorman in the circle danced like a tower. They sped round and round, none crying louder than the two tinkers in the heart of the swirling company, and lightly the doctor's daughter was among them. She drove them to a faster turn of foot; giddy as weathercocks in a hundred changing winds, they were revolving figures in the winds of their dresses and to the music of the scissors and the metal pans; giddily she spun between the dancing hoops, the wheels of cloth and hair, and the bloody ninepins spinning; the candles grew pale and lean in the wind of the dance; she whirled by the tinkers' side, by the scissorman's side; by his dark, damp side, smelling his skin, smelling the seven furies.

It was then that the doctor, the midwife, and the baby entered through the open door as quietly as could be. Sleep well, Pembroke, for your devils have left you. And woe on Cader Peak that the black man dances in my house. There had been nothing for that savage evening but an end of evil. The grave had yawned, and the black breath risen up.

Here danced the metamorphoses of the dusts of Cathmarw. Lie level, the ashes of man, for the phoenix flies from you, woe unto Cader, unto my nice, square house. Mrs. Price fingered her garlic, and the doctor stood grieving.

The seven saw them. A coven, a coven, they cried. One, dancing past them, snatched at the doctor's hand; another, dancing caught him around the waist; and, all bewildered by the white flesh of their arms, the doctor danced. Woe, woe on Cader, he cried as he swirled among maidens, and his steps gathered speed. He heard his voice rising; his feet skimmed over the silver cobbles. A coven, a coven, cried the dancing doctor, and bowed in his measures.

Suddenly Mrs. Price, hugging the black baby, was surrounded at the entrance of the room. Twelve dancers hemmed her in, and the hands of strangers pulled at the baby on her breast. See, see, said the doctor's daughter, the cross on the black throat. There was blood beneath the baby's chin where a sharp knife had slipped and cut. The cat, cried the seven, the cat, the black cat. They had unloosed the spellbound devil that dwelt in the cat's shape, the human skeleton, the flesh and heart out of the gehenna of the valley roots and the image of the creature calming his wound in the far-off streams. Their magic was done; they set the baby down on the stones, and the dance continued. Pembroke, sleep well, whispered the dancing midwife, lie still, you empty county.

And it was thus that the last visitor that night found the thirteen dancers in the inner rooms of Cader House: a black man and a blushing girl, two shabby tinkers, a doctor, a midwife, and seven country girls, swirling hand in hand under the charts that marked the rise and fall of the satanic seasons, among the symbols of the darker crafts, giddily turning, raising their voices to the roofs as they bowed to the cross reversed above the inner entrance.

Mr. Griffiths, half blinded by the staring of the moon, peeped in and saw them. He saw the newborn baby on the cold stones. Unseen in the shadow by the door, he crept towards the baby and lifted it to its feet. The baby fell. Patiently Mr. Griffiths lifted the baby to its feet. But the little mandrake would not walk that night.

# The Dress

They had followed him for two days over the length of the county, but he had lost them at the foot of the hills, and, hidden in a golden bush, had heard them shouting as they stumbled down the valley. Behind a tree on the ridge of the hills he had peeped down on to the fields where they hurried about like dogs, where they poked the hedges with their sticks and set up a faint howling as a mist came suddenly from the spring sky and hid them from his eyes. But the mist was a mother to him, putting a coat around his shoulders where the shirt was torn and the blood dry on his blades. The mist made him warm; he had the food and the drink of the mist on his lips; and he smiled through her mantle like a cat. He worked away from the valley-wards side of the hill into the denser trees that might lead him to light and fire and a basin of soup. He thought of the coals that might be hissing in the grate, and of the young mother standing alone. He thought of her hair. Such a nest it would make for his hands. He ran through the trees, and found himself on a narrow road. Which way should he walk: towards or away from the moon? The mist had made a secret of the position of the moon, but, in a corner of the sky, where the mist had fallen apart, he could see the angles of the stars. He walked towards the north where the stars were, mumbling a song with no tune, hearing his feet suck in and out of the spongy earth.

Now there was time to collect his thoughts, but no sooner had he started to set them in order than an owl made a cry in the trees that hung over the road, and he stopped and winked up at her, finding a mutual melancholy in her sounds. Soon she would swoop and fasten on a mouse. He saw her for a moment as she sat screeching on her bough. Then, frightened of her, he hurried on, and had not gone more than a few yards into the darkness when, with a fresh cry, she flew away. Pity the hare, he thought, for the weasel will drink her. The road sloped to the stars, and the trees and the valley and the memory of the guns faded behind.

He heard footsteps. An old man, radiant with rain, stepped out of the mist.

Good night, sir, said the old man.

No night for the son of woman, said the madman.

The old man whistled, and hurried, half running, in the direction of the roadside trees.

Let the hounds know, the madman chuckled as he climbed up the hill, let the hounds know. And, crafty as a fox, he doubled back to where the misty road branched off three ways. Hell on the stars, he said, and walked towards the dark.

The world was a ball under his feet; it kicked as he ran; it dropped; up came the trees. In the distance a poacher's dog yelled at the trap on its foot, and he heard it and ran the faster, thinking the enemy was on his heels. Duck, boys, duck, he called out, but with the voice of one who might have pointed to a falling star.

Remembering of a sudden that he had not slept since the escape, he left off running. Now the waters of the rain, too tired to strike the earth, broke up as they fell and blew about in the wind like the sandman's grains. If he met sleep, sleep would be a girl. For the last two nights, while walking or running over the empty county, he had dreamed of their meeting. Lie down, she would say, and would give him her dress to lie on, stretching herself out by his side. Even as he had dreamed, and the twigs under his running feet had made a noise like the rustle of her dress, the enemy had shouted in the fields. He had run on and on, leaving sleep farther behind him. Sometimes there was a sun, a moon, and sometimes under a black sky he had tossed and thrown the wind before he could be off.

Where is Jack? they asked in the gardens of the place he had left. Up on the hills with a butcher's knife, they said, smiling. But the knife was gone, thrown at a tree and quivering there still. There was no heat in his head. He ran on and on, howling for sleep.

And she, alone in the house, was sewing her new dress. It was a bright country dress with flowers on the bodice. Only a few more stitches were needed before it would be ready to wear. It would lie neat on her shoulders, and two of the flowers would be growing out of her breasts.

When she walked with her husband on Sunday mornings over the fields and down into the village, the boys would smile at her behind their hands, and the shaping of the dress round her belly would set all the widow women talking. She slipped into her new dress, and, looking into the mirror over the fireplace, saw that it was prettier than she had imagined. It made her face paler and her long hair darker. She had cut it low.

A dog out in the night lifted its head up and howled. She turned away hurriedly from her reflection, and pulled the curtains closer.

Out in the night they were searching for a madman. He had green eyes, they said, and had married a lady. They said he had cut off her lips because she smiled at men. They took him away, but he stole a knife from the kitchen and slashed his keeper and broke out into the wild valleys.

From afar he saw the light in the house, and stumbled up to the edge of the garden. He felt, he did not see, the little fence around it. The rusting wire scraped on his hands, and the wet, abominable grass crept over his knees. And once he was through the fence, the hosts of the garden came rushing to meet him, the flower-headed, and the bodying frosts. He had torn his fingers while the old wounds were still wet. Like a man of blood he came out of the enemy darkness on to the steps. He said in a whisper, Let them not shoot me. And he opened the door.

She was in the middle of the room. Her hair had fallen untidily, and three of the buttons at the neck of her dress were undone. What made the dog howl as it did? Frightened of the howling, and thinking of the tales she had heard, she rocked in her chair. What became of the woman? she wondered as she rocked. She could not think of a woman without any lips. What became of women without any lips? she wondered.

The door made no noise. He stepped into the room, trying to smile, and holding out his hands.

Oh, you've come back, she said.

Then she turned in her chair and saw him. There was blood even by his green eyes. She put her fingers to her mouth. Not shoot, he said.

But the moving of her arm drew the neck of her dress apart, and he stared in wonder at her wide, white forehead, her frightened eyes and mouth, and down on to the flowers on her dress. With the moving of her arm, her dress danced in the light. She sat before him, covered in flowers. Sleep, said the madman. And, kneeling down, he put his bewildered head upon her lap.

# The Vest

He rang the bell. There was no answer. She was out. He turned the key.

The hall in the late afternoon light was full of shadows. They made one almost solid shape. He took off his hat and coat, looking sidewise, so that he might not see the shape, at the light through the sitting-room door.

"Is anybody in?"

The shadows bewildered him. She would have swept them up as she swept the invading dust.

In the drawing-room the fire was low. He crossed over to it and sat down. His hands were cold. He needed the flames of the fire to light up the corners of the room. On the way home he had seen a dog run over by a motorcar. The sight of the blood had confused him. He had wanted to go down on his knees and finger the blood that made a round pool in the middle of the road. Someone had plucked at his sleeve, asking him if he was ill. He remembered that the sound and strength of his voice had drowned the first desire. He had walked away from the blood, with the stained wheels of the car and the soaking blackness under the bonnet going round and round before his eyes. He needed the warmth. The wind outside had cut between his fingers and thumbs.

She had left her sewing on the carpet near the coal scuttle. She had been making a petticoat. He picked it up and touched it, feeling where her breasts would sit under the yellow cotton. That morning he had seen her with her head enveloped in a frock. He saw her, thin in her nakedness, as a bag of skin and henna drifting out of the light. He let the petticoat drop on to the floor again.

Why, he wondered, was there this image of the red and broken dog? It was the first time he had seen the brains of a living creature burst out of the skull. He had been sick at the last yelp and the sudden caving of the dog's chest. He could have killed and shouted, like a child cracking a black beetle between its fingers.

A thousand nights ago, she had lain by his side. In her arms, he thought of the bones of her arms. He lay quietly by her skeleton. But she rose next morning in the corrupted flesh.

When he hurt her, it was to hide his pain. When he struck her cheek until the skin blushed, it was to break the agony of his own head. She told him of her mother's death. Her mother had worn a mask to hide the illness of her face. He felt the locust of that illness on his own face, in the mouth and the fluttering eyelid.

The room was darkening. He was too tired to shovel the fire into life, and saw the last flame die. A new coldness blew in with the early night. He tasted the sickness of the death of the flame as it rose to the tip of his tongue, and swallowed it down. It ran around the pulse of the heart, and beat until it was the only sound. And all the pain of the damned. The pain of a man with a bottle breaking across his face, the pain of a cow with a calf dancing out of her, the pain of the dog, moved through him from his aching hair to the flogged soles of his feet.

His strength returned. He and the dripping calf, the man with the torn face, and the dog on giddy legs, rose up as one, in one red brain and body, challenging the beast in the air. He heard the challenge in his snapping thumb and finger, as she came in.

He saw that she was wearing her yellow hat and frock.

"Why are you sitting in the dark?" she said.

She went into the kitchen to light the stove. He stood up from his chair. Holding his hands out in front of him as though they were blind, he followed her. She had a box of matches in her hand. As she took out a dead match and rubbed it on the box, he closed the door behind him.

"Take off your frock," he said.

She did not hear him, and smiled.

"Take off your frock," he said.

She stopped smiling, took out a live match and lit it.

"Take off your frock," he said.

He stepped towards her, his hands still blind. She bent over the stove. He blew the match out.

"What is it?" she said.

His lips moved, but he did not speak.

"Why?" she said.

He slapped her cheek quite lightly with his open hand. "Take off your frock," he said.

He heard her frock rustle over her head, and her frightened sob as he touched her. Methodically his blind hands made her naked.

He walked out of the kitchen, and closed the door.

In the hall, the one married shadow had broken up. He could not see his own face in the mirror as he tied his scarf and stroked the brim of his hat. There were too many faces. Each had a section of his features, and each a stiffened lock of his hair. He pulled up the collar of his coat. It was a wet winter night. As he walked, he counted the lamps. He pushed a door open and stepped into the warmth. The room was empty. The woman behind the bar smiled as she rubbed two coins together. "It's a cold night," she said.

He drank up the whisky and went out.

He walked on through the increasing rain. He counted the lamps again, but they reached no number.

The corner bar was empty. He took his drink into the saloon, but the saloon was empty.

The Rising Sun was empty.

Outside, he heard no traffic. He remembered that he had seen nobody in the streets. He cried aloud in a panic of loneliness:

"Where are you, where are you?"

Then there was traffic, and the windows were blazing. He heard singing from the house on the corner.

The bar was crowded. Women were laughing and shouting. They spilt their drinks over their dresses and lifted their dresses up. Girls were dancing on the sawdust. A woman caught him by the arm, and rubbed his face on her sleeve, and took his hand in hers and put it on her throat. He could hear nothing but the voices of the laughing women and the shouting of the girls as they danced. Then the ungainly women from the seats and the corners rocked towards him. He saw that the room was full of women. Slowly, still laughing, they gathered close to him.

He whispered a word under his breath, and felt the old sickness turn sour in his belly. There was blood before his eyes.

Then he, too, burst into laughter. He stuck his hands deep in the pockets of his coat, and laughed into their faces.

His hand clutched around a softness in his pocket. He drew out his hand, the softness in it.

The laughter died. The room was still. Quiet and still, the women stood watching him.

He raised his hand up level with his eyes. It held a piece of soft cloth.

"Who'll buy a lady's vest?" he said. "Going, going, ladies, who'll buy a lady's vest?"

The meek and ordinary women in the bar stood still, their glasses in their hands, as he leant with his back to the counter and shouted with laughter and waved the bloody cloth in front of them.

# The True Story

The old woman upstairs had been dying since Martha could remember. She had lain like a wax woman in her sheets since Martha was a child coming with her mother to bring fresh fruit and vegetables to the dying. And now Martha was a woman under her apron and print frock, and her pale hair was bound in a bunch behind her head. Each morning she got up with the sun, lit the fire, let in the red-eyed cat. She made a pot of tea, and, going up to the bedroom at the back of the cottage, bent over the old woman whose blind eyes were never closed. Each morning she looked into the hollows of the old woman's eyes, and passed her hands over them. She could not tell if the old woman breathed. Eight o'clock, eight o'clock now, she said. And the blind eyes smiled. A ragged hand came out from the sheets, and stayed there until Martha took it in her little, padded hand and closed it around the cup. When the cup was empty Martha filled it, and when the pot was dry she pulled back the white sheets from the bed. There the old woman lay, stretched out in her night-dress, and the colour of her flesh was grey as her last hairs. Martha tidied the sheets and attended to the old woman's wants. Then she took the pot away. Each morning she had her meal with the boy who worked in the garden. She went to the back door, opened it, and saw him in the distance with his spade. Half-past eight now, she said. He was an ugly boy, and his eyes were redder than the cat's, two cuts in his head forever spying on the first shadows of her breast. Martha put his food in front of him, and sat sideways with her hands near the fire. When he got up he always said, Is there anything you want me to do? She had never said yes. The boy went back to dig potatoes out of the patch or to count the hens' eggs; and if there were berries to be picked off the garden bushes, she joined him before noon. Seeing the little red currants pile up in the palm of her hand, she would think of the money under the

178

old woman's mattress. If there were hens to be killed she could cut their throats far more cleanly than the boy who let his knife stay in the wound and wiped the blood on the knife along his sleeve. She caught a hen and killed it, felt its warm blood, and saw it run headless up the garden path. Then she went in to wash her hands.

It was in the first week of spring. Martha had reached her twentieth year, and still the old woman stretched out her hand for the cup of tea, still the front of her nightdress never stirred with her breathing, and still the fortune lay under the mattress. There was so much that Martha wanted. She wanted a man of her own and a black dress for Sundays and a hat with flowers. She had no money at all. On the days that the boy took the eggs and the vegetables to market, she gave him a six-penny piece that the old woman gave her, and the money the boy brought back in his handkerchief she put into the old woman's hands. She worked for her food and her shelter as the boy worked for his, though she slept in a room upstairs and he in a bed of straw over the empty sheds.

On a bright market morning she walked out into the garden so that her plan might be cooled in her head. She saw two clouds in the sky, two unshapely hands closing round the head of the sun. If I could fly, she thought, I could fly in at the open window and fasten my teeth in the old woman's throat. But the cool wind blew the thought away. She knew that she was no common girl, for she had read books in the winter evenings when the boy was dreaming in the straw and the old woman was alone in the dark. She had read of a god who came down like money, of snakes with the voices of men, and of a man who stood on the top of a hill, talking with a thing of fire.

At the end of the garden, where the fence kept out the wild green fields, she came to a mound of earth. There she buried the dog she had killed for catching and killing the hens in the garden. Peace in Rest, the cross said, and the date of the death was written backwards so that the dog had not died yet. I could bury her here, said Martha to herself, by the side of the dog, under the manure so that nobody could find her. And she patted her hands, and reached the back door of the cottage as the two hands got round the sun.

Inside there was a meal to be prepared for the old woman, potatoes to be mashed up in the tea. The knife made the only sound, the wind had dropped down, her heart was as quiet as though she had wrapped it up. Nothing moved in the cottage; her hand was dead on her lap; she could not think that smoke went up the chimney and out into the still sky. Her mind, alone in the world, was ticking away. Then, when all things were dead, a cock crew, and she remembered the boy who would soon be back from market. She felt her hand die again in her lap. And in the midst of death she heard the boy's hand lift up the latch.

He came into the kitchen, saw that Martha was cleaning the potatoes, and dropped his handkerchief on to the table. Hearing the noise of the money in the cloth, she looked up at him and smiled. He had never seen her smile before.

Soon she put his meal in front of him, and sat sideways by the fire. As she bent over him, he smelt the clover in her hair, and saw the damp garden soil behind her fingernails. She rarely went outside the cottage into the unusual world but to kill or pick the berry bushes. Have you taken up her dinner? he asked. She did not answer. When he had finished his meal, he got up from the table and said, Is there anything you want me to do? as he had said a thousand times. Yes, said Martha.

She had never said yes to him before. He had never heard a woman speak as she had spoken. The first shadows of her breast had never been so dark. He stumbled across the kitchen to her, and she lifted her hands to her shoulders. What will you do for me? she said, and loosed the straps of her frock so that it fell about her and left her breast bare. She took his hand and put it on her breast. He stared like a fool at her nakedness, then said her name and caught hold of her. What will you do for me? she said. Thinking of the money under the mattress, she held him close and let her frock fall on the floor and ripped her petticoat away. You will do what I want, she said.

After a minute she struggled out of his arms and ran softly across the room. With her naked back to the door that led upstairs, she beckoned him and told him what he was to do. We shall be rich, she said. He tried to finger her again, but she held his fingers. You will help me, she said. The boy smiled and nodded. She opened the door and led him upstairs. You stay here quiet, she said. In the old woman's room she looked at the cracked jug, the half-open window, and the text on the wall. One o'clock now, she said into the old woman's ear, and the blind eyes smiled. Martha put her fingers round the old woman's throat. One o'clock now, she said, and knocked the old woman's head against the wall. It needed but three little knocks, and the head burst like an egg.

What have you done? cried the boy. Martha called for him to come in. He opened the door and, staring at the naked woman who cleaned her hands on the bed, and at the blood that made such a round, red stain on the wall, he screamed out in horror. Be quiet, said Martha; but he screamed again at her quiet voice and ran downstairs.

So Martha must fly, she said to herself, fly out of the old woman's room into the wind. She opened the window wide, and stepped out. I am flying, she said.

But Martha was not flying.

# The Followers

It was six o'clock on a winter's evening. Thin, dingy rain spat and drizzled past the lighted street lamps. The pavements shone long and yellow. In squeaking goloshes, with mackintosh collars up and bowlers and trilbies weeping, youngish men from the offices bundled home against the thistly wind—

"Night, Mr. Macey."

"Going my way, Charlie?"

"Ooh, there's a pig of a night!"

"Goodnight, Mr. Swan"—

and older men, clinging on to the big, black circular birds of their umbrellas, were wafted back, up the gaslit hills, to safe, hot, slippered, weatherproof hearths, and wives called Mother, and old, fond, fleabag dogs, and the wireless babbling.

Young women from the offices, who smelt of scent and powder and wet pixie hoods and hair, scuttled, giggling, arm-in-arm, after the hissing trams, and screeched as they splashed their stockings in the puddles rainbowed with oil between the slippery lines.

In a shopwindow, two girls undressed the dummies:

"Where are you going tonight?"

"Depends on Arthur. Up she comes."

"Mind her cami-knicks, Edna . . ."

The blinds came down over another window.

A newsboy stood in a doorway, calling the news to nobody, very softly:

"Earthquake. Earthquake in Japan."

Water from a chute dripped on to his sacking. He waited in his own pool of rain.

A flat, long girl drifted, snivelling into her hanky, out of a jeweller's shop, and slowly pulled the steel shutters down with a hooked pole. She looked, in the grey rain, as though she were crying from top to toe.

A silent man and woman, dressed in black, carried the wreaths away from the front of their flower shop into the

182

scented deadly darkness behind the window lights. Then the lights went out.

A man with a balloon tied to his cap pushed a shrouded barrow up a dead end.

A baby with an ancient face sat in its pram outside the wine vaults, quiet, very wet, peering cautiously all round it.

It was the saddest evening I had ever known.

A young man, with his arm round his girl, passed by me, laughing; and she laughed back, right into his handsome, nasty face. That made the evening sadder still.

I met Leslie at the corner of Crimea Street. We were both about the same age: too young and too old. Leslie carried a rolled umbrella, which he never used, though sometimes he pressed doorbells with it. He was trying to grow a moustache. I wore a check ratting cap at a Saturday angle. We greeted each other formally:

"Good evening, old man."

"Evening, Leslie."

"Right on the dot, boy."

"That's right," I said. "Right on the dot."

A plump blonde girl, smelling of wet rabbits, self-conscious even in that dirty night, minced past on high-heeled shoes. The heels clicked, the soles squelched.

Leslie whistled after her, low and admiring.

"Business first," I said.

"Oh, boy!" Leslie said.

"And she's too fat as well."

"I like them corpulent," Leslie said. "Remember Penelope Bogan? a Mrs. too."

"Oh, come on. That old bird of Paradise Alley! How's the exchequer, Les?"

"One and a penny. How you fixed?"

"Tanner."

"What'll it be, then? The Compasses?"

"Free cheese at the Marlborough."

We walked towards the Marlborough, dodging umbrella spokes, smacked by our windy macs, stained by steaming lamplight, seeing the sodden, blown scourings and street-wash of the town, papers, rags, dregs, rinds, fag-ends, balls of fur, flap, float, and cringe along the gutters, hearing the sneeze and rattle of the bony trams and a ship hoot like a fog-ditched owl in the bay, and Leslie said:

"What'll we do after?"

"We'll follow someone," I said.

"Remember following that old girl up Kitchener Street? The one who dropped her handbag?"

"You should have given it back."

"There wasn't anything in it, only a piece of bread-and-jam."

"Here we are," I said.

The Marlborough saloon was cold and empty. There were notices on the damp walls: No Singing. No Dancing. No Gambling. No Peddlers.

"You sing," I said to Leslie, "and I'll dance, then we'll have a game of nap and I'll peddle my braces."

The barmaid, with gold hair and two gold teeth in front, like a well-off rabbit's, was blowing on her nails and polishing them on her black marocain. She looked up as we came in, then blew on her nails again and polished them without hope.

"You can tell it isn't Saturday night," I said. "Evening, Miss. Two pints."

"And a pound from the till," Leslie said.

"Give us your one-and-a-penny, Les," I whispered, and then said aloud: "Anybody can tell it isn't Saturday night. Nobody sick."

"Nobody here to *be* sick," Leslie said.

The peeling, liver-coloured room might never have been drunk in at all. Here, commercials told jokes and had Scotches and sodas with happy, dyed, port-and-lemon women; dejected regulars grew grand and muzzy in the corners, inventing their pasts, being rich, important, and loved; reprobate grannies in dustbin black cackled and nipped; influential nobodies revised the earth; a party, with earrings, called "Frilly Willy," played the crippled piano, which sounded like a hurdy-gurdy playing under water, until the publican's nosy wife said, No. Strangers came and went, but mostly went. Men from the valleys dropped in for nine or ten; sometimes there were fights; and always there was something doing, some argie-bargie, giggle and bluster, horror or folly, affection, explosion, nonsense, peace, some wild goose flying in the boozy air of that comfortless, humdrum nowhere in the dizzy, ditch-water town at the end of the railway lines. But that evening it was the saddest room I had ever known.

Leslie said, in a low voice: "Think she'll let us have one on tick?"

"Wait a bit, boy," I murmured. "Wait for her to thaw."

But the barmaid heard me, and looked up. She looked clean through me, back through my small history to the bed I was born in, then shook her gold head.

"I don't know what it is," said Leslie as we walked up Crimea Street in the rain, "but I feel kind of depressed tonight."

"It's the saddest night in the world," I said.

We stopped, soaked and alone, to look at the stills outside the cinema we called the Itch-pit. Week after week, for years and years, we had sat on the edges of the springless seats there, in the dank but snug, flickering dark, first wth toffees and monkey-nuts that crackled for the dumb guns, and then with cigarettes: a cheap special kind that would make a fire-swallower cough up the cinders of his heart. "Let's go in and see Lon Chaney," I said, "and Richard Talmadge and Milton Sills and . . . and Noah Beery," I said, "and Richard Dix . . . and Slim Summerville and Hoot Gibson."

We both sighed.

"Oh for our vanished youth," I said.

We walked on heavily, with wilful feet, splashing the passers-by.

"Why don't you open your brolly?" I said.

"It won't open. You try."

We both tried, and the umbrella suddenly bellied out, the spokes tore through the soaking cover; the wind danced its tatters; it wrangled above us in the wind like a ruined, mathematical bird. We tried to tug it down; an unseen, new spoke sprang through its ragged ribs. Leslie dragged it behind him, along the pavement, as though he had shot it.

A girl called Dulcie, scurrying to the Itch-pit, sniggered hallo, and we stopped her.

"A rather terrible thing has happened," I said to her. She was so silly that, even when she was fifteen, we had told her to eat soap to make her straw hair crinkle, and Les took a piece from the bathroom, and she did.

"I know," she said, "you broke your gamp."

"No, you're wrong there," Leslie said. "It isn't *our* umbrella at all. It fell off the roof. *You* feel," he said.

"You can feel it fell off the roof." She took the umbrella gingerly by its handle.

"There's someone up there throwing umbrellas down," I said. "It may be serious."

She began to titter, and then grew silent and anxious as Leslie said: "You never know. It might be walking-sticks next."

"Or sewing-machines," I said.

"You wait here, Dulcie, and we'll investigate," Leslie said.

We hurried on down the street, turned a blowing corner, and then ran.

Outside Rabiotti's café, Leslie said: "It isn't fair on Dulcie." We never mentioned it again.

A wet girl brushed by. Without a word, we followed her. She catered, long-legged, down Inkerman Street and through Paradise Passage, and we were at her heels.

"I wonder what's the point in following people," Leslie said, "it's kind of daft. It never gets you anywhere. All you do is follow them home and then try to look through the window and see what they're doing and mostly there's curtains anyway. I bet nobody else does things like that."

"You never know," I said. The girl turned into St. Augustus Crescent, which was a wide lamplit mist. "People are always following people. What shall we call her?"

"Hermione Weatherby," Leslie said. He was never wrong about names. Hermione was fey and stringy, and walked like a long gym-mistress, full of love, through the stinging rain.

"You never know. You never know what you'll find out. Perhaps she lives in a huge house with all her sisters—"

"How many?"

"Seven. All full of love. And when she gets home they all change into kimonos and lie on divans with music and whisper to each other and all they're doing is waiting for somebody like us to walk in, lost, and then they'll all chatter round us like starlings and put us in kimonos too, and we'll never leave the house until we die. Perhaps it's so beautiful and soft and noisy—like a warm bath full of birds . . ."

"I don't want birds in my bath," said Leslie. "Perhaps she'll slit her throat if they don't draw the blinds. I don't care what happens so long as it's interesting."

She slip-slopped round a corner into an avenue where the neat trees were sighing and the cosy windows shone.

"I don't want old feathers in the tub," Leslie said.

Hermione turned in at number thirteen, Beach-view.

"You can see the beach all right," Leslie said, "if you got a periscope."

We waited on the pavement opposite, under a bubbling lamp, as Hermione opened her door, and then we tip-toed across and down the gravel path and were at the back of the house, outside an uncurtained window.

Hermione's mother, a round, friendly, owlish woman in a pinafore, was shaking a chip-pan on the kitchen stove.

"I'm hungry," I said.

"Ssh!"

We edged to the side of the window as Hermione came into the kitchen. She was old, nearly thirty, with a mouse-brown shingle and big earnest eyes. She wore horn-rimmed spectacles and a sensible tweed costume, and a white shirt with a trim bow-tie. She looked as though she tried to look like a secretary in domestic films, who had only to remove her spectacles and have her hair cherished, and be dressed like a silk dog's dinner, to turn into a dazzler and make her employer, Warner Baxter, gasp, woo, and marry her; but if Hermione took off her glasses, she wouldn't be able to tell if he was Warner Baxter or the man who read the meters.

We stood so near the window, we could hear the chips spitting.

"Have a nice day in the office, dear? There's weather," Hermione's mother said, worrying the chip-pan.

"What's *her* name, Les?"

"Hetty."

Everything there in the warm kitchen, from the tea-caddy and the grandmother clock, to the tabby that purred like a kettle, was good, dull, and sufficient.

"Mr. Truscott was something awful," Hermione said as she put on slippers.

"Where's her kimono?" Leslie said.

"Here's a nice cup of tea," said Hetty.

"Everything's nice in that old hole," said Leslie, grumbling. "Where's the seven sisters like starlings?"

It began to rain much more heavily. It bucketed down on the black backyard, and the little comfy kennel of a house, and us, and the hidden, hushed town, where, even now, in the haven of the Marlborough, the submarine piano would be tinning "Daisy," and the happy henna'd women squealing into their port.

Hetty and Hermione had their supper. Two drowned boys watched them enviously.

"Put a drop of Worcester on the chips," Leslie whispered; and by God she did.

"Doesn't anything happen anywhere?" I said, "in the whole wide world? I think the *News of the World* is all made up. Nobody murders no one. There isn't any sin any more, or love, or death, or pearls and divorces and mink coats or anything, or putting arsenic in the cocoa . . ."

"Why don't they put on some music for us," Leslie said, "and do a dance? It isn't every night they got two fellows watching them in the rain. Not *every* night, anyway!"

All over the dripping town, small lost people with nowhere to go and nothing to spend were gooseberrying in the rain outside wet windows, but nothing happened.

"I'm getting pneumonia," Leslie said.

The cat and the fire were purring, grandmother time ticktocked our lives away. The supper was cleared, and Hetty and Hermione, who had not spoken for many minutes, they were so confident and close in their little lighted box, looked at one another and slowly smiled.

They stood still in the decent, purring kitchen, facing one another.

"There's something funny going to happen," I whispered very softly.

"It's going to begin," Leslie said.

We did not notice the sour, racing rain any more.

The smiles stayed on the faces of the two still, silent women.

"It's going to begin."

And we heard Hetty say in a small secret voice: "Bring out the album, dear."

Hermione opened a cupboard and brought out a big, stiff-coloured photograph album, and put it in the middle of the table. Then she and Hetty sat down at the table, side by side, and Hermione opened the album.

"That's Uncle Eliot who died in Porthcawl, the one who had the cramp," said Hetty.

They looked with affection at Uncle Eliot, but we could not see him.

"That's Martha-the-woolshop, you wouldn't remember her, dear, it was wool, wool, wool, with her all the time; she wanted to be buried in her jumper, the mauve one, but her husband put his foot down. He'd been in India. That's your Uncle Morgan," Hetty said, "one of the Kidwelly Morgans, remember him in the snow?"

Hermione turned a page. "And that's Myfanwy, she got queer all of a sudden, remember. It was when she was milking. That's your cousin Jim, the Minister, until they found out. And that's our Beryl," Hetty said.

But she spoke all the time like somebody repeating a lesson: a well-loved lesson she knew by heart.

We knew that she and Hermione were only waiting.

Then Hermione turned another page. And we knew, by their secret smiles, that this was what they had been waiting for.

"My sister Katinka," Hetty said.

"Auntie Katinka," Hermione said. They bent over the photograph.

"Remember that day in Aberystwyth, Katinka?" Hetty said softly. "The day we went on the choir outing."

"I wore my new white dress," a new voice said.

Leslie clutched at my hand.

"And a straw hat with birds," said the clear, new voice. Hermione and Hetty were not moving their lips.

"I was always a one for birds on my hat. Just the plumes of course. It was August the third, and I was twenty-three."

"Twenty-three come October, Katinka," Hetty said.

"That's right, love," the voice said. "Scorpio I was. And we met Douglas Pugh on the Prom and he said, 'You look like a queen today, Katinka,' he said. 'You look like a queen, Katinka,' he said. Why are those two boys looking in at the window?"

We ran up the gravel drive, and around the corner of the house, and into the avenue and out on to St. Augustus Crescent. The rain roared down to drown the town. There we stopped for breath. We did not speak or look at each other. Then we walked on through the rain. At Victoria corner, we stopped again.

"Good-night, old man," Leslie said.

"Good-night," I said.

And we went our different ways.

# Bibliographical Notes

"Adventures in the Skin Trade." First part of Chapter I published as "A Fine Beginning" in *Folios of New Writing,* edited by John Lehmann; The Hogarth Press, 1941. Chapters I and II complete in *New World Writing,* Nos. 2 and 3. Chapter I, minus the first part, published in *Adam,* No. 238, 1953.

"After the Fair." *New English Weekly,* March 15, 1934; *New World Writing,* No. 7, 1955.

"The Enemies." *New Stories,* June-July, 1934; *The World I Breathe,* 1939; *Map of Love,* 1939.

"The Tree." *Adelphi,* New Series, 9, 1934; revised version: *Map of Love.*

"The Visitor." *Criterion,* 14, 1935; *The World I Breathe; Map of Love;* etc.

"The Lemon." *Life and Letters Today,* 14, 1936.

"The Burning Baby." *Contemporary Poetry and Prose,* No. 1, 1936; *The World I Breathe.*

"The Orchards." *Criterion,* 15, 1936; *The World I Breathe; Map of Love; New Directions,* 1938.

"The Mouse and the Woman." *Transition,* No. 25, 1936; *The World I Breathe; Map of Love.*

"The Horse's Ha." *Janus,* 1936.

"A Prospect of the Sea." *Life and Letters Today,* 16, 1937; *The World I Breathe.*

"The Holy Six." As "The Six" in *Contemporary Poetry and Prose,* No. 9, 1937; as "The Holy Six" in *The World I Breathe.*

"Prologue to an Adventure." *Wales,* No. 1, 1937; *The World I Breathe; Delta,* Christmas, 1938.

"The Map of Love." *Wales*, No. 3, 1937; *Map of Love; The World I Breathe*.

"In the Direction of the Beginning." *New Directions*, 1938; *Wales*, No. 4, 1938.

"An Adventure from a Work in Progress." *Seven*, No. 4, 1939.

"The School for Witches." *New Directions*, 1939; *The World I Breathe*.

"The Dress." *The World I Breathe; Map of Love*.

"The Vest." *Yellow Jacket*, 1939; *Mademoiselle*, February, 1955.

"The True Story." *Yellow Jacket*, 1939; *New World Writing*, No. 7, 1955.

"The Followers." *World Review*, October, 1952; *New World Writing*, No. 5, 1954.

---

# SIGNET and MENTOR Books of Interest

**100 AMERICAN POEMS**
*Edited by Selden Rodman.* A refreshing new collection of poetry, dating from Emerson up to the present day, with an illuminating introduction by a noted poet. (#660—25c)

**100 MODERN POEMS**
*Edited by Selden Rodman.* An exciting collection of the best work of American, English and European writers. (#M54—35c)

**THE GOLDEN TREASURY**
*F. T. Palgrave, enlarged and up-dated by Oscar Williams.* Great lyric poems of the English language from 1526 to the present—642 great poems, by 193 poets. (#MD90—50c)

**LEAVES OF GRASS**
*Walt Whitman.* A complete edition of the incomparable poems of America's remarkable poet. (#Ms117—50c)

**THE INFERNO BY DANTE**
*Translated by John Ciardi.* One of the world's great poetic masterpieces in a new verse translation in modern English by a celebrated contemporary poet. (#MD113—50c)

**HIGHLIGHTS OF MODERN LITERATURE: A Permanent Collection of Memorable Essays from The New York Times Book Review**
*Edited by Francis Brown.* The world's leading authors and critics discuss modern literature in fifty-eight informative, thoughtful and stimulating articles. (#M104—35c)

**THE CREATIVE PROCESS**
*Edited, with introduction, by Brewster Ghiselin.* Thirty-eight of the greatest minds in the world reveal how they actually begin and complete creative work in such fields as art, literature, science and philosophy. (#MD132—50c)

**THE PAINTER'S EYE**
*Maurice Grosser.* A brilliant analysis of the conventions, principles and techniques of painting from the Renaissance to the present, illustrated with reproductions of 32 masterpieces. (#M159—35c)

**BOOKS THAT CHANGED THE WORLD**
*Robert B. Downs.* The fascinating histories of sixteen great books—from Machiavelli's *The Prince* to Einstein's *Theories of Relativity* — that have changed the course of history. (#M168—35c)

**COMPANY MANNERS**
*Louis Kronenberger.* A penetrating and provocative appraisal by a noted critic of American culture, with special emphasis on art, theater and television as well as individual morals, manners and ideals. (#M156—35c)

**GOOD READING (enlarged, up-to-date edition)**
*Edited by the Committee on College Reading.* A carefully selected guide to 1,250 useful and entertaining volumes which will help you select your own reading program from the wealth of the world's important literature. New 25-page check-list of paperbound titles. (#MD124—50c)

---

**TO OUR READERS:** We welcome your comments about SIGNET, SIGNET KEY and MENTOR BOOKS, as well as your suggestions for new reprints. If your dealer does not have the books you want, you may order them by mail, enclosing the list price plus 5c a copy to cover mailing costs. Send for a copy of our complete catalogue. The New American Library of World Literature, Inc., 501 Madison Avenue, New York 22, N. Y.